Father Figure

Jan-Andrew Henderson

A Black Hart Publication

Scotland. Australia.

First published 2020 by Black Hart

Black Hart Entertainment.
Redgum Close, Bellbowrie, Brisbane 4070.
Janandrewhenderson.com
blackhartentertainment.com

Book Layout © 2020 BookDesignTemplates.com
Cover design by Book Design Stars.

Father Figure by J A Henderson 1st ed 2020.
ISBN 978-1-64826-917-2 (Print)
ISBN 978-1-64826-942-4 (eBook)

Greyfriars and the surrounding area exist as portrayed in this novel and the historical facts in Donny Marigold's journal are accurate.

Father Figure is based on real events.

This book is dedicated to the City of the Dead Guides

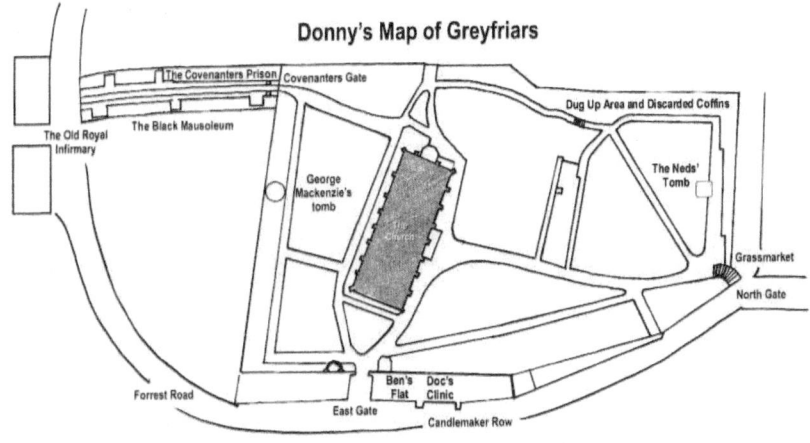

Donny's Map of Greyfriars

Legend has it that Greyfriars Churchyard in Edinburgh is haunted by Sir George Mackenzie, buried there in 1691. King's Advocate to Charles II of Britain, Mackenzie was a ruthless persecutor of a religious group known as the Covenanters and responsible for the deaths of thousands of men, women and children. It is claimed he can never rest in peace because of the atrocities he committed.

It is commonly thought the 'Mackenzie Poltergeist' is named after George Mackenzie. In reality, the term was coined by Ben Scott and has nothing to do with the King's Advocate.

The Wittenberg Region, Bavaria 1635

Flooded fields outside the town of Distel rejected the crimson rays of the setting sun. The water was already gorged with blood, a velvet quagmire pebbled with bodies. Broken limbs, stiffened by rigour mortis, reached out of the murk, demanding attention. It had been raining for three days now and bolts of lightning tore open the sky to the east.

Each flash lit the razed buildings behind the highland mercenaries, silhouetting a porcupine ridge of spikes among the ruins. But this forest was man-made, rough-hewn stakes with the rotting remains of people impaled on their points.

Campbell Menzies led his men towards higher ground, wading thigh deep through the stinking swamp, a throat stinging pall of smoke turning them into ghostly waifs. The mercenaries had tied rags around their faces, obscuring their features, but tense postures and outstretched swords betrayed their mounting fear. One stumbled and fell, vanishing under the fetid surface then reappearing with a cry of horror, using the bobbing, waterlogged bodies as leverage to push himself upright. Every head snapped round and the closest soldier gave a few coughs of laughter, cutting the sound short before his companions detected mania dancing across its edges.

One of the men splashed over to his commander.

"By aw that's holy, Menzies," he pleaded. "We have tae get oot of here. There's naebody left alive. We killed them all."

"We're going nowhere." His leader pointed to a partially denuded hill silhouetted against the sinking sun. "We'll camp up there. It'll be dark soon and we'll drown if we try tae cross this terrain withoot torches."

He kicked out angrily at the incessant rain bombarding the quagmire.

"This downpour would put oot the very fires of hell."

"There's a wee consolation then," his companion grunted. "Since that's surely where we are."

The corpse of a little girl nudged his leg and he pushed it away with his sword.

"It seems like the Lord has sent his tears tae wash away this sin." Menzie's second in command pointed up as a comet streaked across the ravaged sky. "There are bad omens everywhere."

"God has turned his face fae this sorry place and the Protestant scum who blemished it." Menzie's voice was calm and cold. "But we hae riches enough tae never return tae this line of work, if that will salve yir conscience."

Another burst of lightning ripped across the darkening sky, much closer now. The men flinched as the scope of their carnage was illuminated for a brief second.

"Protestant scum? Is that how we justify murdering women and bairns?"

Menzies lashed out, striking the soldier across the head.

"You are my lieutenant," he snarled. "And you'll bloody well act like it. Now get those men tae the hill while we can still see it."

The highlanders pulled themselves up the incline and collapsed on spongy earth, stripping off sodden plaids and using them to wipe their weapons clean of mud and gore. Some sat staring into the gathering night, shivering with cold. Others lay naked and exhausted in the mud. Nobody talked. The storm was increasing in intensity and lightning forked into the swamp every few minutes, creating a sizzling froth.

Thunder boomed after each flash; its din flattened by the expanse of water.

Then they heard another sound. Not the squall - but a more ominous noise, if that were possible, and growing in volume.

The men got to their feet, peering into the gloam. Some crossed themselves half-heartedly.

"The Devil is coming," one whispered.

But it was a vast herd of Westphalian Cattle, panicked by the raging elements, that crested the horizon and galloped towards them - sending up plumes of crimson-flecked water. Great horned heads thrashed from side to side, eyes rolling in panic. A terrified lowing filled the air as if the dead were crying out at this final indignation.

"There are hundreds o them," one man cried. "Whuar were the townspeople hiding thon big bastards?"

"What if they carry the plague?" another joined in. "They're heading straight fur us!"

"Never mind the damned plague," Menzies yelled back. "If they breach this hill, they'll trample us like stalks of corn. Archers tae the high ground! The rest of you, keep those mad beasties at bay!"

The exhausted foot soldiers bunched into battle formation halfway down the hill. Arrowmen scrambled to the top and began to shoot at the stampede, cursing their wet bowstrings. The hail of missiles barely slowed the cattle, blind terror driving the creatures on, until they splashed out of the water and thundered up the incline.

The naked highlanders charged down to meet them, screaming their legendary battle cry. They slammed into the oncoming livestock, swinging claymores through thousands of pounds of bone, muscle and hide. The screams grew louder as the front rank were trampled under jagged hooves or impaled on the Westphalian's viciously curved horns.

But the line held. The cattle slewed to a halt, slipping and sliding, momentum broken by the sheer ferocity of the human assault. They turned back and milled around in the water, churning the mass of bodies to pulp beneath them.

"Cut open the beasts that fell on land." Campbell Menzies stuck his dripping sword in the ground. "Then burrow inside them like tics. Their warmth will keep ye alive till morning."

He gave a sardonic snort.

"Luck must be wi us today."

Kicking over the corpse at his feet, he gave a sigh. It was the gored and broken body of his second in command. The man had fought at his side for two years and saved his life more than once. And his last reward had been a blow to the face.

"You have deserted this place, Lord, and abandoned us too." Menzies raised both arms to the heavens, his emotionless façade finally cracking. "I curse the mither and faither who brought me intae this hellish world. And I curse myself mair for living."

Another bolt of lightning careened into the water and a heifer gave an almost human wail as darkness enveloped her death throes.

Campbell Menzies closed the sightless eyes of his companion and lay down next to the body, absorbing the man's fading heat. He rolled onto his back and crossed scarred hands over his chest. Cool, clean rain filled his eye sockets and ran in rivulets down his face.

Drifting off to sleep, the commander allowed himself the luxury of pretending they were tears.

-Part 1-

Daisy and Donny

A belief is not merely an idea the mind possesses; it is an idea that possesses the mind.

Robert Oxton Bolton

All of this has happened before, and it will all happen again.

J. M. Barrie. *Peter Pan*

-1-

Edinburgh 2002

The sun was sinking as Daisy Lenin entered Greyfriars Graveyard. Light danced along the rim of the surrounding stone wall and found itself trapped in the upper branches of willows and cedars. A sparrow tilted its head at the girl, eyes glittering puncture marks. Gravestones tripled in length as their shadows striped the neatly cut grass and closed ranks to squeeze out the green - night emerging from the ground up.

This was the magic moment Daisy had waited for. Late enough for the cemetery to be deserted but not dark enough to stop her seeing what she was doing. Shouldering her rucksack, the teenager strode across the graveyard, threading between the headstones, trying to look as if she had every right to be there. The bird flitted from tree to tree behind her, drawn to the only other living thing in sight.

At the furthest corner was an area known as the Covenanters Prison, secured by a padlocked iron gate. The prison was a long corridor of tombs pressed against towering walls - jutting out from the main body of the cemetery like a misplaced jigsaw piece.

Glancing around to make sure nobody was watching, Daisy ran round the side of a nearby crypt and retrieved her 'ladder' from its hiding place. It wasn't much to look at, just a ten-foot plank of wood with nails hammered in at regular intervals, but she was sure it would do the trick.

"What you up tae, hen?"

Daisy spun round. A group of youths emerged from behind a nearby mausoleum. One was pulling up his zip. They wore tracksuits or hooded tops and baseball caps veiled their eyes.

"Naughty, naughty," one of them sneered, a cigarette dangling from his lip. "That's trespassing, doll."

"C'mon doon wi us," another added. "We got a nice gaff in a tomb at the bottom of the graveyard." He grinned at the others. "We can hae a wee party."

Daisy leaned the ladder against the wall and quickly climbed to the top, using the nails as footholds.

"Get back here, bitch!" The youths broke into a sprint, heading towards her.

Sitting on the stone arch above the gate, Daisy pulled up her ladder and slid it down the other side. Seconds later she was standing in the prison.

The gang reached the Covenanter's gate and glared balefully at her.

"You're no safe in there, ya stuck up cunt." One of them pulled up his top to reveal a bread knife tucked into the waistband of his jeans. "I'll cut ye when I catch yis, know?"

Daisy ignored them. Leaving the plank in the shadows, she walked the length of the corridor, trying not to look at the black mouths of the mausoleums on either side. Each had a locked gate to stop vagrants and vandals getting in, but it was just as easy to imagine they were keeping the long-dead inhabitants from breaking out.

The youths watched her fading into the gloom.

"C'mon, Marky." One pulled at his leader. "We cannae get over the wall. Let's go an see what's happened to big Ando, eh? He was supposed to be meetin us wi some gear."

Marky shrugged the boy off, staring at the retreating form.

"Aye, aw right. But I'll be keepin mah eye oot fur that one. Wee fucker's no gonnae diss *me* an get away wi it."

He turned and made his way back across Greyfriars, the others trotting at his heels.

Reaching the last tomb, Daisy pulled a hacksaw from her rucksack and went to work on the padlock keeping it closed. Around her, shadows slowly solidified into blackness and she was forced to switch on the battery-operated lantern she had bought earlier.

The faint, hiccupping wail of a siren erupted in the distance and froze her to the spot. Had someone seen her breaking into the prison and called the police?

But there were no occupied tenements at this end of the graveyard and the siren seemed to be circling the perimeter rather than entering. Besides, it sounded like an ambulance. Galvanised into action, she attacked the padlock with renewed energy.

"Ando? Where the hell are you, ye dozy twat?" Marky glanced around the tomb his gang had made their own. In the corner were two deckchairs, their brightly coloured stripes turning to monochrome in the dusk. The remains of a fire had scorched a star-shaped smear on the concrete floor.

"You better no be tryin oot the merchandise before we've had a shot."

He motioned to his companions.

"Stop scratchin yerselves, ye wankers. Get oot the torches an look for him."

The others trooped out. A few minutes later, there was a shout.

"Over here, lads."

Big Ando was lying, face down, at the bottom of a nearby trench, head submerged in a puddle. The others peered down at him, reluctant to climb in.

"Is he dead?"

"Naw," Marky snorted. "He's havin a fuckin paddle. Stupid bastard must have been so wasted, he fell over the edge."

"What are we gonnae dae? Should we call the polis?"

"Oh, aye? Ye've got mair tracks on yer arm than Waverly train station." Marky gave big Ando a disgusted kick in the ribs. "You want the fuzz tae get hold o yer mobile number… be my guest."

"What dae ye think he died of?"

"It wasnae old bloody age."

Marky pointed. A needle floated in the muddy pool next to the pit.

"Check his pockets an grab any stash. See if he's got money an all. Then let's leg it. We'll need tae keep oot the graveyard for a few weeks until the heat dies doon."

He glanced in the direction of the Covenanters Prison and curled his lip.

"It's your lucky night, darlin."

Ben Scott gazed out of the window of his flat overlooking Greyfriars, a pointless exercise, as all he could see was his own reflection in the darkening pane. For three hours he had sat at his computer staring at an unfinished horror and come up with nothing. He blew on the glass and drew a pair of cartoon breasts with his finger on the condensation.

"Maybe I should write a romance."

He opened the window and let a blast of night air cool his face. Beyond the forest of dark headstones, he could hear muted voices, too low to make out what was being said. He glanced across at the screen at the last thing he had typed.

"Say, you remind me of a man."

"What man?"

"The man with the power."

"What power?"

"The power of Hoodoo."

"Hoodoo?"

"You do."

"I do?"

"Remind me of a man."

"What man?"

"The man with the power."

Most people thought the exchange was part of the film *Labyrinth*, where a teenager inadvertently makes a deadly fantasy world real. In fact, it was originally from a movie called the *Bachelor and the Bobby Soxer*, about a high school girl who falls for a playboy. Either way, he had stolen the lines.

"I'm looking out over a graveyard," he sighed to himself. "And I run a ghost tour company."

He closed the window.

"You'd think I'd get some bloody inspiration from *that*."

Standing in the lonely puddle of light, sweat trickled down Daisy's face as she worked on the lock. The bird watched from the top of the tomb, jerking its tufted head from side to side. Somewhere beyond the cemetery, the siren gave a final angry bleep and the sound was extinguished.

The padlock eventually gave way and Daisy replaced it with one she had purchased from the same hardware store as the light and nails. Then she dragged her meagre possessions into the musty interior.

Now that she was safe, the teenager was able to properly take in her surroundings.

The mausoleum was square and bare, with a high ceiling and packed earthen floor. By the light of her lantern, Daisy could see that it was built from granite blocks, mottled with damp patches and the spattered remains of ancient plaster. She hated to dwell on the fact, but the tomb looked like an oversized cell.

Daisy fished a knife from her pocket and clicked open the blade, placing it by her side for protection. She pulled a sleeping bag from her rucksack along with a bottle of water and a cheese sandwich – all the corner shop had left at this time of evening.

She sniffed the bread longingly, then removed the cheese from inside and ate that instead, wiping the slices on the wall so they wouldn't tempt her anymore. She threw them out of the tomb then lay down in the dirt and began to do push-ups.

The sparrow looked warily at the discarded bread, too close to the mouth of the tomb for comfort, yet white and inviting in the darkness. It darted down and landed a few feet from the grubby triangles, then hopped towards the feast, stopping every few seconds to scan the surrounding area.

Daisy heard a squawk over the sound of her own laboured breathing. She edged along the wall of the tomb and stepped outside, penknife held defensively in front of her.

There was nobody there.

The girl looked down and clasped a hand to her mouth. She staggered backwards into the tomb and the penknife fell from her fingers, swallowed up by the darkness.

The bird writhed on the grass next to the entrance, body jerking spasmodically, until it lay still.

From the Journal of Donny Marigold

My name is Donny Marigold and I see dead people. It's a bit of a curse, really.

Take my uncle Eddie. He always claimed his wife ran off with an insurance salesman. But I could see her standing at the kitchen sink, sleeves rolled up and a screwdriver sticking out of her back.

Made Sunday lunch an awkward experience, especially when it was my turn to wash up.

Uncle Eddie drank a lot and used to look uneasily in that direction, so I wondered if seeing ghosts ran in the family.

But it was probably just the spot where he murdered her.

-2-

The ambulance shot up Candlemaker Row, passed the entrance to Greyfriars Graveyard and veered onto Forrest Road, siren wailing. In the back, Chloe Springall bent over a little girl, holding an oxygen mask to the child's waxy face.

"We must be nearly there, honey." The paramedic tried to keep the panic out of her voice. "You try to be calm, eh, Valerie? You've had bad asthma attacks before, so your mum says. That means you know what you have to do. Just keep breathing nice and slow."

Valerie's mother sat rigid on the bench opposite, face ashen, clutching an overnight bag. Her lips worked in silent prayer as if they were the only part of her that dared move. The ambulance rounded another corner, throwing Chloe backwards onto the woman's lap. Valerie gave a choking gasp and her body convulsed.

"What's taking so long, dammit?" The paramedic slammed a hand flat against the partition separating her from the cab. She whirled and crouched over the girl.

"Don't do this, honey! You can make it!" She put two hands on Valerie's chest and began to pump up and down. The girl's mother turned her head away, tears running down her cheeks Chloe tore off the oxygen mask and clamped her mouth over the girl's blue lips. Then back to the little chest, pushing with all her strength.

"Come on, sweetie. Stay with me, Valerie! Stay with me!"

The ambulance slewed to a halt and the siren bleeped once and went dead. Chloe heard the driver leap from the cab and run around the side of the vehicle. The back doors flew open and he jumped over the descending ramp as Chloe pulled frantically at the straps holding the wheeled stretcher in place.

"I radioed ahead and there's a resuscitation unit standing by in Accident and Emergency," the driver panted, helping to free the last fastening. "Let's get you in there, darling."

He and Chloe hauled the trolley down the ramp and into the hospital car park. The paramedic stopped and looked up in confusion.

Around them, the Victorian spires and worn stone carapaces of Edinburgh Royal Infirmary were barely visible outlines, silhouetted by streetlamps from the road outside. There were no lights in any of the windows and no glass in most of them.

"What are you waiting for?" the driver cried, trying to wrestle the trolley from Chloe's grasp. "Let's get her inside!"

"This is the *old* infirmary, Billy!" Chloe shoved him away from the motionless girl. "It's been shut for months. You know that, you bastard! You *know* that!"

She began to thump Valerie's chest again, wincing as she heard a rib give way. The driver stepped back, biting his lip.

The child's mother weaved down the ramp, her face crumpling as she saw abandoned buildings on every side. With an animal cry, she ran at the driver - but her legs gave way before reaching him. The woman crawled towards her daughter and clung to the trolley, stroking the girl's limp hand.

Chloe straightened up, walked over to her companion and struck him across the face.

"Her name was Valerie Darroch," she spat, pointing to the dead girl. "And you just killed her."

The ambulance driver stared across the street. A light wind whispered through the trees poking over the wall of Greyfriars Graveyard, ruffling their leafy tops. He could smell the scent of wet grass mingling with the musty odour emanating from the deserted buildings.

"I've done the new hospital run a hundred times," he stammered, touching the red weal rising on his cheek. For the first time, he seemed to be properly aware of his surroundings.

"Why the fuck did I come *here*?"

From the Journal of Donny Marigold

I suppose I should mention that I can talk to the dead as well, though it can be a trying experience.

I met one guy, for instance, who must have been beheaded and another whose lower jaw was missing. Obviously, I didn't get much of a conversation out of those two. And the chip shop on the High Street has a ghost who shouts a lot in Italian. I thought about buying a phrase book but he waves a garden trowel at me and keeps sticking his head in the fat fryer. He's obviously a mad bastard and I swear it makes the chips taste funny.

It's not that the dead can't learn. There's a Spanish aristocrat up on Salisbury Crags who speaks perfect English. He told me he's had three centuries to learn and can say 'Keep away from the ledge, honey' in fourteen languages. But lots of ghosts repeat the same actions and hardly seem to know I'm there.

Shame really. You'd think the one advantage of being dead is not being tied down. You could go haunt someplace nice like the French Riviera. But ghosts don't tend to stray far from the area they expired and, what's more, they can't seem explain why.

That's why I like Greyfriars Graveyard. It's always had a haunted reputation but I can tell you, for a fact, it doesn't have any spirits. I mean, who actually dies in a cemetery?

Then City of the Dead started their nightly horror walk into Greyfriars and began telling their customers how spooky the place was. All rubbish, of course. But, to my everlasting regret, I ended up joining them.

Then, God help me, I roped in Daisy Lenin too.

And, together, we unleashed hell.

-3-

Donny Marigold was sitting on a bench just inside the cemetery, puffing on a cigarette to keep the night bugs away, the first time he saw a City of the Dead ghost walk.

A small party of tourists entered the main gates, led by a man in a denim jacket and gleaming white trainers. Once he had ushered the group inside, the guide struck up a theatrical pose.

"This is Greyfriars Graveyard, highlight of the tour," he yelled. "And one of the most haunted places on earth! It was built to accommodate vast numbers of dead caused by... eh... the mad cow epidemic of 1635."

Donny's eyebrows went up. Something about that number niggled him more than the fact that the guide was spouting all kinds of nonsense. He stubbed out his cigarette and leaned forwards to listen properly.

"Greyfriars is the scene of many a dark deed." The guide waved vaguely to his left where a startled looking vagrant was raking through a bin. "Like the infamous Massacre of Benbooie, when a shinty match between the Campbells and McDonalds got out of hand after a ball ended up lodged in the goalkeeper's face."

An elderly American woman with a rucksack the size of a small boat raised her hand.

"And when was this?"

"1635."

"Same as the epidemic?"

"It was an eventful year."

This time, Donny laughed out loud. The guide carried on undeterred.

"The most haunted part of the Graveyard is the Covenanters Prison, lair of a dangerous entity called the Mackenzie Poltergeist, which attacks visitors to the cemetery. Now the City of Edinburgh Council keeps the prison locked day and night."

He fished a silver key from his pocket and held it reverently up.

"But we at City of the Dead Tours have obtained sole access!"

The American woman put her hand up again.

"How come the council gave you a key? If the poltergeist is so dangerous?"

"Because we paid 'em." The guide gave a wolfish grin. "This is Scotland, Madam. A true Scotsman will sell you the underpants right off his bum if you offer enough money. That's why we don't wear anything under our kilts."

"What happens if the poltergeist attacks one of *us*?"

"S'all right. The company has insurance."

The woman frowned and put her hand down.

"You could sue us, of course," the guide continued nonchalantly. "Stand up in court and say you were molested by a supernatural presence on a ghost tour. See how far *that* will get you."

There was a smattering of laughter among the group but Donny curled his lip in disbelief. As far as he was aware, the only attacks on visitors to the Covenanters Prison had been from drug addicts who hid at the back. *That's* why the gates were locked. Not that it deterred the junkies, who had simply moved to tombs in the opposite corner of the kirkyard.

The American woman waddled over and sat next to him. She was wearing a Day-Glo jacket that could have been seen from space.

"I think I'll miss out the supernatural part," she whispered. "I only came to see Bruce's grave.

"Robert the Bruce?"

"No, Lenny Bruce." She patted the teenager on the arm. "Of course, it's Robert the Bruce, silly. Don't you know your own history?"

"Enough to know Robert the Bruce's grave is in Dunfermline Abbey."

"Ah." The woman gave a knowing wink. "But the guide said he was secretly buried here after the battle of Stirling Bridge."

"Robert the Bruce wasn't *at* the battle of Stirling Bridge."

"Apparently, he just turned up late."

"You, young man! I sense you are an unbeliever!" The guide waved at Donny. "Would you like to come along and have your scepticism dumbfounded?"

"I suppose so."

"That'll be £8.50."

"I'll pass."

The guide shrugged and carried on in a booming voice. Donny had to admit he was a natural showman. But his historical stories were completely wrong and that gave the teenager an idea.

Eventually, the group moved off. The American woman patted her knees and shot Donny a motherly smile. Uncertain how to respond, he offered her a cigarette. The smile became more pained.

There was a rustling sound outside the graveyard entrance. The woman clutched Donny's arm as a dark figure in a long cloak and a hockey mask stumbled into view. It staggered towards them, tripped over the hem of its cloak and landed face down at their feet, giggling uncontrollably.

"Can I have a drag?" The figure rolled onto its back and reached out a thin white arm. Behind the mask, the muffled voice was soft and feminine.

"I take it you work for the tour?" The woman said disapprovingly, wafting away an overpowering smell of alcohol.

"Either that or I have a really weird-shaped head." The figure took the cigarette from Donny's outstretched hand and tried to push the white vial through the nose slit. A shower of red sparks erupted from the tip.

"Sorry! Sorry!" The figure sat up, brushing frantically at the costume. It spat out the cigarette and pulled off the disguise, revealing a stunning blonde girl, only a couple of years older than Donny. Strands of hair stuck to her sweat-slicked forehead.

"Yeah, I work for the tour. My name's Constance Storm, by the way." The girl retrieved the bent cigarette and placed it none too certainly in her mouth. "It's my turn to be the jumper outer. I sit in the pub until the tour gets here. Run across the graveyard. Shout *Boo*! They go nuts. I get a tenner."

The girl gave a volcanic hiccup.

"That works out at about £7,000 an hour."

"How long you been in the bar?" the American woman tisked.

"Since three o'clock this afternoon."

Donny and the American exchanged glances.

"Listen. I'm a tad unsteady on my feet. Can you jump out instead?" Constance looked up pleadingly. "Otherwise, my boss is going to kill me."

"I'm too old for that, I'm afraid." The woman replied regretfully.

"I was talking to the kid. My eyes are a bit unfocussed."

She began to struggle out of the cloak and promptly toppled over again.

"It's easy. Go on! I'll split the money with you. Just leap out when the guide gives the cue word, then yell and run away."

"Sounds simple enough," Donny agreed.

Constance's mouth turned down at the corners, her trembling lip prompting another shower of sparks.

"I don't even smoke," she complained, throwing away the cigarette. "But doing this freaks me out. Somebody got such a fright last week they threw a Chihuahua at me."

"A Chihuahua?"

"All right, it might have been a handbag. I can't see a bloody thing with that mask on." She finally got out of the costume and handed it to Donny.

"This is no job for a delicate girl like myself. What if someone over-reacts and hacks me to death with a machete?"

"It's a bunch of tourists," the American woman said. "Not a Columbian death squad."

"What? You think *they* don't take holidays?"

"I'll do it." Donny got up and put on the cloak. "What's the cue word?"

"1635."

"There's a shock."

He set off across the graveyard, pulling on the mask. Constance wasn't kidding. The eyeholes narrowed his vision to two pinpoints that wobbled as he walked.

"Jeez," he gasped. "This thing stinks like a pub carpet on Sunday morning."

By now the tour party were inside a large mausoleum in the Covenanters Prison. The teenager edged up to the entrance and listened for the cue, trying to keep his breathing muted as possible.

He needn't have worried. The guide was in full flow, giving a manic performance and ratcheting up the tension. From the sound of it, he was just inside the doorway, which meant the tour group must be standing at the back. Good. Donny didn't much fancy getting a punch in the mouth when he leapt in.

"The Mackenzie Poltergeist is a vicious and unpredictable entity," the guide rasped. "And this mausoleum is where it seems to live. You don't see it but you certainly feel its effects. It will hit or scratch or bite people. Even knock them out." He gave a heartfelt sigh. "I wouldn't be here myself if I could get a proper job. I'm doing a degree in biology at the Open University."

There wasn't a peep from the group. They had been herded into a pitch-black mausoleum in a locked section of a supposedly haunted graveyard - and the only flashlight was in the possession of a tour leader who seemed on the verge of crazy. Donny could understand their fear.

That gave him an idea. The guide was expecting him to jump out on a pre-arranged signal. What if he came in at the wrong moment?

A slow smile spread across the boy's face.

"I've seen things you would not believe," the voice continued. "I remember a time when two Australians were standing at the back. Just where you are, madam."

There was a squeak of fear and a shuffling sound as the woman quickly moved.

"One of them had just gotten out his camera and...."

Donny leapt into the tomb, arms spread, screaming at the top of his lungs.

"JESUSCHRISTALMIGHTY!" The guide flew backwards, hands thrown across his face, colliding with a group of women crammed into one corner. The torch soared into the air, hit the wall and went out.

Donny scuttled out of the tomb while pandemonium erupted. He could hear screaming tourists slapping at each other in a desperate bid to escape their pitch-black confinement.

Grinning from ear to ear, the teenager ran back the way he had come, as the party burst through the doorway and collapsed on the grass outside. Some were sobbing, others laughing uncontrollably, each dealing with an enormous surge of adrenalin in their own way.

After saying goodbye to the shaken party, the guide marched across to the bench. Constance was lying on her side, head in the American woman's lap. Donny sat next to them, trying to look innocent.

"What the hell was that?" the man spluttered. "I almost had a heart attack!"

"Shhhh." The American stroked Constance's hair gently. "You'll wake her."

"It was me." Donny held out the cloak, neatly folded with the mask on top. "Sorry if I gave you a fright."

A man and woman who had been on the tour nervously approached the bench.

"That was off the charts!" The couple shook the guide's hand. "I mean, the stories were cheesy as hell, but what an ending! Scared the pants off me."

"Feel free to go back and look for 'em. I did promise you all a fright, though, eh?"

"So how did you do it?" The man began removing his thick woollen coat.

"Wasn't me." The guide jerked a thumb in Donny's direction. "It was the kid."

"How did *you* do it?" the man repeated.

"Eh… I just jumped in and shouted." Donny looked puzzled.

"I mean, how did you do *this*?" He dropped the jacket and rolled up his sleeve. "I have two layers of clothing on."

Donny's eyes widened.

There was a huge purple welt on the man's skin in the shape of a hand.

From the Journal of Donny Marigold

I figured this was the point to make my pitch. The American woman had left and we'd laid Constance out on the bench to make her more comfortable. Not that she would have noticed. She was snoring like a hog.

"My name's Deek." The guide accepted the cigarette I offered him. "Nice bit of covering just then. You did a good job."

He took a tenner from his pocket and handed it to me.

"Only fair you get paid."

"Thanks," I said. "But I'm from around this area and I've never heard of any Mackenzie Poltergeist."

"Aye, but that lot were all tourists," Deek replied dismissively. "You can tell tourists pretty much anything and they'll believe it."

"I can see ghosts." I ventured.

"Well... anything except that."

"I could give you some proper stories about Edinburgh's past," I persisted. "Really cool stories nobody else knows."

"No offence pal," Deek scoffed. "You look a bit young to be a historian."

I ignored the fact that, like Constance, he didn't seem much older than me. Besides, what could I say? I doubt he'd believe I got my knowledge from dead people who had actually seen the events.

"Knock yourself out, though." Deek dipped into his pocket again and pulled out a business card. "That's my boss's details."

I sent an email with some sample stories and got a reply the next day.

I don't suppose you'd like a job as a jumper outer? Heard you had quite an effect. And the historical stuff you sent is good too. I'll give you fifty quid for it. Got any more?

- Ben Scott. Big Giant Head. City of the Dead Tours.

I was in.

What I didn't realise, at the time, is just how powerful stories can be.

Especially if they're taken the wrong way.

-4-

Myrtle Gibbs felt a little tipsy as she climbed the stairs to her top-floor flat.

All right, she admitted to herself. *I'm completely off my face.*

Every time the girl reached the top of a flight she teetered on the edge and had to clutch at the banister to keep from tumbling back down. Every time the action brought on a fit of giggles and she stopped and leaned against the wall.

When she was drunk, Myrtle was easily amused.

"This is Myrtle Gibbs coming up the stairs," she whispered loudly to herself. "Wondering if she can get in the flat without killing herself or waking everyone in the building."

On the top landing, she dropped her keys and banged her head on the door trying to pick them up.

"I'll be blaming my hangover on that tomorrow." She finally inserted the key in the lock by using both hands and her teeth. "If I remember it happening..."

The door opened and Myrtle sprawled face down in the hallway. She lay for a while, chuckling to herself, until the dust made it too difficult to breathe.

Zig-zagging to her room, she collapsed on the bed and struggled out of her clubbing gear, a task that took on marathon proportions, since everything she wore was skin tight. Myrtle put on her favourite slippers, large furry feet with claws at the tips - then stumbled, still naked, into the bathroom to clean her teeth. She wasn't too concerned about meeting anyone. All her flatmates were female and, if they hadn't emerged from their rooms by now, were obviously out for the count.

"Rawr, rawr, rawr." She clomped back to her room doing a monster walk, a ring of toothpaste smeared round her mouth.

Nobody woke. Shame, really. She'd had a great night and wanted someone to talk at.

She switched off the wall light using one breast, just to see if she could do it. She was feeling her way to her bed when she heard a faint noise at the window.

Myrtle burped loudly. Damned pigeons. Why couldn't they perch on the first floor where there were nice flower boxes to poop in?

She lurched over to the window and pulled open the curtains.

A pair of wings were drawn in condensation on the dark pane.

"Myrtle Gibbs is well puzzled by this strange turn of events." She tried to wipe away the outline but her fingers encountered only smooth glass.

The wings were on the *outside*.

Myrtle tried to focus properly. How was that possible? She pressed her face against the window and squinted into the blackness. She could just make out a crosshatching of vertical and horizontal tubes a couple of feet away.

Scaffolding.

Of course. She recalled workmen arriving that morning to erect the damned thing. No doubt they'd be back at eight tomorrow, waking her up with their banging and clattering.

"That sucks," she hiccupped. "A long lie is one of the fundamental human rights."

There was a movement to her left and an object slammed into the window, the whole pane buckling against her squashed nose.

Myrtle shot back, collided with the bedside table and landed on her butt. She caught sight of manic eyes and a spittle-flecked mouth, open in a silent yell. Thick gloved fingers pawed at the window pointing to the wings. Then they reached down and tugged at the latch.

The girl slid backwards, friction from the carpet burning her skin, heels drumming on the floor as they fought to get purchase. Myrtle tried to scream but her throat had constricted so much that only a strangled string of gasps emerged.

The window slid up and the intruder flopped onto the carpet, a large man with ginger hair. He crawled towards her, reaching out one hand.

"I follow you in the graveyard," he said, head tilted to one side. "You're a dark angel. An angel showing people a doorway to another life."

The woman scuttled through the open bedroom door and slammed it shut with her foot. When her screams finally emerged, they brought flatmates pouring into the hallway. Myrtle lay curled in a ball, on the hall floor, wailing uncontrollably.

Her room was empty, window wide open.

The stranger had fled the way he had come.

A week later, Myrtle Gibbs quit her job as a City of the Dead guide, put her belongings in a taxi and moved back to Livingston.

Her flatmates never saw her again.

From the Journal of Donny Marigold

The graves are so crowded on each other that the sextons frequently cannot avoid in opening a ripe grave encroaching on one not fit to be touched. The whole presents a scene equally nauseous and unwholesome. How soon this spot will be so surcharged with animal juices and oils, that, becoming one mass of corruption, its noxious steams will burst forth with the prey of a pestilence, we shall not pretend to determine.

Hugo Arnot *A History of Edinburgh (1779).*

I figured if I was going to write stories with the tours, I'd better start looking into the history of the place.

Greyfriars Graveyard was founded in 1562, by Mary Queen of Scots, on the grounds of a former orchard. In the daytime, it's really pretty, if you ignore the gravestones and neds drinking meths at the bottom.

(Note: For anyone English, 'ned' is a Scottish term for Non-Educated Delinquent. Think chav, but with less style and more aggression).

Greyfriars was one of the few burial sites in Edinburgh and it was common practise to inter the dead without headstones. Overcrowding, horrific living conditions and daily violence guaranteed the cemetery a continual torrent of bodies. Give them all tombstones and, within a short space of time, nobody would have been able to see the grass.

The cemetery contains approximately 700 headstones but it is estimated that around 450,000 people are buried under this tiny patch of land.

Greyfriars is simply a mountain of bodies.

During the great plague of 1568, thousands of diseased corpses were flung into a huge pit in the cemetery and covered over. 1661 to 1668 saw the interment of hundreds of executed Covenanters. For centuries the body parts of hanged criminals were displayed on spikes at the bottom end, before ending up in unmarked graves.

Nice.

In December 1879, the city authorities gathered together several tons of human skeletons that had been excavated from St Giles' graveyard and dumped them in Greyfriars as well.

Just another statistic, I thought.

I had no idea, at the time, how vital that fact would become.

Since the highlight of the walk was the Covenanters Prison, it seemed like a logical place to research first.

The Covenanters were Scottish Presbyterian Protestants who became convinced they were God's 'Chosen People'. When King Charles I of Britain tried to impose religious reform on Scotland, the Presbyterians feared their monarch was trying to bring about the sneaky return of Catholicism to Scotland. And they weren't having that.

In 1638 hundreds of them signed the 'National Covenant' on a flat tombstone in Greyfriars Graveyard, then rose up in revolt. So many signed with their own blood that their makeshift table was said to resemble a sacrificial altar.

The Covenanter revolt sparked off the English Civil war and led to the execution of Charles I by Oliver Cromwell. But the movement was doomed to failure. Charles II became king of Britain and was understandably pissed off that the Scots had helped kill his dad. He crushed the Covenanter armies and the defeated survivors and their families were imprisoned within the high walls of Greyfriars – an area now known as the Covenanters Prison. They had no shelter, little food and most of them perished.

It was, in effect, the world's first concentration camp.

The remaining Covenanters were ruthlessly persecuted by the King's Advocate - Sir George Mackenzie, ironically, buried in Greyfriars. According to legend, he has haunted the graveyard ever since, unable to rest in peace after the atrocities he committed.

Really? I'd *never seen him.*

-5-

Daisy Lenin had been job hunting for days. But she was only fifteen, abrupt and uneasy around people, and her clothes were grubby from sleeping rough. What's more, she seemed to have acquired a mysterious red blemish on her face in the shape of a handprint, making it look like she'd been given a beating.

The teenager tried staying in a nearby homeless shelter but the place smelled of urine and the other residents were a cadaverous, bedraggled pack with blank, pasty faces and shambling gaits. Besides, she could tell the staff suspected she was a runaway.

Daisy couldn't take the chance of being caught by the police and sent home. She had no choice but to stay in the Covenanters Prison, no matter how terrifying she found it.

In the daytime, however, Greyfriars looked altogether different. Spring detonated sweet-smelling blossoms in the trees and suited businessmen ate lunch in the grass, unwrapping their sandwiches on improvised tabletops of flat tombstones.

Daisy sat near the cemetery entrance, back against a marble marker, demolishing a can of coke and a tuna salad. She had also spent precious money from her dwindling wad of notes on a cheap paperback romance, in a futile attempt to keep her mind busy. But she was a painfully slow reader and found the book hard going.

The girl was still trying to lose herself in a world of bodice ripping and heaving bosoms when a shadow fell across the pages.

Daisy looked up and frowned.

A figure was standing in front of her, hands in both pockets. The sun was directly behind the stranger, turning him into a mere outline, though the posture and shape were definitely male.

Daisy turned back to her book, hoping the intruder would go away, suddenly aware of how unpresentable she looked. The stranger moved behind her, forcing Daisy to shuffle round and squint at him.

It was a teenager, dressed entirely in black. Black leather jacket, black jeans, black T-shirt, black boots – as if he were a shadow himself. Even his shoulder-length hair was ebony, spilling across his forehead like an oil slick. He looked vaguely familiar, Daisy thought.

"What are you reading?" he asked.

"I wanted to buy the Financial Times." The girl clutched the romance to her chest, embarrassed by her choice of material. "But the pages would have blown away."

The teenager gave a bark of laughter, so short that it was almost devoid of humour.

"My name's Donny Marigold," he said. "Know whose grave you're sitting on?"

"No. I'm sure he doesn't care, though."

"John Grey." The boy ignored her comment, not certain if it was sarcasm or genuine. "He was a policeman who owned a dog called Bobby. When he died, the pooch sat on his grave every night for fourteen years until its own death. Dog's famous now. Greyfriars Bobby. There was a bestselling book and Disney film about him."

"Thank you for the information." Daisy opened the novel again in an effort to end the one-sided conversation.

"Course, there was a pie shop around the corner where the owner used to feed Bobby. Plus, lots of bones in the graveyard." The boy crouched down, angling his head to get a better look at the paperback. "And the poor wee dog had to sleep *somewhere*. What was he going to do? Emigrate to Florida?"

"I'm trying to read."

"All I'm saying is there's two sides to every tale." The teenager looked discouraged and, for a second, Daisy considered putting the book down and talking to him. But, although she was desperately lonely, she was wary of any contact with others, especially after her experience in the hostel. Half a dozen residents had sidled up to her and muttered boozy, glue tainted ramblings that passed as explanations for their tattered lives. She resented the way another complete stranger had foisted himself on her.

Besides, she looked a mess. She had to use public toilets to wash and clean up and the results were far from satisfactory. And the handprint, though fading, was still obvious.

"Let me show you something." Donny Marigold motioned for Daisy to give him the novel.

"What?"

"It's a trick." He kept his hand out. "It's good."

Daisy closed the paperback once more and handed it over. The teenager balanced it on one knee and reached into his jacket. He withdrew his hand, fingers and thumb clenched as if he were holding a writing instrument.

"This… is a ghost pen."

"You're strange."

"A common reaction. You can't see the pen, of course, but I can because I can see ghosts."

"I'm going to call my mum and dad if you don't leave me alone." Daisy pulled a mobile from her pocket. She hoped the threat would be enough to drive the teenager away because she had no credit left. Nobody to ask for help, either.

"Fair enough." Donny gave another short burst of laughter and clicked the top of his imaginary pen. "I'll be off. But let me just write something first."

He placed his fingers on the front of the book and moved them up and down.

"Here you go." He handed it back with a flourish. Daisy looked at the cover out of instinct but, of course, there was nothing written there.

"When I'm gone, have a look at page ninety-seven. Ninety-seven is my lucky number."

"You said you were going away." Daisy dropped the novel on the ground and stared into the distance.

"I did." Donny gave her a half smile and got to his feet. "But it was nice meeting you."

He stuck his hands in his pockets again and walked off.

Daisy watched him leave, then went back to her paperback. On impulse, she turned to page ninety-seven.

Scrawled across the top in red pen was a message.

Meet me in the graveyard tonight at 8.00pm. I'll show you a way out of the situation you're in.

Daisy's head shot up, a chill running down her spine.

But Donny Marigold was gone.

From the Journal of Donny Marigold

I had a stroll around the graveyard, sketching out a map of the place. I knew it well enough but wanted to get the layout down on paper.

Greyfriars Church was slap bang in the middle of the graveyard. It meant you could follow a tour for a while, then go round the building and get ahead of it without anyone seeing you. As well as the normal headstones, there were quite a few larger monuments scattered around, the last resting places of those who could afford a more impressive marker than the mere plebs. They also happened to be perfect for hiding behind.

The north end, at the bottom of the hill, was the bit to avoid. Some of the enclosed tombs had broken padlocks and the interiors were littered with bottles and cans. That meant they were being used by junkies and assorted ne'er-do-wells. A little further on was a walled section where the council had dug a pit to repair the sewage and drainage system for buildings in the Cowgate. Not a job I would have fancied, as they must have come across dozens of decomposing bodies from years past. The evidence for that was right in front of me. Against the wall of the cemetery, several cheap coffins, now empty, were piled haphazardly on top of each other - too rotten even to be worth stealing for scrap.

The workers were obviously none too happy with their lot. Though they had finished essential repairs, the area was in an utter state. The cavernous fissure was still there, with mounds of excavated loose earth piled on either side.

Fortunately, the guides stuck to the west of the graveyard until they reached the Covenanters Prison at the end.

I clambered onto a mound, pulled a carrier bag from my pocket and begin to pick out stones. Nothing too big. None that were sharp. I whistled the theme from Peter and the Wolf *as I worked until I had filled the plastic sack.*

"I can come back and do this every day," I chuckled. "Knowing the speed Edinburgh Council work, they won't get around to filling the hole until Christmas. Five years from now."

I'd figured out exactly how to help Daisy Lenin and I was feeling pretty damned pleased with myself about it. Too pleased to pay attention to where I was going, so the soil gave way and I fell and gashed my hand.

-6-

Donny Marigold and Daisy Lenin sat on a bench just inside the graveyard under a star-peppered sky. Daisy hunched over until she appeared almost folded, hands hidden inside her jacket sleeves. Donny lounged back, arms behind his head and legs outstretched. A cigarette dangled from his lips.

"What's the matter with your knees?" Daisy glanced sideways at her companion. "They don't bend?"

"I was trying to look relaxed." Donny sat up quickly. "I'm not used to talking to strange girls, I suppose."

"I'm strange?"

"Well, you *are* staying in a tomb in the Covenanters Prison."

"How do you know that?" Daisy shrank away from the boy.

"A little bird told me."

"How did you do that thing with the book? That's the reason I came. I wanted to know."

"Like I said. It's a trick."

"Oh." Daisy's eyes dropped to her lap. "I don't like tricks."

They sat silently for a while longer.

"I don't like talking to strangers either," the girl muttered.

"You know my name. Donny Marigold." The boy leaned forwards, pulled a hard-backed book from the rucksack between his legs and handed it to her. "I got you something else to read in case you finished your paperback."

Daisy took it and looked at the cover.

Record of Interments in Greyfriars Kirkyard 1650 – 1700.

She opened the book. Inside was list after list of the names and occupations of long-forgotten people buried in the graveyard. Each had a date alongside. Donny watched as Daisy scanned each page, not simply flicking through, but reading the entries properly.

"I like this," she said quietly, without raising her head.

A small group of tourists entered the graveyard led by their guide. He spotted the couple and gave a wave.

"Evening, Donny."

"How's it going, Deek?"

Daisy looked up briefly as the guide began his story.

"Welcome to Greyfriars Graveyard, Ladies and Gentleman. One of the most haunted places on earth."

Donny gave a small smile.

"Every inch of this cemetery is filled with history," Deek continued pointing to a dark window in one of the tenements. "That flat, for instance, was occupied for several months in the 1930s by the author T. S. Eliot. Looking out over the many cats prowling round the cemetery he came up with the idea of writing a book of poetry about them. The result was the collection *Old Possum's Book of Practical Cats* – which was eventually turned into the musical *Cats*. If you don't think that's scary, you've obviously never seen it."

Donny nodded appreciatively.

"Not that we see many moggies in the place these days," Deek continued in a stage whisper that could have been heard as far away as Glasgow. "Recently, s*omething* seems to have scared them all away."

Donny nudged Daisy.

"I wrote that," he said proudly. "Got it off Wikipedia, so it's probably shit. But I've started doing proper research too."

"You work for them?"

"Sort of."

"Is that how you know I'm living in the Covenanters Prison?" Daisy reluctantly shut the book. "The tours replaced the padlock I sawed through, so I've moved to an open tomb at the very bottom. I stay inside and keep out of their way."

"They know you're there. You'll get thrown out eventually." Donny watched the guide lead his party towards the prison. "Unless I can do something about that."

"Like what?"

"It's pretty dark now." Donny bent and fished in his bag again, bringing out a scrap of paper. He switched on a tiny flashlight and gave the sheet to her. She noticed one hand was bandaged.

"This is a map of Greyfriars. So you can find your way around?"

"I live here," Daisy answered flatly. "I already know my way around."

"Of course." He tipped the bag upside down and several pebbles fell out. "Which means you'll be able to get close to Deek's tour party without being seen."

"Why would I want to do that?"

"So you can throw these."

Daisy crouched behind a tombstone, clutching the missiles. The group had their back to her, listening intently to the guide. She remembered Donny's instructions.

No heads or faces. Aim for the same place every time. Right between the shoulder blades.

Daisy stood and launched the first stone. It was too dark to make out individuals properly, so she concentrated on their whispers. The missile hit a large man square in the back. Daisy ducked down, heart hammering, as he turned on the rest of the group.

"Someone punched me! Was that you?"

There was a chorus of denials.

The girl waited until the hubbub had died down, stood quickly and threw another pebble.

"What the hell?" A woman's voice this time. "Something hit my shoulder!"

Daisy curled into a ball, making herself as small as possible. A slow smile spread across her face. Deek moved further away, taking the group with him, and began another story.

Daisy peeked above the headstone. The tour was one massive shadow and even if she stopped hiding, she doubted they'd be able to see her anymore. The girl would just be another blob in the pool of ink filling the cemetery.

Deek was talking loudly and she could barely hear the subdued whisperings of his party. She stood up, closed her eyes and concentrated, tuning out the thundering voice – listening intently to the barely perceived sibilance of the group. In her hand, she felt the weight of the pebble. In her mind, she calculated the distance and angle of trajectory to just below the source of the sound. Eyes still closed, she launched the stone.

"Goddamn it!" The new voice was genuinely frightened. "Something got me too!"

This time a few of the tour party broke ranks, peering behind the nearest headstones for signs of an assailant. But Daisy was too far away and most of the group were reluctant to stray far from the guide.

One man, braver than the others, ventured off on his own. Invisible in the murk, only the crunch of twigs underfoot betrayed his movements.

"I know you're hiding out here, buddy." he threatened loudly in an American accent. "You're gonna be sorry when I find you."

Daisy honed in on the voice, eyes still closed. She threw the stone as high and powerfully as her thin arms would allow.

"It got me," the voice screamed, suddenly far less belligerent. "Something slapped me in the chest! What's going on?"

"I told you the Mackenzie Poltergeist was real." Even Deek sounded afraid, though Daisy couldn't tell if it was just for show. "It's trying to keep you out of the prison because that's where it lives."

Taking a deep breath, he composed himself. "But I'm going to take you in there, anyway."

He led the silent group into the Covenanter's Prison.

Daisy ran back to where Donny was sitting on the bench, smoking another cigarette. He had put on a black cloak in preparation for jumping out. Daisy thought he looked a bit like the Grim Reaper but with a nicer complexion.

"I didn't know I could throw like that." She collapsed onto the seat and a frown crossed her face.

"How did *you* know I could throw like that?"

"I know lots of things, Daisy." Donny took a long drag and exhaled through a grin. "And I think you're safe for a while."

"What do you mean?"

"I'm going to have a word with my boss." The boy picked up the book and handed it back to his companion.

"After that demonstration, I'm pretty sure he'll hire you too."

Hours later, in her sleeping bag in the mausoleum, Daisy suddenly sat up.

Earlier that night, Donny Marigold called her by her first name.

Yet she was positive she hadn't told him what it was.

-Part 2-

City of the Dead

There are few more impressive sights than a Scotsman on the make.

J M Barrie

Take care, lest an adventure is now offered you, which, if accepted, will plunge you in deepest woe.

J. M. Barrie. *Peter Pan*

From the Journal of Donny Marigold

I was getting quite into the history of Greyfriars.

It's in the heart of the Old Town and, in the late 17ᵗʰ century, a whole host of publications appeared painting the area as the capital of weird. Pandæmonium, or the Devil's Cloister Opened. *By Richard Bovet (1683);* Satan's Invisible World D *by George Sinclair (1685) and* The Kingdom of Darkness *by Nathaniel Crouch to name a few.*

One of the most famous stories was that of Major Thomas Weir, a signatory of the National Covenant, who took up residence opposite Greyfriars Graveyard. There, his religious fanaticism reached truly ridiculous levels and he became a fire and brimstone preacher known as Angelical Thomas, *a nickname practically guaranteed to stop him getting girls.*

In 1670, Weir made an astonishing confession. He claimed to have been secretly in league with the Devil and insisted he had met Satan on several occasions.

I wondered if he dressed up or if it was an informal thing?

Of course, nobody believed Weir until his sister Jean backed his claims. She confirmed seeing the Major with a horned monster and topped her confession off by accusing him of having committed incest with her since she was a child.

That did it for the citizens of Edinburgh. Jean Weir was publicly executed, in case being the victim of child abuse hadn't made her sorry enough. Thomas soon followed, the last man in Scotland to be burned for witchcraft.

The final bit of Weir's story puzzled me. All right, lots of people confessed to witchcraft in those days, but they were usually tortured until they did. And the kind of people picked for such treatment were social outcasts and dotty old women who tried to cure illnesses by shoving frogs' legs up peasant's noses.

Why would a religious zealot and self-professed pillar of the community voluntarily admit to being pals with Nasty Nick? Weir was an elderly man by this time and might have been losing his marbles - but his sister backed up the story, even though she must have known the consequences.

It just didn't make sense.

-7-

The City of the Dead staff meeting was in progress, held in Ben Scott's flat overlooking the graveyard. Cigarette smoke obscured the furniture like Victorian fog and wine bottles balanced on every available surface. The original guides - Lee, Deek and Constance - were sprawled in chairs, drinking furiously. Daisy and Donny sat on the floor, backs against the wall, both holding an untouched schooner of beer.

There was a clumping sound on the stairs outside and the last of the regular staff, Oss, burst into the room.

"Sorry I'm a wee bit tardy, guys," he panted, helping himself to a lager from the fridge. "I was getting a full body wax. Wanna see?"

He began unfastening his belt to a chorus of protests.

"Then my bus swerved off the road and hit a Kebab shop. Guess the driver didn't want to see either." He patted his stomach. "So I had a quick snack while I was waiting for him to calm down."

"You're only an hour late, hun." Lee beamed at him and raised her glass. "But I'll need another few bevvies before I can appreciate your super smooth nads."

"They look like Faberge eggs, doll."

"Maybe we should have *that* on the tour."

"Just what your mum said." Oss plonked himself down next to Deek and winked at Donny.

"How's it going, wee D?"

Donny nodded politely. Seeing them all together for the first time, he was struck by how young they all were. None of them looked older than their late teens.

"If I can finally get down to business?" Ben interrupted. There was a chorus of coughing and shuffling, mixed with shouts of "Boring!" and "Not drunk enough yet!"

"The good news is that the tours are finally taking off." Ben lit a cigarette and puffed out a cloud of smoke. "Mainly due to my superb leadership skills."

"Can we have a raise then, boss?" Constance was slumped in the corner, a glass of wine in each dainty hand.

"Please address me as Der Fuhrer." Ben picked up a sheet of notes. "Unfortunately, I consulted my horoscope and it told me you were all going to be killed by a runaway tram, so there's no point in giving you more money."

"How are the new staff doing?" Lee asked. "I take it they're on the tours tonight?"

"Two of them are. Myrtle Gibbs called and quit. Said her house had been broken into, so she was going back to Loch Snechie or wherever the fuck she came from."

The guides shrugged. They found Myrtle irritating anyway.

"How are the others getting on?" Lee persisted.

"Got no idea. Think I want to listen to an hour and a half of drivel out in the cold?"

Donny looked crestfallen.

"You rotter!" Lee spotted the boy's distress and raised her glass. "I propose a toast to Donny and Daisy."

The other guides followed suit.

"Yeah. It's his fantastic script and her pretending to be a poltergeist that's made all the difference."

"To Donny and Daisy." Ben nodded graciously. Donny flushed bright red and Daisy stared at the floor.

"And that brings me to item number two." Ben suddenly became serious. "What the hell are we going to do about Edinburgh Walking Tours?"

The rest muttered to each other. EWT were a large European company who hadn't taken kindly to the rise of a bunch of upstarts. In response, they had begun running free walks at the same time as City of the Dead, from virtually the same starting point. What's more, they had enough money to keep doing it until their smaller rivals went out of business.

"Any ideas?" Ben raised his pen expectantly.

"We could do our walks naked." Deek smiled pleasantly. "Oss could show off his shiny new knacks."

"We *do* want to scare the customers," Lee agreed.

"Aye. Well, have a think about it." Ben put down his pad with a sigh. "We've got sole access to the Covenanters Prison but people love free stuff and EWT have the cash to put advertising everywhere. Have you seen the size of the crowds they're pulling?"

"We could use that to our advantage," Donny broke in hesitantly.

All eyes turned on him.

"At the start of the tour, there's at least ten minutes when City of the Dead and EWT are in the same place, with both guides touting for trade."

"Go on."

"That means we have ten whole minutes to convince that huge crowd on the Edinburgh Walking Tour they'd rather come with us, even if they have to pay."

"Donny's right." Constance slurred. "We have better stories, thanks to him. And we're smarter, funnier and prettier than they are."

She lifted both glasses to her mouth and paused, unsure of which to drink first.

"Well, I am."

"Yeah. I'd pay to see *you* do the tour naked," Oss leered, clinking glasses with Deek. "You as well, Lee," he added diplomatically.

"We can fight dirty too." Donny gave a sly grin. "Make EWT look rubbish, so even more of their customers will come with us."

"And how do we do that?"

"I have a few ideas."

"Like it." Ben tapped the pen against his teeth. "We start stealing enough of their punters and they'll stop going head to head. Especially if all they're achieving is collecting a huge bunch of people for you chancers to poach."

"We're gonna kill 'em," Deek enthused. "We'll teach them to mess with the Dead."

"You should kit us out properly. I'd like a pink Chanel suit." Having made her pitch, Constance's head slumped and Deek caught both glasses before they dropped from her hands.

Ben glanced at Donny, dressed entirely in black and looking appropriately sinister.

"Right! I want all your clothes sizes." He clapped his hands together. "I'm gonna buy you the sharpest gear I can find, just like this kid. Jet black T-shirts, jeans and boots. Plus full-length black leather coats and silver topped canes."

He pointed to each of them.

"Oss? Lose some weight. Lee? Start wearing makeup. Constance? Oh, you're asleep. Deek?"

Deek looked up expectantly.

"Nah." Ben shook his head. "I don't have enough to pay for plastic surgery. You'll have to get by on your personality."

"You said I didn't have one."

"You can borrow mine. I don't use it much." Ben rubbed his hands together gleefully. "Tomorrow we begin operation Kick the Living Shit out of the Enemy."

"Sweet. Can I have a code name?"

"Deek's your *real* name?" The tour boss went to the kitchen to fetch more booze.

"Point taken."

"I'm totally up for this." Oss high-fived Lee. "This is *our* graveyard and we rule in here."

"Got *that* right, hun."

There was a loud thumping noise from above, as if something incredibly heavy was running across the ceiling. The guides looked up, following the sound with their eyes.

As it reached the far wall, the vase of flowers on the mantelpiece exploded.

Shards of glass flew through the air, one piece nicking Oss's cheek. Water and petals fountained over Deek as he threw himself out of his chair. Lee let out a piercing shriek and Constance's head shot up, eyes filled with sleepy panic. Donny and Daisy grabbed each other's arms.

"What the hell are you guys playing at?" Ben stuck his head back into the room. "That vase was a present from my mother."

He tisked at the water spreading across the floor, studded with glittering glass and broken blooms.

"I know it's an ugly old thing, but so was mum."

"We didn't touch it." Lee stammered. "It just shattered."

"Yeah. Right."

"Nobody was near it, boss." Oss pressed a hand to his bleeding face. "I swear."

"There must have been a crack in it or something." Ben returned to the kitchen. "I'll get a bloody mop."

"I think I'd like to go to the pub," Lee whispered. "Suddenly, I'm feeling a bit freaked out."

"Give me a chance to clean this up then I'll come and join you." Ben reappeared with the mop. "Mine's a pint of Stella. Try not to blow it up."

Deek and Oss hauled Constance to her feet and frog-marched her to the door. Lee followed, swiping a couple of bottles on her way out.

"We'd better be off as well." Donny and Daisy got to their feet.

"Just a minute you two." Ben waved them back down.

"I have a little proposition I'd like to discuss."

From the Journal of Donny Marigold

The story of Greyfriars was getting more and more intriguing.

Within fifty years of the Covenanters being wiped out, Edinburgh's Old Town - especially the area surrounding Greyfriars - had undergone an inexplicable transformation. To the astonishment of the world and, presumably its own citizens, the capital changed from a religious backwater to the intellectual centre of Europe. Glasgow, on the other hand, took five centuries to invent Tikka Masala curry. By accident.

Edinburgh's leading lights met in taverns around the graveyard until the building of the 'New Town' in the late 18th century, when they all moved to the nice part of the city. Which is what you'd do if you were smart, I suppose.

A good example of these forward thinkers was David Hume. He was a Christian and a law student until an unknown 'revelation' inspired him to abandon his studies become an atheist and devote his time to just thinking. Nice work if you can get it.

He refused to reveal where this revelation came from but it led him to the verge of a nervous breakdown.

In 1738 he finished The Treatise of Human Nature, *now regarded as one of the most important philosophical works ever published. It was so far ahead of its time, critics called it 'unintelligible' and nobody paid any attention. It's about the nature of the self, free will and, oddly enough, miracles.*

One of David Hume's pals was an Edinburgh judge who lived near Greyfriars, James Burnett. In 1773 Burnett began a six-volume epic called On the Origin of Language. *In it he put forward the unheard of idea that man* evolved *rather than being put on earth by God. A hundred years before Charles Darwin, this theory was so far ahead of its time that nobody took it seriously and Burnett became famous in Edinburgh as a bit of a nutcase.*

He also happens to be buried in the Covenanters Prison.

Also interred in Greyfriars is the unfortunately named William Smellie, who lived just down the street. Between 1768 and 1771 he was the editor and main writer of that behemoth of knowledge, The Encyclopædia Britannica - *while his* Philosophy of Natural History *led to Smellie being described as a 'precursor of Darwin'.*

-8-

Once the others were gone, Ben helped himself to a huge glass of wine, then tilted the bottle in Donny and Daisy's direction. Both held up glasses of beer and shook their heads.

"That was really weird, Ben." Donny pointed upwards. "Before the vase exploded, there was a thumping sound from the roof like someone was moving across it. What's up there?"

"Another flat. But it's empty."

"Are you sure?"

"You'll see for yourself in a minute."

Donny and Daisy looked at each other. Ben sat down and lit a cigarette. He patted his pockets. Took a deep breath. Donny sipped his drink. Daisy put down her glass, still full and folded both hands on her lap. The tour boss tried a reassuring smile, but it turned into an uncertain grimace halfway through.

"Right, you two." He exhaled a worm of poisonous smoke. "What's the real story here?"

The teenagers regarded him blankly.

"You." He stabbed the cigarette towards Daisy. "What the hell are you doing living in a tomb in the Covenanters Prison?"

Daisy glanced away.

"It's cheap." Donny tried to deflect the question. "Got its own garden too. If you ignore the fact that there are loads of dead people underneath."

"Daisy." Ben held up his hand to silence Donny. "Me and my staff get on pretty well. But they have homes to go to. So I'll ask again. Why are you living in a tomb in the Covenanters Prison? You're a runaway, aren't you?"

Daisy stayed silent.

"I don't make judgements." Ben's tone was unexpectedly gentle. "Well… I do, but I've made plenty of bad decisions myself." His voice broke and he cleared his throat. "Donny vouched for you. Maybe he'll do the same for me."

"Ehmmm… I actually don't know you very well."

"I ran away from home when *I* was a kid." Ben tried again. "But after spending a couple of nights dossing on a school roof in Perth, I went home. I was lonely and I was freezing. And I was still at a bloody school."

Daisy gave a small smile.

"I'm not going to turn you in. But if you're going to keep working for me, I need to know the truth."

"You didn't give me the third degree when *I* got hired." Donny began.

"That's because you told me you were seventeen and had your own flat," Ben snapped. "Now I know it's a lie."

"How come?" Donny stammered.

"You're a sweet kid but you haven't offered Daisy your floor to sleep on. And it can't be because you live in some dump. Not when you're wearing a pair of £250 boots. What? Are you just pretending to look out for the girl?"

"I didn't," Donny protested. "I don't…"

"Yes. I'm a runaway." Daisy raised her head, though not far enough to look Ben in the eye. "And I won't go back. I can't."

"Fair enough." Ben turned his gaze on Donny. "And you? Going to man up and come clean?"

"I'm sixteen and I live with my dad." Donny took a gulp of his beer. "But he travels a lot, so I get to do what I want."

"Does that include skipping school? You seem to come and go whenever you please."

"I've got a private tutor. My dad doesn't believe in schools."

"I assure you they exist." Ben smiled. "Unlike my poltergeist."

He stared at the teenagers for a long time.

"That's why you two are essential to the company."

"You're not going to fire us?" Donny regarded his boss suspiciously.

"No way. You've made a deal with the Devil." Ben got to his feet and pulled up the Venetian blind. Outside they could just make out the squat outline of Greyfriars Church blocking the stars.

"You're a great storyteller and Daisy's doing such a good job of being the Mackenzie Poltergeist that we're going to increase her role."

Daisy gave a fine impression of a deer caught in headlights.

"As well as throwing stones, you can make noises in the graveyard. Set traps for the tourists." Ben waved his hand absently. "Whatever. We'll work out the details later."

He tapped the dark windowpane.

"We're well on our way to convincing the public we have a real supernatural entity trapped in the Covenanter's Prison. Sales are going through the roof."

He pulled the blind down with a hiss.

"And here's what I'll do for you in return."

He beckoned for the pair to follow him.

Ben's flat was in an 18th century building, with a spiral stone staircase winding down to the main entrance at street level on Candlemaker Row. But he led the teenagers up the stairs to a single door on the next landing, opened it, and ushered them inside.

"See. Completely empty."

They were standing in a large, sparsely decorated attic studio, with a rafter striped roof. There was a bed in one corner, a computer in the other and a kitchen attached. Ancient latticed windows of thick glass looked over Greyfriars, just like the flat below. There were a pair of binoculars perched on the sill and that gave Donny an idea. He filed it away for future use.

"I got this apartment for next to nothing," Ben said proudly. "The landlords were desperate because nobody who rented it ever stayed long."

He waggled his eyebrows.

"Maybe it's haunted."

"Maybe it's because the flat below has weirdos coming and going at all hours of the night." Donny retorted. "Probably thought they were living above a drug dealer."

"That would make it a pretty desirable property in my book." Ben wiped grime from the windowsill and sat down.

"I was supposed to turn this place into an office but I can't be bothered walking up the stairs." He shook his head in disbelief. "God, I must be more drunk than I thought, doing this."

He pulled a key from his pocket and held it up.

"It's yours if you want it, Daisy. Rent free. In return, you and Donny will keep working for me. And you'll both do anything I tell you, no questions asked."

Daisy looked around the room like a frightened animal inspecting a strange lair. She sat tentatively on the bed and finally smiled.

"I don't know what to say," she whispered.

"It was the guides' idea, not mine." Ben shrugged. "They don't want to come across you lying dead of hypothermia and your eyes pecked out by crows. Bunch of pussies." He lit another cigarette. "We could have blamed *that* on the poltergeist."

Daisy snickered.

"You're not scared of staying in a haunted flat?" Ben asked.

"Ben, she's living in a tomb at the moment." Donny plonked himself down at the computer. "This thing got internet?"

"It does. But I'm not paying you to surf porn."

"I can answer emails and design posters and leaflets and anything else that needs done. Your website could do with a serious upgrade too."

"Really? You could sort that?"

"I'm a fast learner. Just a knack I have."

"The benefits of having a home tutor, eh?"

"Brain the size of a planet and no friends whatsoever." The boy laughed. "I got all the time in the world."

"*I'm* your friend," Daisy said quietly and Donny blushed again.

"What about you, chatterbox?" Ben winked at the girl. "You in?"

"I could do your accounts," she suggested. "I'm very good with figures."

"Oh, sure," Ben replied amiably. "I'll just hand you the combination for my safe while I'm at it."

"You can trust me." Daisy looked crestfallen.

"Let's see how it goes, eh?"

"This is really good of you." Donny was already on the internet and tapping keys. "I could update the website regularly. Make up sightings."

"Jeez, I've created a two-headed monster." Ben leaned forwards, suddenly solemn.

"I don't intend to end up in trouble over this, understand?" His voice roughened. "I'll pay you in cash and if you get caught doing anything dodgy, you were acting without my knowledge. If the police come calling, you told me you were both seventeen and I believed it. That clear enough?"

The teenagers nodded.

"The guides will back me on this. They don't want to lose their livelihood, no matter how much they like you."

He sat back and laced his hands together.

"Do we have an agreement?"

Donny and Daisy looked at each other again.

"We have an agreement."

"Then go get your stuff out of that damned tomb. You'll be spending enough time in the graveyard as it is." Ben tossed the key across the room but the alcohol had impaired his aim and it bounced off the back of Donny's head. Daisy reached out and caught it without even looking.

"That was some move," Ben grinned.

"Ben?" Daisy said timidly.

"Yes, toots?"

"Someone might come looking for me." The girl bit her lip. "A terrible man."

If her boss was surprised, he didn't show it.

"Don't you worry about that," he replied evenly.

"No matter what he's like, he's never going to be as bad as me."

From the Journal of Donny Marigold

You seek for knowledge and wisdom, as I once did; and I ardently hope that the gratification of your wishes may not be a serpent to sting you, as mine has been.

Mary Shelley, *Frankenstein*

By the early 19th century, Edinburgh University Medical School, on the other side of the Graveyard wall, had become the finest in the world. The Anatomy department, for instance, led all other nations in its exploration of how the human body worked. That meant the anatomists needed corpses to practise on.

Greyfriars Graveyard was the hunting ground of the infamous 'Resurrection Men', who dug up newly buried bodies and sold them to the university. The Anatomy department had also become fascinated by the concept of 'Medical Electricity'. The idea that passing a charge through a corpse could be used to bring the dead back to life.

One of the graduates of Edinburgh Medical College was a young man named John Polidori. A few years later, Polidori found himself at a party in Geneva with the famous poets Lord Byron and Percy Shelley and got pally with Shelly's wife. As a drunken bet, all four came up with a macabre idea. They would each write a horror story for the others to read and see which was scariest.

Despite their fame as writers, Byron and Shelly's efforts are forgotten. Polidori, however, penned a short story called The Vampyr. *It was the first modern vampire tale and featured a dentally challenged aristocrat who became the main influence on Bram Stoker's* Dracula.

Shelly's wife, Mary, had obviously been listening carefully to Polidori's stories about his time next to Greyfriars. In 1818, she wrote a worldwide bestseller about a disinterred corpse, brought to life when a doctor passes electricity through it.

She called her novel Frankenstein.

It was as if Greyfriars had been the catalyst for two of the world's most famous horror stories. Actually, it was four, but I'll come to the others in a while.

I've always wanted to be a writer myself and the notion of starting another competition, to come up with scary tales, was a very cool one.

Unfortunately, it wasn't my idea and the person who suggested it had a very different agenda.

I didn't know at the time but it helped begin a chain of events that set us all on the road to destruction.

-9-

The enemy guide walked up the Royal Mile, hunched against a biting May wind and cursing to himself. A light rain was beginning to fall and he wasn't in the mood to spend an hour and a half in the cold, yelling at a bunch of unruly foreigners. The back of his yellow coat bore the logo **Edinburgh Walking Tours**.

Donny and Daisy hid in a narrow close until he passed.

"There goes fucking Big Bird," Donny chuckled. "Couldn't be a better target if he had a bull's eye pinned on his arse."

He reached into his pocket and gingerly pulled out a brown orb. At each end was a hole sealed with a tiny transparent blob.

Donny had spent the afternoon making a batch of bombs out of hens' eggs. With his mouth over one hole, he had carefully blown the yolk out of the other. He then used a syringe to replace the contents with a concoction made by Deek and sealed the punctures with superglue.

"Be careful with this," he warned Daisy. "You break it and nobody will come near us for a week."

"What's in here?" She regarded the fragile sphere with trepidation.

"Ammonium sulphate." Seeing his companion's alarm, he patted her shoulder. "Perfectly harmless, according to Deek. Just stinks to high heaven."

He tossed the egg casually into the air. Daisy, naturally, caught it without looking.

"Gotta go," the boy winked. "May the Gods of throwy stuff lend strength to your arm."

Daisy waited until the Edinburgh Walking Tour guide was almost out of range, stepped from the alleyway and let fly. Not waiting to see if her aim was true, she darted back down the close and ran as hard as she could, only stopping when she was two streets away.

The girl needn't have worried. The egg hit the EWT guide smack in the back of the head. He whirled round, hand reaching into his hair and coming away wet and sticky.

"Aw, God!" He sniffed his fingers to see what the offending liquid was and almost fell over. "That is fucking *horrible*!"

Two tour guides gathered their customers, like opposing armies, by advertising hoardings at either end of Parliament square. On the south side stood Oss, legs apart and twirling his cane like some Satanic cheer-leader. His already imposing presence was made all the more sinister by cats-eye contact lenses.

On the north portion of the square, the EWT guide was finding it hard to concentrate. The smell wafting from the back of his head was making him feel physically sick and the stench wasn't going unnoticed by his party.

"Let's go join that other tour." One man near the front nudged his girlfriend.

"But this one is free."

"So? The guide smells like he's shit himself."

The girl caught a whiff of the pungent aroma and screwed up her face in agreement. The pair broke away and headed for Oss's group, followed by another half dozen, one or two holding their noses.

The EWT guide decided to cut his losses and start before he was abandoned by anyone else. After a short introduction, he shepherded his charges to the steps of St Giles Cathedral and sprinted to the top, making sure he was downwind of his group. It was the spot where City of the Dead always told their first story.

That'll teach them, he thought. He knew the Dead were responsible for his ambush, even if there was no way to prove it.

"Behind you is the Mercat Cross," he thundered. "It has been a meeting place in Edinburgh for almost seven hundred years and official proclamations were made from that spot."

A hand shot up in the crowd. The guide repressed a sigh.

"You have a question?"

Donny stepped forward.

"How long did you say the cross has been there?"

"No, no!" The guide's eyes widened as he recognised the boy. "You're banned from these walks."

"I'm banned?" Donny sounded genuinely distressed. "Why am I banned?"

"Because you're a troublemaker."

The crowd turned to look at him. Donny had abandoned his trademark black and was dressed in slacks and a duffle coat. His hair was parted in the middle and he wore a pair of owlish spectacles.

"He keeps interrupting my talk," the guide explained.

"I *need* to ask questions." The boy pleaded. "It's my school history project and I'll fail if I don't do my research."

The tour party glared at the man. He gritted his teeth and indicated for the boy to go ahead.

"How long exactly has the Mercat Cross been there?"

"I don't know *exactly*," the guide seethed. "About six hundred years."

"But it was only built in 1885," Donny countered. "The original was much further down the street and demolished twenty years earlier." He shrugged at the crowd. "I'm doing a project on how accurately walking tours represent the history of Edinburgh."

Around the corner, a burst of laughter erupted. Oss had begun his tour and was pulling out all the stops.

The EWT guide began again, determined not to be put off.

"If you look round the side of the building you can see a car park, built on top of the old St Giles cemetery. And under parking lot 46 is the last resting place of the famous Presbyterian preacher John Knox."

Donny's hand shot up again. The guide ignored him.

"Not a particularly dignified spot to spend eternity! Huh?" He swept his arm around in an arc. "Yes, you're literally standing on hundreds of bodies."

"That's not right," Donny interrupted loudly. He continued to wave his hand around while the guide tried to look anywhere else but at him.

Another member of the party raised his arm.

"Yes?" the EWT guide could hardly contain his frustration.

"I think the kid has a question, dude. You wanna let him speak?"

The man most certainly didn't, but he had no choice.

"John Knox *isn't* under the car park," Donny said as meekly as he could. "Neither is anyone else. They dug up all the bodies, crushed them down and reburied the whole lot in Greyfriars Graveyard. Two tons worth."

"And just when did this happen?" The guide was determined to catch this little know-all at his own game. "If you're such an expert."

Donny knew the date, of course. 1789. But when he opened his mouth a completely different number came out.

"1635."

Fortunately, the enemy guide hadn't a clue when the bodies were moved and looked suitably crestfallen.

"I'm not an expert," Donny quickly recovered. "I've just read a couple of books on local history as research." He pointed to the corner of the church. "I went on a City of the Dead tour yesterday and *they* got it right."

As if on cue, there was another burst of laughter from just out of sight. Another half dozen tourists peeled away and headed in the direction of the merriment.

Oss had finished his introduction and was ready to go.

"I normally tell my first story on the steps of St Giles," he said. "But some other company has pinched my spot. No fair. Want to help me psyche them out?"

His group nodded. They were thoroughly enjoying themselves and happy to oblige.

"Right." Oss gave his cane a ringmasterly spin. "Follow me and act exactly as I do…"

The EWT guide was slowly building up momentum again when his audience heard a mass of muted giggling behind them.

They turned around and gawped.

Oss was crossing the car park, his sniggering group in tow. All of them running in slow motion.

Donny guffawed out loud. The EWT guide spluttered and stopped mid-sentence.

Oss stuck a kazoo in his mouth and began to parp the theme tune to *Chariots of Fire*. His followers pumped their arms and legs in a grotesque parody of the film's famous race scene, their expressions contorting as they mimicked the exertion of world-class sprinters. Some managed to stay poker-faced. Others were laughing uncontrollably.

"At least I don't resort to cheap gimmicks to entertain my tour!" The EWT guide shouted, finally losing his temper.

"You don't resort to historical accuracy or personal hygiene either," Donny shot back. "I'm going with the other lot. It may cost a few quid but at least they're having fun."

By the time Oss and Donny vanished down Barrie's Close, their tour had quadrupled in size and EWT only had six people left.

From the Journal of Donny Marigold

"Look at what I've got."

I pulled a pair of box-shaped binoculars from my bag and handed them to Daisy. She took them warily as if they might suddenly bite her.

"Can I use your computer?" I asked.

"Of course."

It's human nature, on being handed a magnifying device, to try looking through it, but Daisy simply placed the present on her lap. She really wasn't the inquisitive type.

I jotted down a few historical facts from the internet. Daisy sat glowering at the far wall, which was off-putting, to say the least.

"I got them for you," I said, when the silence had gone beyond uncomfortable and entered ridiculous mode.

"Thank you very much."

"Don't you want to try them out?"

She glanced down at the binoculars in bewilderment.

"Everything in the room is close."

I couldn't tell if she was being serious or not. As usual.

"Then look out the window."

"It's dark."

"That's the beauty of these babies." I got up and unhooked the strap from her knee. Daisy baulked as I leaned over and I felt a flash of annoyance at her ingratitude.

"You have to turn them on." I flipped a switch on the side of the device. "They're infra-red. Cool, eh?"

Daisy stared at me blankly. Honestly, it was like pulling teeth.

"It means you can see in the dark," I explained, exasperated. "Use them when you're out in the graveyard to spot the tours better."

"They must have been very expensive." She flicked her thumbs nervously. "I don't really deserve them."

"You can buy me a Ferrari when you get your next wage packet."

Daisy didn't smile.

"Go on." I handed the binoculars back. "Have a gander at the graveyard. You'll be impressed."

Daisy wandered over to the window, raised the binoculars to her eyes and peered through them.

"Oh," she breathed. "These are good."

Finally! I went back to surfing the net while Daisy stood motionless gazing out into the night, like a diminutive captain waiting for her ship to hit an iceberg.

"Donny," she said finally. "All the tours are over. What's Ben doing in the graveyard?"

"Let me see." I got up and joined her at the window. She moved aside to give me room, handing over the binoculars. I raised them to my eyes and looked out.

It was Ben Scott, sure enough. I recognised the leather jacket, remarkably like mine, and the bouncy walk. He headed for the northern corner of the graveyard, where the ground was still churned up.

Ben flitted in and out of the trees looking cautiously around. He obviously didn't want anyone to see him.

"What's he doing now?" Daisy was whispering, even though Ben was at least forty yards away.

"I've no idea," I admitted. "The shed where Edinburgh Council keep their equipment is in the way. He's out of sight."

"You go back to work." Daisy elbowed me aside. "I'll keep an eye on him."

She really did like the binoculars.

I did as she suggested. At least she'd found something to amuse herself. The poor soul didn't even have a TV in the flat.

"He's back," she said after a while. "He's carrying something but I can't make out what it is."

I returned to the window.

Ben was struggling across the far side of the graveyard, weighed down by a heavy shape hoisted over one shoulder. At this distance, it was impossible to tell what it was. Ben held out one hand in front of his body, waving it around the way a blind man uses a white stick. I realised he wasn't using a flashlight.

Boy. He really *didn't want anyone to know he was there.*

Unfortunately, it meant he *couldn't see anything either. He tripped over a low headstone and vanished in a flurry of arms and legs.*

"Muppet," I grunted. "Should have given him *the bloody binoculars."*

Daisy sniffed indignantly.

"Only joking," I countered quickly. "I just don't know what he's playing at."

Ben was back on his feet, the bundle balanced precariously over his shoulder once more. He eventually found a dirt path leading to the Covenanters Prison and followed it until he got to the locked gates. He unfastened the padlock, let himself in and vanished.

"Ach, whatever he's up to, it's his business." I threw the binoculars onto the bed and went back to the computer. "But let's never tell anyone we were spying on him."

"Why not?" Daisy frowned.

"Because he's quite a scary guy," I chuckled. "The next time he carries something through the graveyard, I don't want it to be my body."

Daisy didn't smile.

-10-

Marky Cotter took a toke of the joint and passed it on. His lads were finally back in their favourite patch, a tomb at the bottom of Greyfriars Graveyard. They drank from plastic bottles of White Lightning, lounging in rickety chairs they had rescued from various skips in the Grassmarket. Despite being in the middle of the city, Greyfriars was dark, walled and isolated and nobody tended to venture in there after the sun had set. The ideal spot for taking drugs and shifting a few bevvies.

Except for the tours.

They could hear the shouting, giggling and screaming. It was downright anti-social. The noise set Marky's teeth on edge and made the others nervous. This was their patch. Something had to be done about it.

Especially that little cunt they'd first encountered at the prison. She seemed to think she had the run of the place now. Marky and his mates would have sorted her out already - but she was obviously working for one of the tours. If they gave her grief, the polis would descend on them like flies over a turd. They got the blame for everything, Marky thought. It wasn't fair.

"Don't Bogart the spliff," he snarled, snatching back the joint from his second in command.

A shadow fell across the doorway.

With a curse, Marky scooped up a torch and shone it at the intruder.

"Evening, lads." Ben Scott stepped into the mausoleum, dressed entirely in black, a silver cane in his hand. It was obvious who he was representing. The youths scrambled to their feet, hands dipping into their pockets.

"You got a right nerve, pal." Marky reached for the flicknife tucked into his back pocket. "You want to fuck off while you can still walk."

"I got a proposition for you." Ben clutched his cane tighter, sweat beading his forehead. "You got a nice wee set up here and I want to help you with that."

Marky's second in command elbowed his way over to Ben and stood toe to toe with him, their faces inches apart.

"You *want* to be shanked, pal?"

"You could hear me out before we get into fisticuffs."

"Let him speak." Marky held up a nicotine stained hand. "*Then* you can chib him."

"I don't mind you guys being here, as long as you leave City of the Dead and its employees alone." Ben refused to back away.

"This is our gaff," Marky said. "You don't know who you're messin with."

"All I need to do to get rid of you is call the police every night and make some crap up. Tell them that you're throwing stuff at us. Behaving threateningly."

"We've never touched your tours. No yet, anyway."

"Yeah. But who do the cops always believe? I'm a respectable businessman and you're a bunch of neds. They'll be down here so often, you'll have to give them their own seats."

"You really think you can come intae our gaff an disrespect us, ya fanny?" Marky motioned to his gang. "Gie this guy a fuckin doin and send him on his way."

"Or we could conduct business and you could make some cash," Ben responded quickly.

"Wait a wee minute." Marky cocked his head at the mention of money. "What are ye proposing?"

"I'm proposing a truce." Ben skirted the second in command and crouched next to Marky. "You leave City of the Dead alone up at our end of the graveyard and we'll leave you alone down at yours. Then we can help each other out with a mutual problem."

"We hae a mutual problem?"

"We do. There's another company coming in here at night. Edinburgh Walking Tours. They're European."

"I dinnae like foreigners," one youth muttered.

"You dinnae like anything, ya raj bastard," another shot back.

"I dinnae fucking like *you*."

"Shut it!" Marky offered Ben a cigarette. "Why's this oor problem?"

"You and me are Scottish. Got a bit of pride in that, know?" Ben's accent became noticeably thicker, unconsciously imitating the youths surrounding him. "No need for us to mess with each other, eh? But you scare the hell out of EWT."

The gang grinned, happy with what they saw as a compliment.

"So Edinburgh Walking Tours *will* do everything they can to get rid of you, even if you leave them alone."

"Asbo nation, eh?" Marky mused sagely. "Abody gies us a hard time."

"I'm suggesting a deal." Ben lit a cigarette. "If you leave us alone, they're fair game for both of us. Let's make sure they regret coming onto *our* turf."

"What's in it fur us?"

"A thousand pounds if you help stop them running night tours in the graveyard."

The youths' grins got wider.

"Plus a ready-made alibi for any time you get into trouble here. I'll swear I walked through the graveyard the night it happened and you weren't around." He smiled broadly. "In return, I can call on you if I ever need a job done that isn't strictly... legal."

"And you'll pay in cash."

"Naturally."

"Where did you grow up, pal?" Marky asked.

"Ardler. The multi-stories in Dundee?"

"Rough place, I've heard."

"It was."

"You ever double cross us an we'll kill you." Marky stared at the interloper and rubbed his mottled chin. "It's our code, know?"

"I understand."

"You want a wee smoke since you're here?"

"Don't mind if I do." Ben put down his cane. "Can't make a habit of it, though. We're not supposed to know each other."

"C'mon you lot, where's yer fucking hospitality?" Marky motioned to his companions.

"Gie the man a bloody chair."

Ben watched his nemesis from the open window of the flat - a tall, gangly EWT guide in the all too common yellow jacket, gesturing to a crowd of twenty or more. Daisy sat behind her boss, drinking tea.

"Doesn't matter what we do," she complained. "We can't put this one off. He's too good."

"I hear you."

Charismatic, loud and funny, Ben had to admit, this guy was really engaging his audience. Small wonder. He had gone on a dozen City of the Dead Tours and memorised the best bits, right down to the jokes.

The guide glanced over at their window and grinned. Ben stared back, his expression unreadable.

Finishing the story, the team leader led his group into the darkness, but Ben knew his rival's route off by heart. The tour boss opened his window and took several deep breaths, gripping the sill until his knuckles went white.

On the other side of the graveyard, The EWT guide reached his preferred spot for the next tale; a flat tombstone rimmed by knee-high iron railings. Standing on it, he was a good two feet higher than his audience, a perfect platform to enhance his performance and give the crowd a better view. The top of the tombstone seemed wetter and darker than usual, but it had been raining on and off for most of the day.

He leapt over the railings and onto the makeshift podium, whirling to face his group.

But, this time, the surface of the stone was slick and slippery and his legs shot from under him. For a second, the guide seemed to hang suspended in the air. Then he slammed down onto the metal railings, arms outstretched in a vain attempt to break his fall. An iron spike sank into the underside of his wrist, and the bone snapped with an audible crack. Another pierced the fleshy upper part of his arm and burst through the other side in a fountain of blood.

The tour party backed away in horror.

"Oh, fuck!" the man screamed, writhing on the oily tombstone in agony. "Call an ambulance! Oh, shit. Oh, God!"

At the open window, Ben lit a cigarette and listened to the cries echoing across Greyfriars.

"He's very loud," Daisy muttered.

"Oh yeah," Ben said softly to himself.

"My boy's certainly scaring them tonight."

From the Journal of Donny Marigold

The first time I met the other woman in my life, I was a bit taken aback.

For a start, she was wearing a blue two-piece bikini and Doctor Martin boots. Her blonde hair was tied in a cobalt ribbon, a weird ponytail that fountained from the top of her head like an explosion. The tip was dyed blue as well, presumably to match her outfit.

She was near the northern end of the graveyard where the ground was most disturbed. And she was dancing. Well, she was jumping up and down and waving her hands in the air.

"Let me guess," I said, strolling over. "You died sometime in the 1980s."

"Why do you say that?" The girl didn't seem surprised that I could see her. But ghosts aren't a very curious bunch, far as I can tell.

"You've got leg warmers on."

"So? They're back in fashion now. Not that I need clothes tips from someone who's dressed like Johnny Cash."

The girl pulled up the blue and black striped tubes until they encased her legs entirely. "What makes you think I've kicked the bucket?"

"There's a dagger sticking out of your chest."

"It looks pretty neat, though." The girl pulled the knife from between her breasts and pushed it into the top of one stocking. "I'm Grizzle."

"That's a pretty name," I said tactfully. "I'm called Donny. What are you doing?"

"Dancing on my husband's grave." She gave a dainty stamp. "He's buried around here somewhere."

This perplexed me. The girl looked to be around my age. A bit young to be a widow or even married at all.

"Did he kill you?" I asked. Ghosts don't care much for beating around the bush.

"He sure as shit did. Thought I was cheating on him, the asshole." Grizzle wrinkled her snub nose. "Don't know how *he found out."*

"Tell me your story," I said, sitting down on the grass next to her. "I'm a good listener."

So she did.

-11-

"My husband was called Mr Menzies. Nobody knew his first name, not even me." The girl plopped down next to Donny. "He was a highland mercenary who fought in the Thirty Years War. You probably never heard of it."

"It was a 17th century conflict." Donny leaned back on his elbows. "Took place in the area now known as Germany and was one of the great bloodbaths of all time. That's about all I know," he added modestly.

"Wow." Grizzle squinted at him. "I bet you don't get invited to many parties. Can you recite the Periodic Table?"

"History's my thing," Donny retorted. "And I probably get invited to more parties than you. Being alive and all."

"You want to hear my story or are you going to keep ogling my boobs?" The girl waved her fingers in front of the teenager's face. "My eyes are up here, pal."

"Sorry." Donny flushed. "I just expected a 400-year-old ghost to be wearing something more... demure. A corset maybe, or a peasant dress."

"I'm dead, my friend." Grizzle dismissed the comment with a wave of one dainty hand. "I can wear a Mariachi outfit if I want. Who's going to see?"

"Eh... Me?"

"I'm still trying to get my head around that one. But enough about you." The girl gave an impish grin. "I don't get to talk very often. It's a bit of a novelty."

"I'll shut up."

"I was selling winkles in the Cowgate when Mr Menzies returned from the conflict in Europe and bought a house overlooking the graveyard. I must have caught his eye. I *was* considered a bit of a looker if I do say so."

"I wouldn't argue with that."

"That's nice of you." Grizzle batted her long eyelashes. "But anyone with more than three teeth was pretty hot back then. Anyway, Mr Menzies asked for my hand in marriage."

She stroked her ring finger, now absent of any wedding band.

"I was thirteen and he was in his forties. A huge man with scars all over his body and a pointy beard like the very Devil. But he was exceedingly rich, so my parents agreed. They thought it would get me out of a life of poverty and maybe give them a chance of sponging a few quid for themselves."

"I take it things didn't turn out that way?"

"He didn't want a wife. He wanted a servant and someone to give him an heir. For two years my husband beat me, abused me and used me." The girl looked at the ground. "Then he killed me."

"I'm sorry."

"Not as fucking sorry as I was."

"Why did he treat you so badly?"

"Once, when he was drunk, he told me something happened to him in a town called Distel. An 'incident' he called it, though he refused to elaborate."

She pulled the knife from her stocking and pared her nails, trying to keep the tremor from her voice.

"Mr Menzies told me that, after what he had done, his soul couldn't be saved. Nor did he want it to be. He wouldn't even permit himself a Christian name any more."

She gave Donny a sad little smile.

"He told me that, if he and his companions were not irredeemably evil, then all human beings must be capable of doing what he did, and that was unacceptable to him. He believed himself to be a monster. *Had* to believe it. And he acted accordingly just to prove his argument."

"Holy hell," Donny breathed.

"Yeah, he was a warped bastard."

"No wonder you were dancing on his grave." Donny moved his bum gingerly away from the spot he'd been sitting. "I'd have dug him up and dragged his corpse down the High Street doing the Hokey Pokey."

"That wasn't a dance of celebration, Donny." The girl looked around apprehensively. "It's a spell my granny taught me to ward off the dead."

"Better watch it doesn't backfire and make *you* disappear," Donny said cautiously. "If your hubby's been buried for more than three hundred years, I doubt he's going to pop up now."

"Oh, but he is." The girl struggled to her feet and pointed her weapon aggressively at the ravaged ground. "I can feel it."

The knife trembled in her outstretched hand.

"Mr Menzies is on his way back."

From the Journal of Donny Marigold

After meeting Grizzle, I looked up the 30 Years War on the internet to get more info. It made for grim reading. It was basically a world war from when the world was smaller.

It was a religious conflict between the Catholics and Protestants, *involving most of the European superpowers of the time. All the armies, no matter what their religious persuasion, were heavily reinforced by foreign mercenaries and expected to be self-sufficient. So they fed, clothed, sheltered, pleasured and paid themselves by looting every town and village they encountered. The few surviving inhabitants then succumbed to a plague caused by the mass of unburied bodies.*

One-third of all the people in central Europe died during the war, which resulted in the deaths of over seven million in Germany alone. That means a larger percentage of the civilian population died in the 30 Years War than in World Wars I and II put together.

A terrible statistic, sure, and I could see how it got Mr Menzies all screwed up.

But nothing to do with Greyfriars.

Right?

Wrong

-12-

'Doc' Menzies lay on the top bunk of a tatty iron bed, whistling softly to himself. In one hand, he riffed a pack of cards deftly through his fingers. Each time he stopped, the Ace of Spades rose slowly from the centre of the deck and then sank back down again.

"Ye never fail tae amaze me, man." His cellmate sat on a stool near the barred window twiddling his thumbs.

"It's just a trick, Angus. I can make them fart as well." Doc scraped the cards across the stone wall, creating a load rasping sound. "Goes down a treat at children's parties."

"Ah mean getting paroled this quick," his companion said dolefully. "Ah wuz sure you'd be in fur another few years at least."

"I've got an honest face."

"Suppose." Angus locked his fingers together and ran them down the scar on his own acned cheek. "No that it'll dae ye much good."

"What's on your mind, Angus?"

"Big Sottie's no very chuffed by this unexpected turn o events, know?"

"He's not pleased for me? We used to get on quite well." Doc flicked his wrist and the cards disappeared. "He should applaud a fellow inmate beating the system."

"You can beat the system all ye want, but beatin *him* certainly isnae the done thing." Angus glanced furtively at the cell door. "He's never lost at poker afore."

"That's because he cheats. And everyone lets him get away with it."

"Are ye surprised? He's built like a fridge full o concrete and has a dozen of Glasgow's finest hard men lickin his arse." Angus got up and paced the cell, his wiry body tense. "He wants his money returned and he wants you hurt fur takin it in the first place. Man's lookin to get his respect back."

Angus squinted at him.

"Why did you do it? You got a death wish or something?"

"It's not my fault Sottie suffers from low self-esteem." Doc sat up and swung his legs over the edge of the bunk. "I need all the money I can get if I'm going to be set loose on the civilised world. I got a mission, you know."

"You've been good tae me Doc, I winnae deny it." Angus shuffled miserably on the spot. "But I cannae be here when he and his cronies arrive. They'll take me apart an all."

"I presume I won't get much help from other inmates if I ask out in the yard?"

"Not against *him*. They'll just turn their backs." Angus looked suitably abject at his own inability to stand up for a friend. "Word is, he's making his move at four thirty today. That's when maist of the guards will be watching the big match."

"Thanks for the heads up." Doc yawned loudly. "What time is it now?"

"Two o clock." Angus held up his watch. "They'll all meet in his cell an come fur you, wherever ye are."

"Then I need a favour." Doc leaned forwards and pulled an Ace of Spades from behind his cellmate's ear. "A last request if you like."

"Dinnae." Angus shook his hand off. "You can stop this! Go hit a screw or throw a hairy fit or somethin. Get yersel put in solitary."

"And mess up my parole? No thanks." Doc held up two fingers. "See this?"

"No."

"That's because it's a ghost pen." The man scribbled a few imaginary lines on the card. "I want you to take this to Big Sottie. Tell him Doc Menzies says *no need to go looking for me at half four. I'll come for you at 16.35*. It has to be those exact words. *16.35*. Think you can remember?"

"Aye, right. He'll use mah heid tae clean the cell floor."

"No, he won't. Trust me." He thrust the card at Angus, who reluctantly took it. "Then make yourself scarce. Get your hair done. Whatever."

Doc lay back on his bunk and closed his eyes.

"I'll be fine."

At ten to five Angus burst into the cell, shaking with excitement. Doc Menzies was still lying on his bed, breathing softly.

"You are *so* jammy!" The convict leapt onto the bunk and landed on top of his cellmate. "Big Sottie's dead! He hung hisself from the light wi his belt."

"What time?"

"Eh? About ten minutes ago." Angus grinned through crooked teeth, his face inches from Doc's. "His fat fucking posse are runnin around like chickens wi their heads cut aff."

Doc opened his eyes and squinted at his companion.

"Much as I like you, Angus, this is closer than we ever need to be."

"Mah bad." The younger man slid off the bed and gave a cheesy grin. "But whit did you dae Doc? What did ye dae tae make this happen?"

"Me? How could I possibly have done anything?" Doc smiled back, the cards miraculously appearing in his hands.

"Now, how about a game of snap?"

From the Journal of Donny Marigold

I found one excellent story that I knew I could use for the tours.

In a legendary incident, body snatchers in Greyfriars pulled an old woman from her last resting place and found, to their delight, she had rings on her fingers. They were happily hacking off the digits when she sat up and gave a yell – prompting the horrified grave robbers to leg it, and probably take up a new career.

Turns out that, in 19ᵗʰ century Edinburgh, you didn't need a death certificate to be buried. You simply had to look dead. In the disease-infested slums of the Old Town, the citizens were interred as fast as possible, sometimes before it was properly confirmed that they had actually kicked the bucket. One Victorian estimate stated that 2% of the population were buried alive. Some even had bells installed in their coffins, so they could attract attention if it happened to them.

Of course, the guides loved the tale and started telling it to their customers right away.

Me? I decided I'd like to be cremated.

-13-

John Walters III strolled into the graveyard, singing softly to himself. Though the sky was dark and the night air chilly, it was obvious summer was stamping its mark on Greyfriars. Flowers carpeted the grass and the trees were thick with leaves, rustling in the moonlight. The cemetery felt altogether more pleasant than on his last visit.

Walters was a researcher for a pharmaceutical company in Dayton, Ohio and travelled the world to medical conferences, where he kept the leading lights up to date on advances in the latest retroviral drugs. It was a job that frequently took him away from home, but he didn't mind. Being alone in a foreign country gave him the chance to make a bit of money on the side. That's why he never used his own name.

He had thoroughly enjoyed the graveyard tour last time he was in Edinburgh. He loved creepy stuff.

And what had happened afterwards? He'd *really* liked that.

The guide, Lee, had told a story about citizens being buried alive in Greyfriars. Some people were even interred with handbells in their coffins so that they could sound an alert if they woke up six feet under.

"Was anyone ever rescued?" Walters inquired, genuinely fascinated.

"I doubt it." Lee stamped her foot on the ground. "With all that earth on top, you couldn't be heard down there with a megaphone."

"Then how do you know anyone was buried alive at all?"

"Because gravediggers moved the bodies around due to overcrowding," the girl whispered melodramatically. "They found scratch marks on the coffin lids, as if the inhabitants had tried to claw their way out."

The audience shuddered at the thought.

"That was probably due to decomposing corpses becoming bloated with gas." Walters figured he may as well share his medical expertise. "Which would splinter coffin wood if it was rotten enough."

"But it's not nearly such a fun story to tell on a ghost tour, is it?"

Walters was a tall, handsome man and years of selling at conferences had taught him when to be knowledgeable and when to be disarming.

"I apologise." He gave a small bow. "I'm only a salesman. I'll stick to my area of expertise and stop questioning yours."

"Thank you." The guide flashed him a charming smile of her own. "Then buy me a drink later and tell me more about dead bodies."

Oh yes. John Walters III liked travelling just fine.

Now he was back in Edinburgh for another conference and back in the graveyard. A flat tombstone loomed out of the dark, looking like a sacrificial alter. He patted it affectionately as he passed.

The graveyard seemed deserted but, at the bottom, he spotted a light in one of the mausoleum doorways. He crept up, holding his breath and peered into the interior.

There was a small fire burning in the corner and half a dozen youths, male and female, were crouched around it. All had pasty faces and emaciated bodies. Empty bottles of cider and a half dozen syringes glittered on the dusty tomb floor.

A dozen pairs of antagonistic eyes turned towards him.

"What you lookin at, ya cunt?" Marky snarled. "Piss off."

It was definitely time to switch to charming mode.

"Sorry fellas," Walters said pleasantly. "Wrong tomb."

"You mental? Away an beat it afore ah rip yer jaw."

"Aye, ya big fanny," a girl in a grubby pink tracksuit joined in. "An dinnae be fetchin the polis. Or ye'll get a serious fuckin gubbin, know?"

"Didn't catch most of that." Walters backed out of the tomb. "But I get the general impression I should go."

He turned and strolled into the night. God, he loved this town!

He stopped and lit a cigarette. It was cold tonight, despite the time of year and, unlike his last visit, he was only wearing a thin jacket. In one of the lit windows surrounding the kirkyard he could see a young girl running on the spot. As he watched, she switched to doing star jumps.

"Takes all sorts, I guess."

Walters looked at the illuminated dial of his watch. He must have missed the last tour but that was his own fault for staying in the pub too long. Shame. He had hoped to bump into Lee again.

As he rose, he spotted an area of churned up earth to the west. He sauntered over and peered into a huge hole. At the bottom was an open coffin, aged and damp with rot.

"There's something you don't see every day."

He leaned over to take a closer look. Didn't see a figure creep from behind a tombstone behind him, plank of wood in hand.

But he felt it smack across the back of his head.

He woke in utter darkness. He was lying on his back, surrounded by the overpowering smell of earth and rot. He reached up his hands and hit wood. He searched both pockets for his mobile phone but it was missing.

Walters gave a strangled sob. He began to scream, clawing at the coffin lid until his nails broke and splinters lodged in his fingers. The wails subsided into gasps as he realised the air was growing stale and difficult to breathe. He groped around the confines of his own prison, looking for a gap. Some way out.

His hand fastened on a cup shaped object and he groaned.

It was a small bell.

Whimpering softly he began to shake it, aware the faint sound would never be loud enough to attract attention.

He was already a dead man.

Long before the sun came up, the ringing had faded into silence.

From the Journal of Donny Marigold

Eric Pike, head of Edinburgh Walking Tours, sauntered into the café, looking relaxed and friendly. He shook Ben's hand warmly and gave me a patronising smile. Settling into a chair opposite, he waved away the waitress and leaned forwards. An eager beaver. Ready to smooth things over.

He wasn't even fooling me and I'm only sixteen.

"I'm on business in Edinburgh, so I thought I'd come and talk to you personally," he said obligingly. "Try and find a bit of common ground. I mean, all this nonsense of vandalising each other's signs and throwing away leaflets is... is... "

"Your fault."

"Very... regretful." Eric breezed right over that one. With his boyish good looks and square chin, I got the feeling he considered himself unflappable.

Oh dear.

"Look. We're both in the same business and there's plenty of customers to go around."

His pocket beeped loudly. He removed a Blackberry with more buttons than the lift in the Empire State Building, switched it off and placed the device on the table.

"I've had a sharp word with my staff and they've promised to stop disparaging your tours to our customers."

"You've been disparaging our tours?" Ben removed a cheap, battered Nokia from his own jacket and put it down next to the Blackberry. "I didn't know about that part."

"Our guides got overenthusiastic and they've been severely repri-manded." Eric Pike fixed me with a steely gaze. *"I think it's only fair you have a word with your people to do the same."*

"Eh? He's not my people." Ben jerked a thumb at me. *"He's a trainee reporter studying journalism at Napier University. I can't get rid of him."*

"I'm looking for an in-depth story for my dissertation." I framed an imaginary banner in the air. **"Big European Company Bulldozes Strug-gling Local Business."**

Eric Pike sized me up. I certainly looked older than my age but a bit young to be at college. Then again, if I was just a school kid, why wasn't I at school?

"I hardly think that's fair." The EWT boss tried to sound reasona-ble. *"True, we run tours at the same times as you and in the same locations. But we have a right to do that, without you interrupting us all the time."*

"In my book, everyone has the right to free speech, which my com-pany are exercising," Ben replied calmly. *"Anything else, you have to fight for."*

"It's legitimate competition, Mr Scott."

"It's mean-spirited and greedy and you know it." Ben still hadn't touched his coffee.

"Mean-spirited!" The EWT boss could hardly believe his ears. I could see his composure slipping by the second. *"You disrupt our tours and throw eggs at our guides. You string wire across the bottom of stairs you know my tour party will go down."*

I tried not to smirk. That had been my idea too.

Eric Pike placed both hands on the table. One was adorned with a large, gold wedding ring.

"But forget all that trivial stuff. We have one girl in a cast after someone broke her leg in the cemetery and a guy in hospital because oil was poured over the tombstone where he always stands."

"Your guides stand on the tombstones?" I got out a pencil and pad. "Isn't that a bit disrespectful?"

"If you had the slightest proof of those accusations, I'd be talking to the authorities instead of you." Ben dropped a lump of sugar into his cup. "Let's just chalk it down to the poltergeist. It's good for business."

"We're bigger and richer than you, Mr Scott." Eric Pike replied coldly, finally dropping the act. "All our guides carry mobile phones with cameras and sooner or later we will catch you up to something."

"Aw, we already tried that." Ben picked up his Nokia. "All Donny got was footage of you going back to your hotel with some drunk teenager you picked up in a bar."

The EWT boss turned white. I almost felt sorry for him.

"So, let's say you stop running tours at the same time as ours and keep out of Greyfriars at night altogether." Ben put the phone back in his pocket and calmly sipped his drink. "In return, our clip won't turn up on the internet where your wife and kids can see it."

As we walked back towards the graveyard, Ben put a hand on my shoulder. I could feel it trembling through my jacket.

"You saved our asses," he said gratefully. "You're a bloody star."

"It was your idea to spy on the big boss rather than his minions," I replied modestly.

"But I didn't think you'd find anything." He hit my arm lightly. "Maybe you should try being a reporter. You're smart, you've got nerve and your writing's good."

"Thank you." I was a bit taken aback. "I've always wanted to be an author."

"You should then. Your scripts are funny and exciting. Well... as exciting as history gets." We passed the statue of Greyfriars Bobby and stepped out onto the road to avoid a gaggle of Spanish teenagers taking pictures of each other.

"I used to write too," Ben said. "Even had a couple of plays put on."

"You did?" Now I was astonished.

"That's in the past." Ben smiled thinly. "Let's just say I recognise talent when I see it."

I was touched. My boss didn't seem the type for compliments. Still... I figured since we were sharing.

"If Eric Pike hadn't agreed to your demands," I asked. "Would you really have put that film on the internet?" We danced a little jig across Candlemaker Row to avoid the number 22 bus. "Knowing what it would do to his wife and kids."

"Maybe they deserve to find out the truth."

"Would you though?"

"Who knows? He believed I would." Ben punched the air, unable to contain his glee. "That's what counts."

"He probably assumes you're capable of anything." I couldn't keep the disapproval out of my voice. "Look what you did to his guides."

"Hey! I didn't do anything." Ben reached his front door and fished out a key. "What kind of guy do you think I am?"

I studied his face, trying to work out what kind of guy he really was.

"So it's a coincidence?" I decided on one more push. "That your main rivals keep coming a cropper whenever they set foot in Greyfriars?"

"Just hold on, Woodward bloody Bernstein." Ben opened his door and a crack of light raced up the dark spiral staircase. "It's the Mackenzie Poltergeist who attacks people in the graveyard, isn't it?"

"You made that stuff up, Ben. That's what you always say."

"I know." The tour boss smiled disarmingly.

"I must be even better than I thought."

-14-

Daisy Lenin crouched behind a headstone munching an oatcake and brushing the crumbs carefully from her leather coat. Like the rest of City of the Dead, she was now clad entirely in black, down to her steel toe capped boots. From her hiding place she could see Ben Scott in his flat, usual glass of wine in hand, chatting to Donny. She unclipped a walkie-talkie from her belt, another present from the boy. She worried about all the money he spent on her but he just brushed off her protests.

She pressed the button on the side and spoke quietly.

"Hello Donny. Over."

Donny approached the window, twin radio in his hand.

"See you in the flat after I've jumped? Over." He pointed upwards.

"I will. Over and out."

In the distance, Lee's lilting accent rolled across the deserted grave-yard.

"As you can see, it's very dark in here and I have the only flashlight. So... if you hear this noise - *eeeeeeea-ooomphh!* It means someone has fallen over a gravestone."

There was a ripple of laughter.

"Make sure they're still conscious. There's nothing worse than waking up at three in the morning in the cemetery, thinking *what am I doing here? Who are these people around me drinking methylated spirits? Where are my clothes?*"

More laughter. Louder this time.

"Ready?" Lee spun her cane between her fingers. "Then let's go."

Daisy clipped the walkie-talkie back on her belt and picked up a stone from the pile in front of her.

The laughter was about to stop.

By the time the group entered the Covenanters Prison, their mood had certainly changed. It was all down to Daisy, who had been launching missiles from behind gravestones at least twenty yards away. Lee had no idea how the girl could be so accurate without seeing her prey but she didn't much care. Word of the Mackenzie Poltergeist was spreading and she had at least forty people on her tour. No problem. She had a loud voice. And she got paid a percentage of the takings, so the bigger the bunch the better.

The party halted inside the prison, enjoying a brief respite. Daisy couldn't get in here without being seen, so she had gone back to her flat. It would be Donny's turn soon.

The gates were protected by a stout padlock on a chain. Lee unfastened it, ushered the party in, wrapped the chain back around the bars and pretended to snap the padlock shut, giving the false impression that they were trapped inside. Who was going to check? But the guide was inexplicably glad that their only escape route wasn't really blocked. She was surrounded by people and knew the poltergeist was an invention but the girl couldn't shake the idea that being stuck in this narrow strip of walled land was a really bad idea.

She turned to the punters and spread her arms. Shrouded in black leather, the effect was positively vampirish. Behind the woman, two gently waving ash trees mirrored the motion, reaching up to bat the moon with spindly fingers.

"This is where the tour changes. This is where I get serious." The guides knew Donny's script so well that they had begun to embellish it, putting in personal touches to make the scenario more believable.

"This... *thing* that's waiting for us displays many classical poltergeist symptoms, hence its name. Anyone know exactly what those are?"

There were one or two grunts but nobody seemed motivated enough to put their hand up. Probably in case Lee picked on them.

"Poltergeists are considered to be physical manifestations of subconscious rage or emotional disturbance. They're often associated with teenagers who, as we all know, are a pretty manic bunch anyway."

A young boy at the front gave an exaggerated gulp and Lee pointed at him.

"Take this kid here. What's your name, son?"

"Nigel." The boy had a strong Liverpool accent.

"With a name like that you probably have plenty of pent-up rage as it is." Lee arched an eyebrow. "So! Say Nigel and his family decide to have a holiday in Edinburgh. The boy doesn't want to go and leave his mates but there's nothing he can do about it. He gets angry and his rage creates a poltergeist. In paranormal terms, he is called the *focus*."

Nigel shot an *I told you so* look at mum and dad. Both were wrapped in identical green parkas with furry hoods.

Result! Lee thought.

The parents looked at each other and gave resigned groans.

"A poltergeist makes noises, moves things. Tries to make the adults uncomfortable. And the child doesn't get the blame. Perfect."

Nigel seemed to be enjoying this aspect of the story immensely.

"But a poltergeist doesn't want to *hurt* the family – just punish them. Because, if it injures them, the child will be alone. And he doesn't want that, not even subconsciously."

"Speak for yourself," Nigel said snidely. His father gave the boy a cuff on the back of the head.

"The Mackenzie Poltergeist isn't like that." Lee lowered her voice. "It *will* hurt you. It *has* hurt people in the past. It doesn't care if you go away and never come back. Because we'll bring in a new group of victims the next day. This poltergeist is stronger than any entity we've ever heard about. Cuts and scratches and bites and burns are found on people after the walk. Others are knocked unconscious."

The tour party pressed in closer. This was the part of the night they were really interested in.

"And we think we know why. We believe Mackenzie is the first ever poltergeist with multiple focuses. There may not be one on this tour, of course."

She winked at the boy.

"But there might. We bring so many people in here that some groups will certainly have a potential catalyst in their midst. And let's face it, you have to be pretty nuts to begin with, paying to wander round a haunted graveyard in the middle of the night."

The boy folded his arms and glared daggers at his parents again.

"This gives our supernatural chum a power and freedom no recorded poltergeist has ever had."

Lee narrowed her eyes.

"If you want to put in biblical terms, the Mackenzie Poltergeist is Legion."

She gave a mock salute to the Black Mausoleum, a few feet away.

"Ok. Raise your right hands."

The party followed suit, perplexed.

"Repeat after me. *I completely absolve City of the Dead Tours of anything that might happen to me in the Covenanters Prison. Amen.*"

This time the laughter was subdued.

"We're about to enter its lair and everyone is going in together. When you get inside *go right to the back* – because it always attacks at the front of the tomb. But don't worry about being molested when you enter. It only wallops people trying to get out."

All eyes were wide. Lee strolled over to the Black Mausoleum and kicked open the gate. Her teeth gleamed white in the darkness.

"After you. *I'm* not going in first."

And she meant it. The tomb gave her the absolute willies.

The crowd filed into the edifice, friends and strangers pushing at each other, some removing cameras from around their necks in readiness. All of them breathless with anticipation and, in some cases, genuine fear. They crammed themselves into the back so tightly that a chorus of squeaks and gasps rattled round the midnight interior of the mausoleum.

"See? Told you you'd all fit. You can't say people don't get to know each other on *this* tour."

Lee glanced back at the prison entrance. She knew Donny Marigold was out there somewhere, waiting until everyone was out of sight, before opening the gates of the prison and creeping down to jump out. The guide grinned again and followed the crowd into the darkness.

"This is the Black Mausoleum. This is where everything happens." She swung her flashlight around the bleak, dank interior of the tomb. "It doesn't look like much but it's where the Mackenzie Poltergeist lives. We are now on a time limit. We know from experience that the entity takes a little while to get going and usually have about 10 minutes before it's strong enough to attack. But don't worry, I'll have you out in nine."

She shone the flashlight on her wrist.

"Damn. My watch has stopped."

"Oh, yeah?" A youthful Australian stepped into the pool of light and peered at the timepiece. "Let me see."

Lee held out her hand.

"The second hand isn't moving." He still sounded sceptical. "It's some sort of trick, though. Your watch just doesn't work."

"It's at the correct time isn't it?" Lee shook her wrist. "Ten fifteen? It must have just stopped."

The tour party tried to check their own watches but it was too dark. Some took out mobile phones and looked at the display.

"It just past 10.15," one of them muttered.

"Then Mackenzie is here." Lee allowed a tremor to creep into her voice, even though it *was* a trick. All the guides watches had been deliberately broken and they set them to the correct time when they pretended to lock the gates. It was a simple but effective deception.

"How come *you* still take the tour if this thing is so dangerous?" The Australian was reluctant to give up on his argument.

"Because I get paid a lot," Lee replied calmly. "And the longer I talk about my employment choices, the more time is ticking away."

"Shut up and let her tell the story!" A frightened female voice emerged from the back.

"Thank you." Lee shone the light under her chin. Cheesy, but it worked too. The guide's enormous eyes lit up with a lambency that was positively demonic and her face suddenly looked startlingly angular.

"So let me tell you all the weird things that have happened in this place...."

From the Journal of Donny Marigold

I have endeavoured in this Ghostly little book to raise the Ghost of an idea.

Charles Dickens

In 1841, the novelist Charles Dickens paid a visit to Edinburgh. According to legend, he wandered into a graveyard, where he found a gravestone bearing a rather disturbing inscription.

Ebeneezer Scroggie. Mean Man.

Dickens was intrigued. What kind of guy was so nasty that even his headstone slagged him off? It obviously got him thinking.

The next year he wrote A Christmas Carol. *It's the story of Ebeneezer Scrooge, an evil old dude exploring why he became a monster and realising he was wrong in his most deeply held convictions.*

But Dickens had read the inscription incorrectly. It actually said **Ebeneezer Scroggie. Meal Man**. *The poor sod was an Edinburgh corn dealer.*

It's a nice anecdote but, as usual, there was more to this story than you see on the surface.

A Christmas Carol *isn't like Dicken's other books. For a start, it's a novella rather than a whole novel, as if he was in a hurry to get it over with. It only took him a month to finish. And, though Dickens had made a career out of bad things happening to innocent kids, he certainly wasn't a horror writer. Yet* A Christmas Carol *has three of the most vivid supernatural beings ever to grace the pages of English literature – the ghosts of Christmas past, present and future.*

It was radically different in another way. The most Christmassy book of all time never mentions Jesus. Instead, it's a celebration of ordinary people, with turkeys and presents and dancing and everything that was disliked by the clergy. Christmas had always been a sombre, low-key affair, a celebration of the birth of Christ, rather than an excuse to sit in front of the telly stuffing your face and watching reruns of The Great Escape.

A Christmas Carol *changed all that. Dickens was the most famous writer in the world and his books had a huge influence on the public, whether they were educated or plebeian. The massive success of this 'Ghostly little book' changed the way we thought of the festive season forever. From that moment Christmas began to morph from a strictly religious ritual into a secular holiday.*

I hadn't realised Dickens was such a screwed up guy. He was a control freak, suffered from bouts of clinical depression and seemed to be looking for answers his books couldn't provide. He was fascinated by mesmerism and taught himself hypnosis, relishing his newfound ability to directly influence others. He also converted from Anglicism to Unitarianism, a doctrine stressing that rational thought, reason and science were not abominations in the eyes of God.

What the Dickens?

Sorry. I couldn't resist that.

-15-

Lee talked for eight minutes, giving Donny time to creep into the prison and inch his way up to the tomb.

"The Mackenzie Poltergeist acts like a predator," she concluded. "It will pick off the weakest in the group. But its conception of 'weak' is not the same as ours. On one tour there was a little kid to one side of me and a wee old lady on the other. But it was the Ozzie guy in the middle who went down. He wasn't scared beforehand. In fact, he was questioning everything I said, so it serves him right."

The Australian gave a cough of derision and was quickly shushed by the others. With her back to the mausoleum doorway, Lee caught a barely perceptible rustle outside. Donny was in place and ready to jump.

"If you're not the kind of person the poltergeist dislikes, you can walk right out of that door and nothing will happen to you. Anyone want to try?"

Everyone shook their heads. A pointless gesture because the guide couldn't see them in the gloom.

"But if you *are* the right kind of person and you stay in the middle of the group, Mackenzie will separate you from the crowd before it attacks. And I'll explain how he does it."

That was the cue line. If the group thought the guide was going to continue with her story, they would be totally unprepared for Donny jumping out. Besides, Lee didn't *have* an explanation for the actions of a fake spook.

She clenched her fists, waiting for the chaos. Ready to scream out loud and add to the shock.

Nothing

Lee frowned.

Still nothing.

"Ehmmm. Some say the first sighting of this spirit was in 1635." The guide fell back on her old, wildly inaccurate keyword. "Yes. 1635."

There was a gasp from her audience. They began to back away from her.

About bloody time, Lee thought angrily. *What the hell is he doing?*

She admired the fact that Donny was inventive in his tactics, but nothing worked better than a straight up leap into the mausoleum, with the jumper outer yelling and waving his arms. She'd seen grown men scream like a girl.

But this was good too. Some of the crowd were actually whimpering. Lee sorely wanted to turn and see what Donny was up to, but she had to play along.

"What?" she asked innocently. "Is something behind me?"

She removed the flashlight from under her chin and shone it at the nearest face, a tough looking man with a goatee. His eyes were billiard balls and his mouth worked silently, as if he were chewing something unpalatable. A hissing sound escaped his lips and he pushed himself back until the sheer mass of milling bodies stopped him retreating any further.

Lee played the flashlight across the front of the group, astonished by their reactions. Some of the women had their eyes tightly shut, gripping each other to stay upright. One or two had begun crying.

"What?" Lee repeated, hairs rising on the back of her neck. "What's behind me?"

Something wasn't right.

There was nowhere left for the crowd to go, yet still they tried to move back. Nigel turned and burrowed his way between the bodies until he vanished completely. The Australian stumbled and fell, pulling down the woman next to him. The vacuum unbalanced the jostling group and another couple toppled over and landed on top of them.

"Jesus!" One woman screamed. "Oh God, stop it!"

This was getting out of hand. Lee whirled, shining the flashlight at the entrance.

The doorway was empty.

"Oh, you wimps!" The guide tried to make light of the situation, though she couldn't repress a shudder. "Whatever you saw, it's gone now. But let's get out of here before Mackenzie decides it's time for round two."

The tour party surged out of the tomb, chattering like starlings. One or two sank to the ground, breathing heavily.

"That was great!" the Australian whooped. "That was bloody great!"

The father in the green parka grabbed Lee by the arm.

"That *wasn't* great," he snarled. "You almost gave my kid a heart attack."

Nigel was clutching his mother's waist, head buried in her coat. His shoulders heaved up and down.

"It wasn't my fault," he whimpered. "I didn't do it."

"It's just a guy in a mask," Lee stammered. "The gate isn't really locked so he sneaks up the prison and appears in the doorway. It's a ghost tour. He's *supposed* to give you a fright."

"Was he supposed to give me *this*?" The man pulled back his parka hood and Lee winced. A hand-shaped bruise covered his forehead.

"That thing was big," his wife moaned. "*Really* big."

She clutched her son tighter.

"And it had horns."

It took Lee half an hour to get out of Greyfriars. Some people wanted to congratulate her. Everyone was looking for an explanation for what they had seen. One or two showed her images on their digital cameras.

"We took a dozen pictures of that thing," they whispered. "Not one of them shows anything."

"It's pitch-black outside. Even a flash wouldn't penetrate that," Lee protested. Then she realised what an opportunity she was missing.

"Or perhaps Mackenzie doesn't want you to record the evidence."

The Australian even asked her for a date.

Lee barged into Ben's flat, threw herself down on a chair and held out her hand. Ben passed her a glass of wine. Donny was reclining on the couch, looking guilty.

"That was fucking *intense*." Lee downed her drink and held it out again. Ben obligingly refilled it.

"Spill the beans, hun." The guide raised her wine in a toast to Donny. "What did you do to these people? They're all raving about the tour and how they're going to tell everyone they know about the Dead." She shrugged. "Except for one family, who'll probably have to go into therapy."

"I missed the jump, Lee." Donny looked crestfallen. "I'm sorry."

"My fault." Ben jerked his thumb at the clock on the wall. "Damn thing stopped at 10.15 and we were so busy talking, I didn't even notice."

"Piss right off!" Lee's glass stopped on the way to her lips. "I do my job well. You don't have to pull any crap to hype up *my* presentation."

"Lee," Donny shook his head slowly. "I never left this flat."

"He didn't," Ben assured her. "He was here the whole time. So was Daisy."

Daisy nodded in assent. Lee hadn't even noticed her, sitting silently in the corner.

"Oh." The guide nodded towards the window. "Well… something very unusual happened back there tonight. The group said a creature with horns looked into the tomb."

"It'll be a drunk guy wandering up to see what was happening in the prison," Ben replied dismissively. "You know it happens sometimes."

"And he was wearing a Viking helmet?"

"Why not? He'll have been part of a stag party," Ben laughed. "That's why he had horns. Get it?"

Lee raised a middle finger to him.

"You're right." Ben put on a poker face. "It couldn't possibly be a bloke in a silly hat. It's most probably a Minotaur on the loose."

"They said it was huge."

"Ever seen a guy in a stag party who wasn't? They drink about fifteen pints a day."

"OK, I'm being stupid." Lee drained her glass again. "I guess I'm just really good at this. Got the punters so worked up they went nuts at the slightest thing."

"Never doubted it." Ben grinned at Donny. "Maybe we should get rid of the jumper outer completely."

"*That's* not in my script," the boy grumped.

"I think I'll stay here for a while and party, if that's OK?" Lee helped herself to more wine. "I really don't want to go home right now."

"Be my guest. Are you sure you're all right?"

"Course I am, hun." Lee's hand trembled as she raised the wine to her lips. "It's just that... well... everyone was staring out of the tomb and having a total freak at what was outside. I was the only one looking in the opposite direction."

"And?"

"I swear, for a moment, I saw something standing behind *them*."

From the Journal of Donny Marigold

I have no parents save one, whom I do not acknowledge.

James Hogg, *The Confessions of a Justified Sinner*

In 1824 James Hogg wrote a book called Confessions of a Justified Sinner. *It was heavily critical of religious fanaticism, especially the idea that everything is predestined by God. Which meant those picked to be saved could do whatever the hell they wanted without being held responsible for their actions.*

The book revolves around a journal found in a graveyard, which turns out to belong to one Robert Wringham.

The obsessively devout Wringham is befriended by a mysterious, shape-shifting figure, who leads him to murder and, finally, takes him over. This would make Confessions *the first book ever written about demonic possession. Or maybe poor old Bob has a split personality, which would make* Confessions *the first book ever written about schizophrenia. It's up to the reader to decide.*

I don't think Hogg knew which was which himself.

The story seemed to scare Hogg, who published it anonymously. It was also so far ahead of its time, it sank without trace, which was turning out to be a fine Edinburgh tradition. But it eventually became famous and a huge influence on the likes of Robert Louis Stevenson and other horror writers.

Parts were set in and around Greyfriars and Hogg frequently lodged in Candlemaker Row.

-16-

Donny sat at the computer in Daisy's flat, a near empty bottle of Pinot Grigio at one elbow and a sheaf of papers next to the other.

"Where did you get the booze?" The girl sat on her bed sipping a mug of tea.

"Ben gave it to me cause I'm making a sightings list of all the things happening in the prison. It's pretty impressive."

"It would be more impressive if you weren't making it up."

"I'm *not*. Well… not anymore." Donny unscrewed the top of the bottle and poured himself a final glass. "The guides are getting the punters to write down their experiences at the end of the tours. There's dozens of them. I'm putting them on the website now."

He swivelled round on the chair.

"Want me to set you up a Hotmail account, while I'm at it?"

"Why? I've only got one friend."

"People really *are* getting hurt, though. They're even emailing pictures of their injuries." Donny shook his head, bemused. "It's like all the stuff we pretended is coming true. How wack is that?"

"You must have a lot of sightings. You've been sitting there for two hours."

"Sorry. Am I getting in your way?"

"No. I like you being here."

"I'm also writing a journal." Donny scratched his neck awkwardly. "I have this bizarre idea that I might find an explanation for what's going on. I want to turn it into a book."

"An explanation?"

"Nothing definite yet. I'm just feeling my way. So don't read it."

"I won't. I'm not much of a reader." Daisy glowered at him over the rim of her mug, steam obscuring her eyes. "How come you drink and swear so much?"

"We should get the newspapers involved. About the poltergeist." Ignoring the girl's question, Donny turned back to the computer and typed some more. "It would be fantastic publicity."

"I don't want publicity, Donny. What if they put my picture in the paper?" Daisy took her tea into the kitchen and topped it up. "I may as well hand myself in to the cops."

"You could take a few nights off. You deserve it." Donny held up the sheaf of printed papers. "Anyway, things are happening without you causing them."

"We're full up these days. We've got enough customers."

"So we put on more tours. More tours mean more money."

He scratched his neck awkwardly.

"And I've... kind of run out of cash."

"I could sell the stuff you gave me."

"Daisy!" The teen looked shocked. "They were presents."

"I would give the money to you."

"I'll manage." Donny took another slurp of wine. "But thanks."

"Do you drink and swear because Ben does?" The girl got up, opened a kitchen drawer and rummaged inside. "I know you look up to him."

"Tact isn't your strong point, is it?" Donny blustered, trying to cover his embarrassment. "Ben treats me like an equal. He doesn't ignore me."

"But he doesn't want you to be like him. He doesn't want anyone to be like him."

Donny went back to typing, not ready to think about that. From the drawer, Daisy took out a squishy eyeball that she had bought in a joke shop, a tube of superglue and a Stanley knife. Sitting back down on the bed, she began to cut the eyeball in half.

"Can you really see ghosts?" she asked.

"You're a genius at changing the subject. Know that?"

"I learn fast talking to you."

"Yes, I can see ghosts." Donny started a new entry. "I don't expect you to believe that."

"Why wouldn't I?"

"Nobody else does."

"Yeah. But I'm peculiar." It sounded like a joke, but you could never tell with Daisy.

"How come you never talk about your parents?" Donny kept his back to the girl.

"Probably the same reason you never talk about yours." Daisy finished separating the eyeball, put both halves on the covers and slid onto the floor. "I still want to know how you do that thing, where you wrote an invisible message on my book? Why won't you tell me?"

She reached under the bed, pulled out a pint-sized figure and carefully placed it on the bed, propping it up against the wall.

"A proper magician isn't allowed to reveal his tricks," Donny grunted, writing again. "It's a rule."

Daisy squeezed some superglue onto the rubbery backs of the severed eyeball.

"All right," Donny said, his voice flat. "My mum's dead."

"Oh." Daisy was immediately contrite. "I'm sorry."

"My father's a big-shot banker. Jets all over the world." The tapping of the keys faltered. "He gives me an allowance instead of his time. But, like I say, I've spent it."

Donny swivelled around again.

"You going to tell me about your parents now?"

He gave a start and almost fell off his chair.

There was a ventriloquist dummy sitting beside Daisy. It wore a Paisley patterned shirt, green cravat, blue jeans and tiny children's trainers. Topped by black candy-floss hair, the pink painted head seemed too big for its malnourished body.

And it didn't have eyes.

"This is Bunny Wunny Woo," Daisy said. "I found him in the loft."

"What the hell were you doing in the loft?"

"Looking for a good place to hide."

"I won't even ask." Donny lit a cigarette and puffed a cloud of smoke towards the diminutive intruder. "Did you give him that stupid name?"

The girl picked up the dummy and sat it on her knee. She pulled back the collar, revealing a scrawny unpainted wooden neck.

"It's written on a tag."

"What are you doing with him?"

"I'm fixing him up. His arms and legs were broken but I glued them all back together."

Daisy took the two halves of the joke shop eyeball and stuck them in the dummy's eye sockets. It goggled at Donny like an electrocuted sprite.

"There. He's finished."

"Yikes," Donny breathed. "It was creepy before. Now it would give Charles Manson nightmares.

"Charles who?"

Daisy wiggled the head at her friend and spoke from the side of her mouth. Her voice came out much lower than normal, the speech slow and slurred, as the girl struggled to annunciate without moving her lips.

How do you do?
I'm Bunny Wunny Woo
My eyes were broken
My jaw was too
But now I'm fixed and as good as new.

Donny's eyes widened. He had heard that monotone voice before. A tight fist of fear tightened in his stomach.

"Living above a graveyard is getting to you, toots." Donny turned back to his typing, trying to keep the quiver out of his own voice. "What do you want that nasty thing for?"

"Daisy's going to look after me," the dummy lisped in that familiar drone. "Be my mummy."

Bunny Wunny Woo rubbed his painted red nose against her cheek.

"I'm going to talk for her."

"You are giving me serious creeps, girl."

Donny tried to concentrate on the keyboard but behind his back he could hear the click of wood on wood as the doll danced a little jig.

"I hope to God you still have your hand up his bum and he's not doing that on his own." The teenager tried to sound nonchalant. "I can tell he's staring at me."

"He never blinks and never looks away," Daisy said in her normal voice. "He's not shy. He's funny and clever."

She gave the doll a hug.

"Everything I want to be."

"There's nothing wrong with you." Donny gave up and turned back to the girl. "You're quiet, that's all."

"I'm stupid." Daisy buried her head in the manikin's nappy hair. "I can't look *you* in the eye most of the time."

"Hey!" Donny came over and sat next to her. "I like you just the way you are."

"Thank Oo." The sound came out muffled by the manikin's tangled thatch.

Her bare arms, wrapped round Bunny Wunny Woo, were lightly freckled and covered in fine down. Daisy shifted her leg shyly, moving it closer to Donny's, so slight a motion he couldn't tell if it was deliberate. The boy leaned towards her.

Daisy didn't move away.

Her dark hair, fusing into the doll's, smelt of cherries. The back of her neck was exposed and the boy couldn't take his eyes off the smooth white skin.

"I feel safe here," Daisy muttered. "For the first time ever."

Donny reached out and put his hand gently on the girl's back. Daisy relaxed against him for a second. He moved his hand to her neck and her shoulders tightened.

The dummy's head swung round, the malign orbs of its newfound eyes boring into the teenager.

"Daisy doesn't like to be TOUCHED!"

The boy jerked his hand away.

"I'm sorry," he stammered. "I didn't mean to upset you."

He scrambled to his feet and struggled into his jacket,

"I… eh… It's late anyway. I have to be going."

Daisy kept her head buried in Bunny Wunny Woo's hair.

"Goodnight Donny," the dummy said in that familiar expressionless drawl, following the boy's movements with its head. "Daisy has exercises to do."

"Daisy? Are you all right?" Donny paused with his hand on the door.

The girl nodded silently, her face still hidden.

"Donny?" It was the mannikin again.

"You have some last pearl of wisdom?" the boy retorted, regaining some of his composure.

Oh boy, he thought. *I'm replying to the fucking doll.*

"Daisy knows what it's like to be a dummy." The wooden monstrosity tilted its head. "We're scared of being used and then abandoned."

"I'll think that over once I've taken my weirdness pills." Donny pulled open the front door. "Goodnight, toots. Sleep well."

"I doubt she will," Bunny Wunny Woo mouthed, his unblinking bug eyes still fixed on the teenager.

"I doubt it very much."

From the Journal of Donny Marigold

I was having a good old rant to Grizzle about Daisy Lenin.

"Once she's finished scaring the hell out of the customers she goes back to her flat. When I'm crossing the graveyard to jump, there she is, in the attic window. Always holding the damned doll. It looks like they're talking to each other."

"That any more unusual than chatting with a ghost?"

"Probably not." I pulled my jacket tighter. It was getting colder at night as autumn began to bite. "Sometimes she's dancing with it in her arms. How crazy is that?"

Grizzle lay on her back across a flat gravestone, pondering what I'd said. Today she was wearing a scarlet basque, fishnet stockings and Wellingtons with little flowers on them.

"Has she changed?"

"She's much more confident. Started to make jokes and join in when people are talking."

"Do you love her?"

"What?" I spluttered. "I don't even understand her."

"You must like her a bit." Grizzle swung her legs over the edge of the tombstone and sat up, rearranging the basque to cover her boobs. "I mean you're out here with a babe like me and all you can talk about is some other girl."

"I like you too," I said, honestly. "But you're dead."

"Dead cute."

"That's true." To be honest, I was finding it hard to take my eyes off her cleavage. "But there's the age difference. 350 years."

"I'm not an old-fashioned girl." Grizzle treated me to a knowing leer. *"I'm experienced."*

"And deceased," I repeated.

"Men! You'll use any excuse not to commit." Grizzle folded her arms. *"I have feelings, you know."*

"You do?"

"Yes. And you've just hurt them." She puffed out her cheeks in exasperation. *"You're the first good-looking boy I've met in three centuries. Being able to see me is a definite plus, by the way."*

"You think I'm good-looking?" I was unexpectedly pleased.

"Yes. And all you can do is rabbit on about some other gal. It never occur to you that I might be a teeny bit jealous?"

To be frank, that thought hadn't crossed my mind.

"I love hanging with you," I said honestly. *"You're not like any other ghost I ever came across. But how can we be anything more than friends? I can't even, like... kiss you."*

"You sure about that?" Grizzle tilted her head at me, blonde curls spilling over one eye. *"What if you could?"*

Her outfit had laces all the way up the front with a little bow covering the knife wound that killed her.

"I most certainly would," I replied. What the hell? Nobody's perfect.

"Come sit beside me." Grizzle patted the flat tombstone she was perched on, then clenched her fists and took a deep breath. *"Just give me a minute. It's going to be difficult but I know I can do this."*

I sat next to her. I felt shy and excited and more than a little afraid.

Unlike Daisy, Grizzle didn't smell of anything. Probably a good thing, considering how long she'd been dead.

"You won't turn into a rotting corpse or anything, will you?" It wasn't the most romantic approach, but I couldn't help myself. *"Your lips won't fall off?"*

"You certainly know how to spoil the moment."

"I'm sorry. I'm a bit nervous."

"I'll only be in control for a short while." Grizzle closed her eyes. *"So if anything goes wrong, get the hell away from me."*

"Now who's ruining the mood?"

"C'mere." She put her arm round the back of my head and pulled me towards her. *"Don't think. Just do."*

Her lips were cold when they touched mine. But it was a kiss. A passionate kiss too. I put my arms round her and our bodies pressed together.

I was snogging a ghost! I wondered briefly where this came on the scale of sexual perversion but, by this time, I really didn't care.

Grizzle broke away first.

"Damn!" She gasped. *"I can't keep it up."*

"I'm not having that problem myself," I laughed.

"Not so nervous now, eh?" She tried to pinch me on the arm but her fingers went straight through. *"Damn! I'm back to normal again. I need more practise."*

"I'm all for that." I fumbled for my Marlboro Lights. *"Holy hell, I want a cigarette."*

"Think what you'd be like if we actually have sex." Grizzle gave a bashful grin. *"You'll get through a whole packet."*

I almost coughed up a lung. I glanced up at Daisy's window, suddenly guilty. But she obviously wasn't interested in me. Not in that way. And, if she caught us in the act, the only person she'd see would be me.

That *would take some explaining.*

"I guess we're back to talking for now." Grizzle stretched and blew a perfect smoke ring, even though she didn't have a cigarette of her own - which I thought was pretty funny. I was starting to really like this girl.

"Tell me about yourself," she said. *"What you like and dislike."*

"I love history, as you know," I began. *"But I'm good at making up stories and what I'd really like to be is a writer..."*

My God. It never occurred to me that I was the dummy now.

-17-

"I've missed playing with my food. Porridge has definite artistic limitations."

Doc Menzies turned his plate around twice, admiring its contents. Then he began to rearrange his breakfast. Two fried eggs for eyes. A bacon rasher for a mouth. Beans for hair.

The woman opposite sniffed loudly. Large black sunglasses obscured her expression.

"Prison wasn't so bad, in the end." Doc's breakfast leered up at him, each item now separate. "I learned to look after myself."

"So I see." His companion glanced dispassionately at the ex-con's wiry body. He looked to be a stone lighter than the last time they were together. "I can't believe you got released so early."

"You didn't press charges and stuck up for me. The parole board took that into consideration."

"Plus you could talk your way out of a greasy barrel."

"It was still a long time without... you know what." Doc speared an eggy eye with his fork. "I don't want to seem indelicate but even the table legs are turning me on."

"But I'm not, eh?" The woman crossed her own shapely calves. A single untouched coffee and a bowl of fruit sat on the table beside her carefully manicured hand. The nails were long and crimson. "Not that it matters anymore."

"I'm sorry how things turned out, Hannah." Doc watched as yolk bled into the foody face. He pushed the plate away, no longer hungry. "You know that."

"You've come to the wrong person for forgiveness." Hannah pulled back the curtains and peered out of the window. "Had any trouble from the police? They like to keep an eye on parolees."

"They're all out fighting obesity or whatever they do nowadays." Doc glanced at his companion while her attention was diverted. Long dark hair curling down to a strong jaw. Pert nose and a perfect complexion. It reminded him of Daisy.

"You're probably right." Hannah let the curtain drop back into place, relaxing as the shadows darkened around her. "I don't think they even bothered to look for our daughter when she ran away. She took off right after I said you were getting out."

"Are you sorry?"

"After they hauled you off to jail, it made me ill just to look at her." Hannah stuck out her chin defiantly. "But I tried."

"I knew you would."

"You may think you love her, Doc, but what you did isn't love. It's twisted obsession."

"What was Daisy eating when she left?"

"See what I mean?"

The waitress sauntered over and Hannah turned her face away.

"Can I have a milkshake and the cheque?" Doc indicated for the girl to take his breakfast. "Strawberry, please."

"What was she eating?" he repeated once the waitress had gone.

"Salads mainly. No bread. No potatoes. No carbs." The woman glanced at her own Spartan salad. "Nothing she thinks will make her fat."

"And dancing?"

"Like a fiend. Plus ball games and exercises." Hannah gave a snort of disgust. "She wouldn't dream of breaking the regime you instilled in her. She's too afraid."

The waitress plonked a milkshake next to them and went back to watching TV over the bar.

"I don't want to be indelicate," Doc continued. "But we need to talk about money."

Hannah reached under her seat and slid a Prada handbag from the shadows.

"Here." She drew an envelope out of the bag and placed it on the table. "Ten thousand in cash."

"Thank you."

"Everything else is mine, Doc. The house. The car. The bank accounts. That was the deal."

"I'll stick to it. You know that much about me."

"What we had was far from perfect." Hannah signalled for the check. "But I loved you and I loved Daisy. You ruined it all."

"I can't change the past, baby. At least you're wealthy now."

Hannah's retort was cut off by the waitress bringing the bill. The woman removed her sunglasses to read it and the server tried not to stare at her face. One of Hannah's eyes was pulled down, bulging grotesquely, as if it were melting onto her cheek. The scar that crossed it began under her hairline and coursed down one side of her face, pulling the lip up into a crimped and lumpy sneer. Lipstick had stained the top of a permanently exposed incisor, like some messy vampire.

Hannah paid the woman, daring her to comment. She scurried away with a barely repressed judder.

"You did this, Doc." Hannah thrust her face towards him. "I know you went to prison for it but I'll never forgive you."

Doc slurped his milkshake loudly.

"You're a cold one, know that?" The woman replaced her sunglasses. "You got something bad inside you, deep down. I'll never understand…"

"What do you want me to do when I find Daisy?" Doc interrupted, removing the money from the envelope and sliding it into his pocket.

"Whatever you like. She's your problem. Just make sure I never see either of you again."

"And you call *me* cold."

"She's changed more than you could imagine, Doc. It's not natural."

Hannah got up and smoothed down her dress.

"She scares the shit out of me."

-Part 3-

Changes

Nothing is so painful to the human mind as a great and sudden change.

Mary Shelley. *Frankenstein*

No matter how hard we try to be mature, we will always be a kid when we all get hurt and cry.

J. M. Barrie. *Peter Pan*

From the Journal of Donny Marigold

In the 19th century, a guy called Robert Chambers moved into a house down the street from Greyfriars. Until that point, Chambers had intended to become a minister but, shortly after arriving in the area, he abandoned religion and decided to become a writer. His books sold relatively well and Chambers seemed destined for a life of modest fame. Nothing controversial. Nothing inflammatory.

Then, in 1844, he published a book called Vestiges of the Natural History of Creation. *It was like nothing else Chambers had ever written and he did his damnedest to make sure nobody would ever find out he was the author. He had his wife transcribe it to disguise his handwriting and insisted that it be published anonymously. It took forty years before Robert Chambers was unmasked.*

It was as if he was ashamed of what he'd written.

Vestiges *claimed that all life, including mankind, was a product of evolution. It was so controversial it caused a national outrage and was loudly condemned. The church blasted the book as immoral and scientists couldn't understand where he'd got these radical ideas from.*

Chambers called his theory of Evolution 'Transmutation', arguing that life could be created by spontaneous generation. In a way, he was absolutely right. Modern scientists now agree that, millions of years ago, inanimate matter was sparked into life by chemical reactions in some primordial soup.

But the theory of Transmutation goes further than that. It states that life, in theory, can similarly be created **at any time and at any place**.

All it needs is the right conditions.

-18-

Daisy woke to the sound of screaming. The clock by her bed read 2.00 AM. Groggy and disoriented, she listened as the heart-wrenching wails subsided into staccato sobbing.

It was a woman and it was coming from downstairs.

The girl sat up, trying to piece together jumbled fragments of the last few hours. She was still fully clothed, mouth parched and dry.

She remembered Donny had come up after his jump to use the computer and the two of them gossiped as he wrote. The boy seemed to be able to concentrate on several things at once and Daisy was in awe of that ability. Plus it meant he could talk to her without having to turn around. He was still embarrassed by the incident when he put his arm round her.

She wished she hadn't been so vehement in her rejection, using that stupid dummy voice to cover her own awkwardness. It was as if something unbidden had taken control of her, forcing him away. Now he would probably never try to touch her again.

"I always wanted to be an author," he said, tapping furiously. "And I finally have something to write about. It's only diary entries so far but I think I can turn what's happening here into a horror novel."

"Don't kill me in it," Daisy retorted. "Or make me a ghost."

"It's not that kind of book." The teenager replied quickly. "I just believe there's more to this graveyard than meets the eye. May as well use it."

Then he had become engrossed in his efforts and Daisy, sitting on the bed behind him, had drifted off.

Her recollections were shattered by footsteps pounding up the stairs and the rattle of a key in the lock.

Ben Scott burst into the room, shaking with fury.

"Where the hell did you get this?" he shouted, thrusting out his arm.

In his hand was Bunny Wunny Woo.

Daisy glanced at the empty chair where the dummy had been sitting, confused and frightened.

"Where did you GET him?" Ben repeated, taking a menacing step towards her bed and shaking the doll like a rattle. Bunny Wunny Woo's head bobbed from side to side as if warning her to keep quiet.

"I found him in the loft." Daisy pulled the covers up to her chin. "I fixed him up."

"Then you put him in my *hallway*!" Ben slammed his hand against the wall and Daisy gave a squeak of fear. "What? Did you think it would be FUNNY!"

"I left him on that chair." The girl clutched the blanket, knuckles white. "I didn't do anything wrong."

"Didn't do anything wrong!" The tour boss lowered his arms, breathing heavily. Bunny Wunny Woo hung upside down, his black hair brushing the floor. The corner of Ben's mouth twitched as he tried to keep himself under control.

"I've been good to you," he hissed. "And you do THIS to me!"

He flung the dummy across the room and it bounced off the computer.

Almost before it hit the ground, Daisy was out of bed and scooting across the floor. She scooped up the Bunny Wunny Woo and clutched it to her chest, cramming herself into the corner of the room, head pressed against the wall.

"Don't hurt me!" she whimpered. "I've no idea what I've done."

"I want that thing destroyed." Ben's voice was thick with emotion. "I should have done it myself years ago."

He punched the wall again and Daisy gave a terrified groan.

"Get rid of it!"

"I just wanted something to call mine." The girl kept her head lodged against the plaster, rocking backwards and forwards. "I don't have any photographs or music or TV or stuff other girls have. I spend all my time in this room. I don't have friends. Donny only comes up to use the computer."

"Aw, hell. He comes up to see Daisy Lenin, you little idiot." Ben sat down on the bed and put his head in his hands. "And I'm your bloody friend. Or I was until you pulled this stunt."

"You frighten me." Daisy curled herself round Bunny Wunny Woo, trying to make herself as small as possible. "All people frighten me."

"So you made yourself a buddy?" Ben sighed. "I don't know if that's genius or insanity."

"I'll get rid of him," the girl said quietly. "Just don't send me away."

Ben raised his head and looked at his tenant, gripping the doll as if it were her only child.

"Keep the damned thing, then," he rasped. "I did, God help me." His voice softened. "I'm sorry I shouted at you. You didn't deserve it."

Suddenly, he began to cry.

Daisy uncurled herself slowly and looked round.

Huge gulping sobs racked Ben's body. He pressed both hands over his face, fingers digging into his cheeks. His breath came in hiccupping gasps and he bent double, moaning softly.

Daisy slid the dummy away and shuffled forward on her knees. Ben ignored her, lost in his own misery. She hauled herself onto the bed next to her boss, tapping thin fingers agitatedly against each other.

Ben sniffed several times, sucking back hot salty tears filling his mouth.

"I didn't mean to scare you," he whispered.

Slowly Daisy reached out, grimacing, ready to leap away at any second. But Ben seemed barely aware that she was there.

Closing her eyes, she put her arms around him and held on until his misery subsided.

After a while, the tour boss wiped his nose on one sleeve and raised his head. Daisy quickly moved away.

"I've never asked what happened to you and I'm not going to start now." He got to his feet. "All I ask is that you afford me the same courtesy."

"I'm not a curious type."

"You're not, are you?" Ben gave her a lopsided smile. "That's a good quality."

He patted her knee.

"You never tell anyone you saw me cry, ok? Bad for my tough reputation."

He went to the kitchen and splashed cold water on his face.

"And don't let anyone see Bunny Wunny Woo again. Keep him hidden. Promise?"

"I promise."

"You're a good kid." Ben wiped his face dry and headed for the door. "I'm glad you're here."

Then he was gone

Daisy waited for her heart to stop thundering. Finally, she got undressed, sat Bunny Wunny Woo on his chair and switched off the light.

Lying in the dark, she could still hear someone whimpering. She went to the window and looked down.

A woman sat on one of the flat gravestones a few yards away. She was naked except for a long black leather coat draped over pale, thin shoulders. Dishevelled blonde hair stuck up in all directions and she puffed furiously on a cigarette, the light illuminating her tear-stained features in short bursts.

Daisy backed away, holding her breath.

It was Constance.

From the Journal of Donny Marigold

Ben Scott didn't talk to me for a week. He blamed me for putting Bunny Wunny Woo in his hallway, as a practical joke after Daisy had fallen asleep. I protested my innocence but he didn't believe me.

He's not a very trusting sort.

I found myself at a bit of a loose end. Ben hired a part-time jumper outer claiming that I needed a rest and couldn't be working every night. It made perfect sense, but I knew it was really to punish me. Daisy, on the other hand, suddenly found herself in possession of a CD player and a TV. Don't know what she did to suddenly warrant that.

My tutor wanted me to spend more time at home studying. I pointed out I was doing plenty of that at the National Library or using the internet in Daisy's flat.

She could hardly complain. My grades had rocketed despite the fact that I wasn't doing many lessons with her. I'd always been good at history and English but suddenly I excelled at physics and biology too, probably thanks to Deek helping me. She wasn't going to rock the boat, as long as I was getting high marks.

I took to wandering around the outside of Greyfriars to see what was there. At the north end was the old Kirk House, now a homeless shelter, providing the main supply of junkies and vagrants for the cemetery.

Just outside the eastern gates was the Bedlam Theatre, which used to be a mental asylum. On the opposite side of the graveyard was Herriot's School which started off as a hospital. Over the wall from the Covenanter's Prison was Edinburgh Royal Infirmary. It was deserted now, a desolate citadel of Victorian spires and courtyards, replaced by a purpose built hospital on the outskirts of the city.

My God, there were an awful lot of sick and crazy people in Greyfriars' past.

Behind the south wall was Edinburgh University Medical Department, which had seen most of its branches moved to other locations. The only disciplines still taught there were anatomy and biochemistry.

Somehow that didn't surprise me.

I wandered around Forrest Road to the buildings directly behind the Covenanters Prison and the Black Mausoleum. Read a plaque on the door.

Oh boy.

It was once Edinburgh University's Artificial Intelligence Department.

Every time I thought I was putting the jigsaw together, I found another piece that might or might not fit.

It just made me more determined to work out the picture.

After a week, I was forgiven and allowed back into Ben's flat.

On the surface, things looked the same. The guides still hung out with each other after the tours, drinking and talking. But there was a tension that had never been there before. They seemed subdued yet strangely alert. Their faces betrayed the sort of look a rabbit might have if it suspected a fox was around.

Daisy, on the other hand, had been promoted. Ben put her in charge of finances and wages. She was great with figures and we now had a lot of money to deal with. He seemed to trust her more than me.

Good. It meant she stopped pretending to be the poltergeist. Autumn had arrived with a vengeance, it was bitterly cold in the graveyard and she didn't seem able to throw things as accurately as she once had. She even hit one poor guy in the head with a stone.

The truth was, Daisy didn't have to pretend to be a ghost anymore. The number of 'attacks' on our customers had become alarmingly frequent. And they were real.

Which only made the crowds bigger. Ben kept hiring new guides but they never seemed to last long. Only Constance, Oss, Deek and Lee remained permanent fixtures. Only they were allowed to come up to Ben's flat after the tours.

But they were subtly changing.

Lee was abstaining from cigarettes and alcohol, which was making her irritable as hell. Constance, on the other hand, had begun smoking and was drinking more than ever. Oss and Deek tried to keep up the banter they had always enjoyed, yet both were tired and pale and their bickering had an unpleasant edge to it. I guess the strain of doing so many walks was beginning to show. Or, maybe, the things happening on their tours were taking their toll.

Ben seemed ever more distant, too concerned with the cash he was making to notice the mood swing in his staff. He was becoming less like their friend and more like their employer.

On reflection, I think he could see fine what was going on. He just didn't want to deal with it.

As for me? I was putting together a theory about the Mackenzie Poltergeist that almost defied belief. I kept it to myself, but it stopped me sleeping at night.

Daisy was different too. She spent more and more time in Ben's apartment and no longer needed Bunny Wunny Woo for support. She laughed often and looked people in the eye when she spoke. She was vivacious and lively and everyone loved her.

I guess you could say she had blossomed.

I couldn't get her out of my mind.

-19-

Rachel Rouge had just been fired. From a strip job at one of the scuzziest joints in town, of all places. She couldn't believe it.

"I'm the best pole dancer you've ever had," she ranted at the manager. "The best you're ever going to have."

"Aye, you're good, hen," the man admitted. "But you've got an attitude."

"An attitude!" Rachel grabbed a gin and tonic sitting on the bar and downed it in one go. "The way I move I should be carried up to the stage in a fucking Sedan Chair."

The owner of the drink turned back from ogling the next act and puzzled over his empty glass.

"See what I mean?" The manager signalled for the barman to give the bemused customer another round. "You bit a guy's nose last week."

"You didn't see where he'd shoved it."

"The other birds manage to handle awkward customers."

"Listen… I could hold on to that pole with just my stomach muscles if you'd let me. No bloody hands." She cast her eyes around the bar again and the men hunched protectively over their pints. "Most star turns in Las Vegas can't do that."

"The clientele just want to see tits, doll. If they were interested in fancy moves, they'd stay home and watch *Strictly Come Dancing*."

"What do you think these are?" Rachel jiggled her bosoms violently and their nipple tassels spun in a sequined arc. "They're not for helping me take off."

"It was the head honcho's decision," the manager said defensively. "You're a fantastic dancer and you've got a body tae die for…"

"But?"

She'd already guessed the answer.

"It's your face, babe." The manager shrugged. "You're no pretty, are you?"

"None of the girls here are oil paintings," Rachel began, already knowing what the retort would be.

"They're a plain bunch, aye." The manager decided to take the shortest route out of the argument. "But you've got a face like a bulldog chewing a wasp."

Once the manager had retired to his office, Rachel fetched her bag of clothes and sat down at the bar, nothing but glitter paint, tassels and a silver thong covering her embarrassment. The customers who had heard the exchange concentrated their attention on the stage or peered into their drinks.

"Did you hear what that pillock said to me?" Rachel asked the barman. He nodded sympathetically.

"Then pretend you didn't and give me a double. Put it on my tab."

She managed to get through half a dozen vodkas before the manager came out again. Throwing the fur coat over bare shoulders, Rachel picked up her bag and headed out of the door, flipping him the bird as she left.

She stomped up Candlemaker Row, still seething. Fired from a pole dancing job! How low could she damned well sink? She was talented, Goddammit! Her voice had a four-octave range. As a kid, she'd taken years of ballet lessons and only left when one of the other girls described her as Bela Lugosi in a tutu.

She'd graduated from drama college with the dream of making it as an actress. Then worked bar jobs and waited tables, always expecting her big break to be just round the corner. Pole dancing had been a way to earn extra money at night and actually have men ogle her. From the neck down, anyway.

Pathetic.

The only film role she'd successfully auditioned for was as a zombie in some low-budget horror. Probably because she didn't need much makeup. That and a pole dancer in some crime show, but only cause she knew how to do it. Even then she was filmed from the back.

Casting directors all agreed she could act. She just couldn't act pretty.

As Rachel passed the entrance to Greyfriars, she heard faint laughter from the back of the cemetery. Must be one of those ghosty tours.

She'd had a colleague who used to stay in a flat overlooking Greyfriars and Rachel had always been fascinated by the place. She'd even written asking for a job. The walks would all be at night, so she could still go to auditions and an actress was probably the perfect person for that kind of thing.

She hadn't got a reply.

Rachel had never been on a ghost walk, so this would be a good opportunity to have a peek at exactly what they did. Maybe try again in her attempts at getting hired.

Hell, her face might even be an advantage. It certainly looked scary enough.

She chuckled at the thought and turned into the cemetery.

The gravel path was lined with little lampposts, though they hardly dented the blackness. Rachel shivered a little, despite her thick coat. The air was clear and crisp and making her feel more than a little tipsy.

The line of lights ended twenty feet north of the Covenanters Prison and muted voices rumbled somewhere inside. Rachel moved onto the grass, frost crunching under her stilettos, and sat down on a low wall, making sure the fur coat was tucked under her bum. She shivered again and stamped high heels on the ground.

This was a stupid idea. She was drunk and it was cold and who knew when the tour would come out of that walled bit?

Gradually her eyes were drawn to the lamppost. It was an old-fashioned type, thin as a washing pole and only a couple of metres high, topped with a little carved crosspiece and imitation gas lamp. Rachel pulled an iPod from her bag, tucked it into her tasselled bra and stuck in the earphones. *Johnny and Mary* by Placebo blasted into her head, one of her favourite songs. One they never let her dance to in the bar because it was too raunchy.

Idiots.

A slow smile spread across her face. The drinks were certainly taking effect.

Why the hell not? She had to keep warm somehow.

After Donny had jumped out, Oss wrapped up his tour and led the group out of the Covenanters Prison. Nothing had happened tonight, which was becoming an increasingly rare occurrence. But Oss was relieved. He was tired of chasing screaming customers round the tombs and assuring them the livid mark on their face was all part of the show.

Donny was standing just outside the Covenanter gate. He had taken off his mask and stuffed it in his pocket, his attention focussed on something just round the corner.

"What you hell are you doing, wee D?" the guide whispered, holding up his hand to stop the group. "Everyone can see you."

Donny didn't reply. Oss stepped forwards to find out what the teenager was staring at.

"Oh," he said, lowering his arm. "Now, *that's* something you don't come across every day."

In a brittle patch of illumination, a nearly naked woman was spinning round and round one of the lampposts. Her shapely arms and legs were stretched out as if she were defying gravity. She was holding onto the pole with only her stomach muscles. Face obscured by whipping black hair, her skin matched the grass below, glittering in the amber light as if covered in golden frost.

The tour party crowded behind Oss in silence, not wanting to destroy the moment. Some of them began to take photographs.

"Is that the poltergeist?" one man muttered.

"Don't be a bloody tube." Oss was too awed to be polite. "That's the most perfect thing I've ever set eyes on."

Putting a finger to his lips he led the group away, all of them staring back over their shoulders at the drunk woman.

Rachel Rouge's best friend reported her missing a week later. The police made a few inquiries, but on finding out she had just been sacked from a strip club, quickly wound down operations. She would doubtless turn up somewhere. Some other town. Some other fleapit.

She never did.

From the Journal of Donny Marigold

In 1825 Charles Darwin attended Edinburgh Medical School on the other side of the wall from Greyfriars Graveyard. There's no doubt he had heard of Hume's pal, James Burnett and his oddball publication outlining human evolution. People in Edinburgh were still taking the mickey out of him, even though Burnett had been dead for over 20 years.

Darwin also read Robert Chambers' Vestiges, *which put him off publishing his own theories until he was certain he was right. In fact, it took Darwin almost a lifetime to pluck up the courage to publish his great work. For twenty-five years, after leaving the Greyfriars area, he suffered from bouts of hysterical crying, panic attacks, depression and nervous tension.*

In 1859 he finally unleashed On the Origin of the Species - *containing his painstakingly worked out theory of Evolution. His idea destroyed one of the cornerstones of religion, the biblical story of Creation. Darwin was understandably wary of calling anyone a monkey's uncle. As a young man he had been fervently religious, considering a career as an Anglican minister - though, like Dickens, he eventually became a Unitarian.*

He was right to worry. The Origin of the Species *caused apoplexy among the general public and poor old Charlie was lambasted as a menace to society. How could a Christian come up with such a dangerous and blasphemous theory?*

Fortunately, Darwin had been backed by another scientific giant. An Edinburgh resident called James Hutton had already published a book proving the earth developed over millions of years, in direct opposition to church teachings.

Darwin and Hutton's works (along with another Scot called Alfred Wallace) were the greatest blows ever delivered to Christian ideology. Darwin became legendary and Hutton is celebrated as the 'Father of Modern Geology'. He also happens to be buried in the Covenanters Prison, where a small plaque marks his final resting place.

A few feet away is the unmarked grave of the man who started the whole thing, James Burnett.

I guess that's how natural selection works.

There were, of course, scientists who tried to subvert these ideas and defend religion. One of the most celebrated was Edinburgh geologist, Hugh Miller. In 1847 he wrote Footprints of the Creator, *which argued that proof of biblical events like the great flood could be found in rock formations.*

Miller might have continued his attacks. Instead, he committed suicide after insisting he was being hounded by an invisible supernatural entity.

-20-

A crowd packed the Black Mausoleum, the more cautious ones crammed against the walls, the rest sardined into the centre. Though winter had arrived, there had to be at least thirty people on the tour. They were all silent. Expectant.

"Just what is this thing we call the Mackenzie Poltergeist?" Constance stood with her hands on her hips. She had dyed her hair black to match her outfit and the result was striking. She looked like she had just stepped off a Harley Davidson.

"We have one explanation that, weird as it sounds, seems to have caught on with the paranormal community. Does anyone know what pheromones are?"

A few of the crowd shrugged and the rest had to follow suit, as everyone's shoulders were pressed together. Constance chuckled, a sound distinctly at odds with her rock chick appearance. The new theory was Donny's, of course, but it sounded suitably sciency.

"Pheromones are hormones that insects produce and secrete in the air. Then their buddies pick them up using a sort of chemical telepathy. That's why an ant colony is like a giant brain even though individual ants are thick as mince."

The tomb smelled of damp and sweat. Constance had downed a few drinks before she began and the aroma made her feel slightly nauseous.

"Human beings, it has recently been discovered, also produce pheromones. It's still an unexplored field of biology but we emit them, for example, when we are sexually aroused."

A few males near the front looked at her lasciviously. She sighed and carried on.

"If we *are* capable of transmitting and detecting pheromones, it explains a lot of erratic human behaviour, especially if you get a crowd of people together all feeling the same thing."

The fact that she was addressing just such a gathering wasn't lost on the tour.

"It explains mass hysteria. Violence at football matches. Love-ins like Woodstock. The Nuremberg Rallies. Religious gatherings where everyone dances like an idiot. That would cover Raves as well. Anywhere that emotions take over from common sense, really."

"Like on this tour," one dissenter muttered, a large man in a long Oilskin coat.

"But insects produce another kind of pheromone," Constance continued, undeterred. "The Alarm Pheromone. They secrete it when they feel threatened and it makes other ants agitated too. Sends them into a frenzy and they'll attack anything that moves."

The group suddenly stopped shuffling against each other.

"We think this poltergeist is a human pheromone cloud that has become so dense that it is able to interact with people." Constance knew her lines off by heart, so half her brain was concentrating on the doorway. Donny would have reached it by now and be waiting just around the corner.

"So... we get a bunch of people into an enclosed mausoleum in a graveyard every night. Like you lot, for instance. We make you afraid. You release alarm pheromones but they can't go anywhere, so they build up in concentration, maybe even join with the emissions from the night before. Finally, there's enough to actually overload a member of the tour party. It might make you hear things or feel cold or sick or even knock you out. It could even cause a psychosomatic reaction that would mark your skin."

"Rubbish!"

It was Oilskin again.

Constance ignored him. The bulk of the party were on her side and Donny would jump soon and give that sceptical bastard the shock of his life.

"If the pheromone theory is true, it makes the poltergeist sound like nothing more than a chemical reaction." Constance lowered her voice. "If it weren't for one thing. This entity seems to have some sort of self-awareness."

There was a loud raspberry sound from the darkness.

"I think I just made an emission." Oilskin fanned the air. "And it sure as shit wasn't pheromones."

"Aw, man. That is rancid!" one woman complained.

Several people laughed. The spell was broken. Constance was losing them.

"This thing has begun to grow and to learn," she said, struggling on. "I'm convinced of it. As it increases in power it gets more... interactive. The more it scares you, the more you produce pheromones. The more pheromones you create, the stronger it grows and the more self-aware it becomes."

She lowered her voice to a whisper.

"It's evolving."

But the tension was broken. One or two people were still laughing quietly. Constance wished Donny would jump out now, but she knew he would wait. Give her the chance to win the crowd back.

"So you don't want to make it angry or you..."

Constance stopped mid-sentence. Her eyes rolled back in her head and she collapsed.

The crowd shuffled forwards. The guide didn't move.

"Is she all right?" A woman whispered.

"Of course she is," Oilskin complained. "This is just a con."

Constance lay crumpled on the ground, arms and legs at an impossible angle, eyes wide open.

"Stop it, now," another woman joined in. "That's not funny."

"What's wrong with her?"

The crowd began to retreat. One or two broke away and knelt beside her, waving their hand in front of her face.

"Nobody can lie in that position without moving!"

"Do something!"

"Oh, God. She's not breathing."

Constance was as immobile as a headstone. The wisps of hair across her nose and mouth didn't stir.

"I think she's dead," one crouching man whispered. "Is anyone here a doctor?"

"Stop it!"

"Someone call the police!"

Constance's head snapped up and one or two people in the front row screamed.

"What happened to me?" she rasped.

"You collapsed. Are you all OK?"

"Oh no," she choked. "That means it's *here*."

"Come on!" Oilskin protested. "You're not falling for this crap, are you?"

"Something touched me." A child's plaintive voice drifted out from the back of the tomb. "Something's been touching my back. I want to leave."

"Get that boy out now!" Constance commanded, struggling to her feet. "I don't know what it did to me but it means we've gone over ten minutes."

The crowd solemnly parted to let the crying boy out.

Only it wasn't a child who emerged from the gap.

A large man in a puffer jacket elbowed the boy out of the way. He stumbled for the door of the mausoleum, sweeping Constance aside.

Just as he was reaching sanctuary, Donny jumped into the tomb.

The man screamed and veered to the right to avoid him. His face slammed into the stone corner of the doorway and he slid sideways, skin peeling off, as his forehead scraped along the wall. He landed on the muddy floor and rolled onto his back, groaning. Blood poured from an enormous gash in his head and turned his face crimson.

The crowd gave a collective gasp.

The man jumped up, fists raised, as if he was trying to defend himself.

"Leave me alone!" he shrieked. "I was looking for wings!"

Donny tore off his mask and the tour party retreated back into the tomb, pushing at each other. Constance skipped quickly away, almost falling in her haste to distance herself.

The large man ran again. This time there was no Donny in the way but blood had gotten into his eyes. He stumbled and his face slammed into the rough stonework with an audible crunch. He reeled back, arms outstretched, as if he had been crucified, and sank to his knees. Constance clasped a hand to her mouth.

The man began to crawl out of the tomb towards Donny, moaning loudly. He pulled himself to his feet, throwing off the boy's helping hand and staggered away into the darkness of the prison.

Constance turned back to the crowd, eyes glittering and black hair falling over her face like a veil. She pointed her cane at Oilskin and giggled, a sinister gurgle that sounded as if she were on the verge of a breakdown.

"Want to try farting again?" she whispered. "See what Mackenzie does to *you*?"

"I won't be the only who's scuppered, then," the man said quietly, glancing at his crying companions.

"Half the people here just crapped themselves."

Donny walked Constance back to Ben's flat.

"What the hell happened in that tomb tonight?"

"I don't know." Constance opened the front door. "You coming up?"

"Nah. I'll let you two alone. You going to tell Ben what happened?"

"What's the point? He refuses to believe any of this stuff is real." Constance tucked the cane under her arm and leaned against the wall. "I suppose that dude could have just freaked out, but you don't really believe that, do you?"

"Nope." Donny took a packet of Marlboros from his pocket with trembling hands. "But I can see ghosts. You believe *that*?"

Constance removed a cigarette from his packet and stuck it behind her ear.

"I'm starting to."

Donny waited until the door had closed then walked into Greyfriars Bobby's pub, next door to the graveyard. He planted his elbows on the bar, lit a cigarette, and ordered a glass of white wine. The barman looked at him suspiciously and considered asking for ID. The teenager held his stare.

The barman poured the drink. The kid might be fresh faced but his eyes were old. You couldn't fake that.

Donny took the glass and made his way to a booth in the corner. There was one other occupant, a man in his forties. He moved along to give the teenager some room.

"How you doing, boy?" he raised his glass. "Been a while."

Donny took a gulp of his wine and leaned his head back against the red leather.

"Hello Doc," he said.

"I wondered when you'd finally turn up."

From the Journal of Donny Marigold

"What the hell is haunting this graveyard?" I sat down on a low wall next to Grizzle and lit a cigarette.

"Apart from me, you mean?" Today she was wearing a tunic, mini skirt and shiny tights, all in Lincoln Green – with hair to match, naturally. She also had on thigh-high leather boots. I'm a sucker for thigh-length leather boots. I briefly imagined Daisy wearing that outfit, then immediately felt guilty. Guilty about Daisy and guilty about Grizzle.

This place was messing me up royally.

"Are you supposed to be Peter Pan?" I asked.

"Yup," the ghost nodded merrily. "It's almost panto season."

"It's September."

"I've always wanted to see a panto."

"Oh no, you haven't!" I said immediately. Couldn't help it, really.

"Oh yes I have!" Grizzle gave a delighted squeal. She leaned forwards and kissed me on the cheek, one hand on my knee.

"Feel that?" She tightened her grip. "I've been practising."

"On who?" I felt a momentary flash of jealousy.

"Not the kissing part, stupid." Grizzle patted my cheek. "I like it when you get all macho and protective, though."

"Stop putting me off." I removed her hand. "I'm serious, Grizzle. What's this thing in the Covenanter's Prison? Is it a ghost? A poltergeist? A demon?"

"What makes you think I'd know?"

"You claim to have been here for three hundred years." I folded my arms in exasperation. "I think you might have noticed a supernatural entity happy slapping people on your turf."

"Don't ask so many questions," Grizzle said solemnly. "Leave it be."

"I'd love to, if my job didn't involve me waltzing to its lair every night and watching people take a pasting. What if it turns on one of the guides?"

"How many people used to come into the graveyard at night before the tours started?" Grizzle asked.

"Nobody."

"And now?"

"Hundreds," I admitted.

"Then, if no guides have been hurt, maybe you're giving it exactly what it wants. People to interact with."

"By interact, you mean molest."

"These attacks are the reason your walks are so busy. So, you've both got what you wanted. It's a symbiotic relationship."

I didn't like the thought of having any kind of relationship with the poltergeist and told her so.

Grizzle looked at the ground and clicked her heels together nervously.

"I'm not going to mess with the Mackenzie Poltergeist, to give it your dumb name. Live and let live is my motto, even if I'm dead."

She leaned her head on my shoulder.

"What about your husband?" I changed tack. "He appeared yet?"

"I'd love to see a panto." Grizzle picked a bit of lint from her tunic and studied it carefully.

"Stop being evasive." I reached out and took her hand. "You're a spirit. You don't get fluffy."

"Oh yes I do!"

I decided to go for the short sharp approach.

"Mister Menzies wouldn't happen to be related to Doc Menzies, by any chance?" I asked.

It certainly had the desired effect.

"You have to stay away from Doc Menzies!" Grizzle squeezed my hand until it hurt. "He's bad news!"

Didn't I know it.

"You have my word." I gave a scout-like salute. "Want to explain why, though?"

"Call it woman's intuition."

"Good enough for me," I said. "I promise."

"I can tell you're lying," Grizzle grunted. "That will end badly for everyone, mark my words."

Of course, she was right.

-21-

More new staff were conducting the tours that night so the regulars could attend a get-together at Ben's flat. Balloons bearing the logo 'Carphone Warehouse' had been taped to the walls and the tour boss presented everyone with paper crowns, which only Deek consented to wear.

"What's the occasion, hun?" Lee asked. "Why all the secrecy?"

"It's Daisy's birthday." Ben poured them all a glass of champagne. "Sweet sixteen."

He glanced at the girl's jet black attire.

"Well... as sweet as someone who looks like a vampire can get."

Daisy grinned.

"Why didn't you tell us, babe?" Constance gave the girl a hug. "We would have brought presents."

"I didn't want to bother anyone."

"She told Donny and he told me," Ben said.

"Donny got me this!" Daisy held up a silver heart-shaped pendant. "I love it."

The boy blushed.

"That is *beautiful*. Looks expensive too." Lee turned to Ben. "What did *you* get her, hun?"

"Eh? I'm supplying the bloody champagne."

"The legal drinking age is 18."

"I'm running a tour company, not a nunnery." Ben poured himself a glass of bubbly. "Besides, Daisy doesn't drink much, so there's more for the rest of us."

"Rotter!"

"Ben lent me the money for the pendant." Donny broke in. "I didn't have nearly enough but I wanted to get Daisy something special."

"Oh, you big softie." Lee kissed her boss on the cheek.

"Listen. I thought I might go over a few points." Ben got out his notorious clipboard. "Since we're all here."

"Isn't this a birthday party?"

"It is. But I thought you'd respond better to criticism while you're drinking my booze."

"Eh? What have we done wrong?"

"Nothing. In fact, you're doing too good a job." Ben paused, trying to find the best way to phrase his doubts. "You're scaring the hell out of the customers and that's great for business. But it's getting a tad extreme."

"You're not kidding," Constance said morosely. "I had a woman slapped so hard last week her glasses broke."

"I know." Ben grumped. "I had to pay for a new pair. I'll bet they fell off when the jumper outer came in and then got stood on."

"It was too dark to see," the girl admitted.

"Daisy's not doing her terror tactics anymore and Donny has toned down the jumps, but it's not making any difference." Ben shook his head. "The punters are still going nuts in the Black Mausoleum. The bruises and scrapes they get when they panic and bump around in the dark are starting to look pretty serious."

He folded his arms and glared at his staff.

"The council and church are making noises. I don't want to be shut down."

"We could let Deek do more shifts," Oss suggested. "He's rubbish."

"Oh yeah?" Deek blew a puff of smoke in his friend's direction. "I've had fifteen people collapse. You've only had ten. And that's just your body odour."

"That hurts, Big D." Oss farted and waved the smell in Deek's direction.

"No, THAT hurts!"

"Nice to see you're all taking this to heart."

"We're not doing anything, hun." Lee held her nose daintily. "Honestly."

"You're not there, boss." Deek agreed. "You don't see what happens. The people who get marked are standing on their own. There's nobody near them."

"It's all psychosomatic. There's always a couple of nutters on the tours, desperate for a bit of attention."

"Even that doesn't fit. Some of the people with marks on their bodies don't believe a word of what we're saying. They aren't even scared until something happens to them." Oss scratched his lip thoughtfully. "And what about the dead birds we keep finding in the mausoleum entrance?"

"When I see a dead bird, I don't normally assume a damned poltergeist killed it." Ben threw his clipboard on the bed. "My first guess would be a cat."

"We don't see any cats in the graveyard these days. And there used to be lots of them."

"You don't see them because their idea of a good time is creeping around in the dark and crapping on the flowers, not following noisy tours to hear about Greyfriars Bobby."

The guides stayed silent.

"Come on guys!" Ben was incredulous. "You're not saying you believe your own PR?"

"Of course not." There was a chorus of grunts and shaking heads.

"But we can't explain what's happening," Oss ventured. "Not rationally."

"If you were the rational type, you wouldn't be trying to light the wrong end of your cigarette."

"Damn."

"I believe." Donny piped up from the corner. "I think the poltergeist is real."

"Me too," Daisy added.

"No offence, toots." Ben wagged a finger at the girl. "But you agree with everything Donny says. And *he* claims he can see ghosts."

"I can speak to them too. Don't forget that."

Ben groaned.

"What if the kids are right?" Constance was still crouched by the window, her glass untouched on the sill. "What if there really is something supernatural in the Covenanters Prison?"

"Let me put it to you in a way you can understand." Ben crammed a party hat on his head. "I'll even wear this so you know I'm serious."

Lee sniggered and put on a paper crown as well.

"Ready to receive your wisdom, hun."

"Before we came along, nobody got attacked. Nobody fell down. Nobody had ever heard of a poltergeist. In case you had forgotten, we invented the bloody thing."

Ben rolled his eyes theatrically.

"People get hurt. People collapse. People find cuts and scratches. That's cause people are stupid."

"Can't argue with that boss. I had one ask me why the castle was built so close to the train station."

"They get a sneaky slap from the guy standing next to them, they have a fainting fit, or a bump from hitting the wall when Donny jumps out." Ben was in full rant mode. "And they think that's proof of sodding life after death, or evidence that two thousand years of science is barking up the wrong tree?"

He ticked off each point on his fingers.

"We made up the poltergeist. We made up the name. We made up explanations for what it is. We made up the stuff it does. WE MADE IT UP!"

He pulled out a sparkly box from under his chair.

"Now, who wants to pull a fucking cracker?"

An hour later, the party was in full swing. Everyone, bar Donny, had put hats on and brightly coloured streamers, bits of cracker and plastic toys littered the floor. Even Lee had begun drinking, declaring that it was a celebration, after all.

Only Constance remained subdued, glancing out of the window now and then, as she slowly sipped her wine.

"I have a money-making idea, I've been wanting to float," Ben said eventually.

"I'm interested in any sentence that contains the word money," Oss replied glibly.

"How about doing a séance? Just for a select few customers who are really into the supernatural."

"You mean the total weirdos?" Deek now had three hats on his head, the lowest one slipping over one eye. "We could charge a bucket load for that."

"It's a great idea, hun." Lee slapped him on the knee. "I'd love to do a proper séance."

"Are you kidding?" Constance countered. "It's freezing out there. On the rare occasions when it's not raining."

"It wouldn't be in the Covenanter's Prison," Ben said. "There's empty premises next door we could use. I have the key."

"How did you manage that?"

"I murdered the occupants," the tour boss chortled. "We could bring them back and ask if you don't believe me."

Constance shot him a dirty look but Ben didn't notice.

"Thought we might do a trial run, just us lot. See how things turn out."

"Absolutely. When?"

"Some night when there's nothing good on TV."

"Fair enough."

"I have a request as well." Donny clinked a pencil against his glass. "Only it's a bit weird."

"Not happening unless you wear a hat, Wee D."

"Find me a black one and I will."

"You can have whatever you want," Ben said magnanimously. "As long as it doesn't cost anything."

"You know I've been writing about the tours, yeah?"

"The famous journal nobody's ever seen?"

"Well… I'm thinking about turning it into a horror novel. About City of the Dead and the poltergeist. I always wanted to be an author, you know."

Ben winced.

"Nice one." Deek hiccupped. "If I come across as a knob-end you can call my character Oss."

"What do you need from us?" Ben held up his hand to quieten the others.

"I want each of *you* to write me a horror story."

"A *bit* weird? That's well out of left field."

"There was a party like this, long ago, and the people at it all did the same thing," Donny replied stubbornly. "Two of the stories became famous and I think they were inspired by Greyfriars." He jabbed a thumb at his companions. "We're storytellers, aren't we? I'd like to see if we can repeat that."

"You talking about the origins of *Dracula* and *Frankenstein*?" Constance asked. The other guides looked impressed.

"That's the one."

"I'm in," Ben said finally. "Who am I to stand between you and your literary masterpiece?"

"Thank you."

The tour boss looked around at the others.

"You up for it? We owe the kid, after all."

"Don't see why not."

"Then pull on it." Ben held out a cracker to the boy. "I'm in."

Donny reached out and pulled.

There was a loud bang. Deek and Oss leapt up and Lee clutched her stomach defensively.

The sound hadn't come from the cracker. It reverberated against the window next to Constance and a splash of red blossomed on the pane, along with the imprint of a pair of wings. The girl toppled backwards with a squeal and landed on the floor, knocking over her drink.

Oss and Deek ran to the window and pulled it up. The others crowded round and looked out.

"Aw no!"

"Poor thing flew into the window," Ben said uncertainly. "Maybe it was sick."

The broken body of a seagull twitched on the ground below them, flapping weakly as it died.

From the Journal of Donny Marigold

If you are clever and you know your business you can fake a bone as easily as you can a photograph.

Arthur Conan Doyle. *The Lost World*

Between 1876 and 1881, Edinburgh resident Arthur Conan Doyle studied at the Medical School, next to the graveyard, where he became friends with Robert Louis Stevenson. It was also when he started writing properly.

He is famous, as everyone knows, for his stories about Sherlock Holmes - a man who prized reasoning and logic over everything else.

Here's a strange thing, though. Despite creating the most rational character in literary history, Doyle was convinced of the existence of supernatural beings. For much of his life, he travelled the world looking for evidence of paranormal events and eventually became one of the world's leading champions of Spiritualism, the idea that humans could communicate with the 'other side'. He also suffered from severe depression and fits of hysteria.

What was up with these writers who hung around Greyfriars? What was torturing them so much? I can see ghosts, but that's just the way it is. I don't have a hissy fit about it.

Then I found something else.

Arthur Conan Doyle used to live near a village called Piltdown and had befriended two scientists, Charles Dawson and Arthur Woodward, who happened to be carrying out geological excavations nearby.

Because of that friendship, Conan Doyle frequently gained access to the site when nobody else was around.

At the time, it didn't seem odd. Doyle was a respected doctor and an amateur anthropologist and geologist.

Dawson and Woodward then began to unearth prehistoric bones and teeth at the site. They used the fossils to construct the now famous Piltdown Man - a human skull with a Simian-like jaw. This was accepted to be absolute proof that man was descended from apes and the final nail in the coffin for those who still doubted Charles Darwin's claims about human evolution.

In 1952 the discoveries were found to be fake. Dawson got the blame, yet I wasn't so sure he was the culprit. The Piltdown jaw was actually an Orang-utan's with the teeth filed down - and it had been cleverly broken to hide the fact it didn't really fit the rest of the skull.

Conan Doyle was an expert on jaws, having inherited a vast collection of casts from a dentist whose house he lived in.

The Piltdown bones were chemically stained to make them appear much older than they actually were.

Conan Doyle was an accomplished chemist.

The other fossils found at the site turned out to have come from different parts of the world. They matched the places that Arthur Conan Doyle had visited on his obsessive quest to find genuine paranormal occurrences.

For God's sake, the man believed in Fairies! So why would he want to fake a missing link and give Charles Darwin a much-needed helping hand? Did he think science and the supernatural, somehow, went hand in hand?

What was going on in his mind?

-22-

Billy Cream was on his third whisky when he heard knocking. He turned down the TV and shuffled into the hallway to open the door.

Recognising the outline in the pebbled glass, he stopped dead. The knocking began again.

Billy pressed himself against the wall and held his breath. The letterbox creaked open and a pair of pale blue eyes scanned the hall.

"Hello, Billy." One of the eyes winked. "Going to let me in?"

"Fuck off."

"I'll huff and I'll puff."

"I've got nothing to say to you."

"That's a shame. I have a bottle of very fine McCallan and a newspaper article I'd like to discuss."

"I want to be left alone."

"Or I could go tell the neighbours who you are," the voice said happily. "You probably don't need the aggro."

The pale blue eyes were unblinking.

"I might even be able to help you again. Go on. Do yourself a favour."

Cursing quietly, Billy Cream opened the door.

Doc Menzies gave him a pat on the shoulder and stepped inside.

The men slouched opposite each other, in cheap Ikea couches, the bottle perched on a coffee table between them. Billy drained his whisky and poured another.

"Get in a fight?" Doc asked. "You seem to be missing a couple of teeth."

"I went on one of those tours of Greyfriars. Don't even know why." Billy touched his cut and battered face self-consciously. "Freaked out a bit and hit a wall."

"Looks nasty. Good job you've had first aid training."

"I'm totally messed up, Doc. I've never been the same since you came into my life."

"You had problems long before that. You just don't remember." Doc removed a newspaper clipping from inside his jacket and placed it on the table. Billy didn't even glance at it. He knew the words off by heart.

Ambulance Driver takes Dying Girl to Closed Hospital

An ambulance driver drove a seriously ill girl to the Old Edinburgh Royal Infirmary, even though it had been closed for several months. Despite regularly ferrying patients to the new Edinburgh Royal Infirmary at Little France, Billy Cream (22) drove Valerie Darroch (12) to the abandoned hospital near Greyfriars Graveyard. The girl subsequently died of a massive asthma attack in the deserted grounds.

Mr Cream blamed the pressures of work on a 'temporary mental breakdown', insisting that he could not recall what happened. According to the paramedic who accompanied the ambulance, Mr Cream seemed 'totally confused' by what he had done.

The incident is now being investigated by both the police and Lothian Health authorities.

"Pressures of work?" Doc raised an eyebrow. "You're not a bomb disposal expert. You sit on your arse and whiz around town going *Nee Naw*."

"I wasn't drinking. The breath test proved it." Tears welled up in Billy's eyes. "The mother of the kid is suing me."

"What made you go to Greyfriars?"

"I don't know." The big man sagged visibly, sinking further into the couch. His white T-shirt had a rusty stain down the front, matching his dirty ginger hair. "What are you doing here, anyway? I didn't even know you were out of prison."

His eyes brightened briefly.

"You're not thinking of setting up the old business? I can't get hired for love or money."

"That's the kind of trouble I don't need anymore." Doc took a pack of cards from his pocket and began to shuffle them. "Like you, I'm out of options. But I have some unfinished stuff to take care of before I consider my next career move."

"Didn't think you were here for a social call." Billy stretched thick arms along the back of the coach and looked nervously over his shoulder. "How long are you going to stare at my decor before you decide to comment?"

"It does leap out at you." Doc got to his feet, the cards magically vanishing. He walked around the room, hands behind his back, like an art gallery patron.

There were photographs of children on every wall. Some in frames, others thumb tacked to the plaster. Most looked like they had been taken in the graveyard.

"You could do with a couple of landscapes. Just for a bit of variety." Doc stopped at three of the larger pictures.

"I see you have Myrtle Gibbs and some other City of the Dead guides beside the kids. There's Daisy. And Donny Marigold as well."

"Eh?" Billy Cream frowned. "He isn't called Donny Marigold."

"Why have you turned them all into birds?"

On every picture, Billy had drawn wings, sprouting from the backs of the children. Some were tiny pencil marks, no more than a cluster of badly executed feathers. Others spread beyond the confines of the paper, unfurling across the walls in crimson and blue paint.

"They're not birds. They're angels."

"Oh." Doc stroked his chin. "I wouldn't know. Never having seen one."

"I have." Billy's drink trembled on the way to his mouth. "I see one every night when I try to sleep. The little girl I killed."

The glass clinked against his teeth and he used both hands to steady it.

"In my dreams she's trying to get to heaven. But the wings are too small and she's carrying something that pulls her down."

"Like a Tesco bag?"

"Something terrible. It's hidden inside her." Billy's head began to droop. "All these children are like that. I can see it in their eyes."

"None of them are looking at the camera. Seems like you've been doing a bit of stalking."

"I can tell anyway. You taught me how."

"And here's Bunny Wunny Woo." To the left of Daisy the dummy peered intently out of a gold frame. "He count as a kid?"

"Reminds me of you. Got the same nasty stare."

"What else do you see, Billy?" Doc stroked Daisy's image and his finger squeaked on the glass. "What do you think is happening to you?"

"I have urges." The man began to cry. "I can't control them."

He jerked involuntarily, whisky spilling down the front of his chest. He rolled his eyes, head lolling back across thick shoulders.

"I'm sick."

"I wouldn't argue with that."

"That's not what I mean." Billy tried to raise his head but the motion was slow and uncoordinated. "Have you poisoned me, Doc?"

"It's a little concoction that I added to the whisky. Easy to put together if you have my background."

"What will it do?" Billy's speech was slurred now. The glass fell from his fingers and landed between his legs, spilling amber liquid across his jeans.

"It'll relax you. Look at the state you're in." Doc sat on the coffee table opposite Billy and took the man's head in his hands. "I need you to look me in the eyes."

"I don't want to!" Billy shut his eyes tightly. "I'm scared!"

He tried to pull himself upright but no longer had the strength.

"Shhhh.... I understand. I really do." Doc held the man's chin tightly and stroked his hair. "You're a good, decent bloke but you can't live like this any more. I don't know if it will work, but I'm going to try and fix you."

Half an hour later, Doc let himself out of the front door, hair plastered to his head with sweat. He had pulled the curtains closed and wiped down the furniture. In a carrier bag were the remains of the whisky and the pictures from Billy's wall of City of the Dead staff. Doc whistled a few bars of *Peter and the Wolf,* then glanced up and down the street to make sure there were no twitching curtains.

Not much he could do about it if there was.

He put his head down, just in case, and walked briskly out of the neighbourhood.

A week later, the police found Billy Cream's body hanging from the light in his living room, like some fat angel in a cheap pantomime. The coffee table lay on its side and his nose had bled onto the mottled carpet as he slowly swung in spirals.

It had spread out and soaked in until it looked like a pair of wings.

-Part 4-

The Stories

It's like everyone tells a story about themselves inside their own head. Always. All the time. That story makes you what you are. We build ourselves out of that story.

Patrick Rothfuss

"Do you know," Peter asked, "why swallows build in the eaves of houses? It is to listen to the stories."

J. M. Barrie. *Peter Pan*

From the Journal of Donny Marigold

When I arrived at the flat after my jump there were a pile of papers lying on the computer table. Daisy sat on the bed hunched over a note-pad, pencil clenched in her fist. She didn't look up when I came in. I tried to take an upside down peek and got a glimpse of crude childish handwriting, with words and sometimes whole sentences scribbled out.

"Nosey!" Daisy shielded the pad with her arm and scowled at me. "You can't see till I'm finished."

"Can't see what?"

"I'm writing a story, like you asked" she grunted through gritted teeth, scoring out the line she had just completed. "I hate it."

"I didn't know you'd do one too." All the same, I was pleased she was trying.

"Everyone else is giving it a go." Daisy put the pencil in her mouth and chewed vigorously, "I'll show I'm as clever as them. I can manage."

I sat down at the computer and picked up the sheaf of A4. There was a handwritten paragraph on the cover.

Here's what you asked for. Hope it's OK, hun. Please don't let people read it. Felt good to put it on paper though! - Lee

"You looked at this?" I held up the bundle.

"It says not to."

"That's very honest. What are you writing about?"

"You told everyone you wanted a horror story." Daisy tapped her chin thoughtfully and started writing again. The end of her pencil

looked like it had been attacked by woodpeckers. "So mine is about why I ran away from home. It's the closest I can get."

"You don't have to do that," I said quickly. I didn't want her reliving those kinds of memories. "Why don't you write about something nice? Like when you were a kid."

"Could you be more patronising?"

"Sure. I could have patted you on the head."

Despite my rather witty comeback, I was more impressed by Daisy's remark. She was picking up a fine old vocabulary.

"I can't write about my childhood, Donny." She kept her head down. "I don't remember."

"What? None of it?"

"Not a thing." Daisy straightened up, hair flopping over her face. She blew noisily through the strands, then swept the locks back with her hands. Her fingers were mottled with black lead. "I must have blocked it all out for some reason."

"Then you really don't need to go upsetting yourself."

I suddenly felt incredibly sorry for her. I'd forgotten how much she'd been through.

"I'm not really a magician you know." I felt I should share something with her in return, though I didn't know how she'd take it. "That trick with the book? And the ghost pen? You still want to know how I did it?"

"Yeah." Daisy brightened. "I'd given up asking."

"I saw you in the supermarket, buying your lunch. Recognised you from the graveyard. You'd just stuck a paperback in your basket."

"It wasn't very good. The hero was called Dirk Manly or something like that."

"When you have a handle like Donny Marigold, you'd swap a leg to be called Dirk Manly."

"Names are very important," Daisy said solemnly.

"Anyway, I found another copy on the shelf and wrote a message on page 97. Then I swapped it for the one in your basket when you put it down to go get a salad."

"Simple as that?"

"Simple as that," I admitted, a bit sadly. *"No magic involved."*

"And you followed me back to the graveyard?"

"Yes." I winced at the memory. *"Creepy isn't it? I didn't know how else to make an impression."*

"I'm glad." To my surprise, Daisy gave a broad grin. *"You saved me. Just like Dirk Manly would."*

I could feel myself going red. She was staring at me but I couldn't read her expression. I never could. She didn't look away this time and neither did I.

"Close your eyes." Daisy put down her pen and paper. *"And don't move."*

"Ehm, sure." I shut my eyes and laced my fingers together. *"You're not going to hit me with a frying pan for being a stalker, are you?"*

"Just promise you won't move, whatever happens. OK?"

"I promise."

I heard a shuffling sound. For a moment I had a horrible vision of Bunny Wunny Woo crawling from under the bed wielding a carving knife.

Instead, I felt lips pressed softly against mine.

I tasted cherries and sweet tea and almost jumped. It was like an electric shock. I shuddered as a strand of fine hair drifted across my cheek. It took all my willpower not to kiss back, but I kept my word. Soft breath danced over my face and there was the briefest touch of a hand on my face. Then another kiss, fleeting as a hummingbird's wing.

My head spun. In my whole life I never felt anything so precious.

When I opened my eyes, Daisy was back on the bed. Her hands were pressed to her mouth, eyes wide with astonishment at her own boldness.

"I'm sorry!" she gasped. *"Was that all right?"*

"Nah, I hate it when beautiful girls kiss me."

"Beautiful!" Daisy giggled and swung her legs backwards and for-wards. "I'm not beautiful."

I stared at her again and she still didn't look away. I couldn't believe how much she had changed. Black polo neck, black mini skirt, black tights moulded to shapely legs sliding into knee length leather boots. Black liner emphasising her sky-blue eyes. For the first time, I noticed she had silver studs in her ears and rings on fingers tipped with bright red nails.

Beautiful? Hell, yeah. She was beautiful.

"I did it!" She slapped her hands on the bed in delight. "I didn't think I could, but I did."

"I'm that repulsive?"

"Absolutely not!" She glanced at me impishly. "Maybe I need some more practise."

"Consider me available at any moment."

"Thank you." Her shyness suddenly returned. "I do need time, though. I'm sorry."

"Daisy Lenin. You take as long as you need." I picked up Lee's story and put it in my bag. "We have all the time in the world."

We didn't, of course. But I was dumb enough to hope.

That night I slept properly for the first time in weeks.

-23-

Lee's Story

Constance and I were shopping in Princes Street.

"I need something new to wear on the tours," I said. "What goes with mud splatters?"

"Overalls?"

"How come you haven't got anything yet? You get within a hundred yards of Harvey Nicks and it's like you're caught in a tractor beam."

"I'm feeling fat." Constance pulled up her skirt and waved a shapely leg in the air. "My ankles are too thick."

"Then wear boots." I'm fond of Constance - but her obsession with appearances is a bit annoying. "You should think yourself lucky. I used to look like a balloon with feet."

"Eh? You're a great shape. Curvy, is all."

"I am now." I rummaged about in my bag and handed over a photograph. "Check this, though."

The picture was me. An obese teenager glowering despondently at the camera. I was wearing a shapeless mustard jersey, baggy jeans and Wellington boots.

"I can't see you." Constance kept her face straight. "You must be hiding behind this huge, fat chick."

"Very funny."

"This is really you?" She handed the photo back. "How'd you manage to lose so much weight?"

There was a tinge of envy to her voice that I took secret pleasure in.

"I had a diet of cigarettes and alcohol. It was very strict."

"You won't be wanting an ice cream then?"

"Didn't say that." I stuffed the picture into my bag. "If you're pay-ing, I'll have a double mint chocolate chip."

We sat on a bench, under an overhanging tree, slurping our cones. Coronas of light danced round the translucent leaves, spattering the pavement with uncertain bursts of spring sunshine. Behind us, the mile long valley of Princes Street Gardens dipped down from the street and stretched out to the railway lines, before rising steeply to the formidable heights of Edinburgh Castle. Though the gardens were just off Edin-burgh's main thoroughfare, they were so large and verdant it gave the impression a chunk of countryside had been dropped into the town cen-tre.

"I got to tell someone," I said. "I had a one night stand."

"Ooooh! Spill the beans."

"The guy was a pharmaceutical salesman from America. I'll proba-bly never see him again. Didn't even get his number." I screwed my face up. "We had sex on a flat gravestone!"

"Oh my fucking God." Constance looked astonished. "Let's hope you're not pregnant or the kid will end up with a forked tail."

"Very tactful, hun."

Children's laughter drifted up to us in short, hysterical bursts. Con-stance twisted and peered through the railings.

"Let's go down into the gardens and sit on the swings. They'll hold your weight now." Constance pulled me to my feet. "C'mon. It's a lovely day."

We walked down from the street towards the play park. Constance took off her shoes and strolled barefoot through the freshly mown grass, inhaling the sharp tang. Then she sprinted for the swings.

"Finish our ice creams and work them off fighting each other for bargains, eh?"

Constance tried to get as high as she could, eyes closed, swinging her long legs with an agitated intensity, as if she were trying to break free of some earthly bond and fly. I sat motionless, hands clasped on my lap.

Finally, she slowed down.

"I've been to this park once or twice before," she said. "Used to come here with a little kid."

A cloud shuttled across the sun and Constance shivered.

"I don't really care for this place, to be honest." She threw the cone over her shoulder, narrowly missing a courting couple. "We shouldn't have come here."

I glanced sideways at her.

"Why not?"

Before I could reply, a small figure darted between the swings, chasing a tennis ball. It was a young boy in a bright red jacket and freckles to match. His little legs wobbled as he bent over, trying to scoop up his toy, but it vanished under the roundabout before he could reach it.

He stopped and looked around for help. His lip trembled and he burst into tears.

"Hey! Don't cry, kid. I'll get it for you." Constance hopped off the swing, jogged over to the roundabout and got down on her knees, pressing the side of her head to the ground. "Wait! I can see it."

She reached a thin arm under the wooden base and felt around. The child stood beside her, sniffing gratefully. Constance pushed further, her whole arm under the roundabout now, up to her shoulder. And I knew. I knew something was going to burst out of the earth and grab her.

"I'm touching it! Almost… Almost…"

I dropped my ice cream and ran towards her.

"Get away from there!" I grabbed Constance by the scruff of the neck and pulled her backwards. "Get AWAY!"

Her knees scraped along the tarmac as I dragged her up and into a sitting position. In her hand, she clutched the tennis ball.

"What the *hell* is wrong with you?" She handed the ball to the grateful child and rubbed her stinging knees. "It's a roundabout, not a meat slicer! What did you think was going to happen?"

"I don't know. It's just…" I helped her up and smiled sheepishly, trying to think of a suitable lie. "I don't like small, dark spaces. It's a phobia, I suppose."

"You're kidding."

"I want to leave."

"You should have told me." Constance put her shoes back on. "My sister had a phobia about the wardrobe in her bedroom. But that's cause I used to hide inside and jump out when she opened it."

"You're a natural for the tours then." I took her hand and led her towards the exit. "Let's get out of here."

"Wait a minute." Constance stopped. "If you don't like small dark spaces, how come you took a job that takes you into the Black Mausoleum every night?"

I couldn't answer that.

I still can't.

From the Journal of Donny Marigold

I met Doc Menzies in the pub. Ordered my usual glass of wine. I don't drink beer anymore.

"Did you ask the guides to write a story, like I asked?" Doc got right to the point.

"I did. And they agreed." I took a sip. "I still don't see why."

"Stories are very powerful, Donny." Doc tapped his nose. "People tell the truth when they have to set it down on paper for posterity."

"What help is that to you?"

"All in good time. Just email them to me as they arrive."

I should have queried it further but I had more pressing matters on my mind. Like the bombshell I was about to drop.

"I'm going to tell Daisy about the arrangement you and I had." I saw no point in beating around the bush either.

"That's not a good idea," Doc replied nonchalantly. "How'd you think my daughter will react when she finds out you and I are pals?"

"We're not pals. I worked for you."

"And that'll go down better? I'm a monster and she hates me, remember?" Doc frowned. "Didn't you get any crisps?"

"I can't lie to her anymore."

"You really care about Daisy, huh?"

I decided to go for complete honesty.

"More than you could imagine. Going to get all protective now?"

"Not when it's your round."

"What are you doing here, Doc?" I asked, exasperated. "If you keep hanging around the graveyard, like some phantom, she'll eventually bump into you. You need to tell her you're here or piss off."

"And leave you to look after her? How's that going to work out if you've spent all the cash I sent?"

I wasn't sure how he knew that, but I wasn't going to be side-tracked.

"I'll find a way."

"Actually, from what I've heard, you're the best thing that ever happened to my daughter." Doc took a slow sip of his pint. "But you don't have the whole picture."

"Then show it to me."

"Not all at once. And there's a good reason."

"Don't be so bloody evasive. I'm tired of puzzles."

"I'll get my own crisps then," Doc got up and went to the bar, throwing a worried look back. It wasn't an expression that sat naturally on his face and I wondered if he was faking it.

"You want another Pino Grigio?"

"No. I have to jump out in a minute."

"Good."

I sat, stewing, until Doc returned. He opened the packet and began to munch.

"Want one?"

"I want answers."

"Tell you what. I've written you a horror story too. It explains a lot."

"Who told you I was good for Daisy?" Doc seemed to know far too much for someone just hanging around and watching.

He leaned forwards, his eyes boring into mine and I could smell the beer on his breath.

"Once you've read my tale, you tell me how exactly I approach my daughter. Because either I get the door slammed in my face, or I break her heart."

I had a million more questions but it was time for me to go to work. And I knew Doc would be gone when I got back.

Instead, I went up to Daisy's flat after my jump. I had my own key now and let myself in. But she was lying on the bed asleep. Her hair fanned out across her face and she was breathing softly, one hand squashed against her cheek. I pulled the covers up and kissed her forehead. As I moved her hand, it clasped mine and held on tightly.

"If you knew I loved you," I whispered. "Would you let me go?"

Then she relaxed and I was free.

Only, I didn't want to be free of Daisy Lenin. Not ever.

As I turned to leave, I saw another printed manuscript on the computer desk. Another note on the cover.

You asked for a horror story, Wee D. Well, this is the closest I can get. And it's true. How screwed up is that?

Your friend. Oss.

-24-

Oss's Story

I used to work part-time as a data entry analyst at the Edinburgh University Artificial Intelligence Department, when it was just over the road. Bet you didn't know I was that brainy. Anyway, one day I had a message left on my computer from the girl who sat at my desk during the evening shift. I replied and soon we were writing to each other every day.

I kept all of our email correspondence, but this is just the... highlights, I suppose you'd say. I think it might be a ghost story. By coincidence, it also explains how I came to be at City of the Dead.

FROM DOUGLAS, ELLEN TO OSS, VICTOR.

Hi there stranger. And I mean stranger. I think you use my computer on the day shift. Station number 4? I am thoroughly bored in this place, so I hope you don't mind me writing. I am on the night shift. In other words I'm the only one here so, naturally, I have a bone to pick. You keep leaving half empty coffee cups on the console.

FROM DOUGLAS, ELLEN TO OSS, VICTOR.

Hello, hello... and greetings from the day shift. Sorry about the coffee. I need a lot to keep my hair standing on end. Keeps the supervisor sweet if she thinks I look like Einstein.

How could you complain about the fascinating life we lead at Edinburgh University Artificial Intelligence Unit? Since my own intelligence is mostly artificial, I feel right at home. Safe and happy in my teak-tinted Formica cubicle - surrounded by the sullen co-workers whom I have come to think of as valued friends - even though we're not allowed to talk to each other. And call me Oss.

FROM DOUGLAS, ELLEN TO OSS, VICTOR.

Greyfriars must be very pretty out of your window. Everything is dark when I am on. Yesterday I thought I saw a Heelan coo. Hard to say what it was doing in the graveyard. Either that or it was a big Yorkshire terrier with horns.

All I see are the ghost tours running in there. I get to hear the same story twice a night, right below my window and have become quite an expert on the Mackenzie Poltergeist.

FROM DOUGLAS, ELLEN TO OSS, VICTOR.

I never heard of any poltergeist in the graveyard. Though I think my supervisor might be possessed by Hitler. She has the same moustache.
Love, Victor

FROM DOUGLAS, ELLEN TO OSS, VICTOR. FROM OSS, VICTOR TO DOUGLAS ELLEN.

OK. Questions. Do you like dogs or cats?

Slightly less indifferent to dogs. My first ever girlfriend had a pug that used to fall down the stairs. I liked the pug whenever it fell down the stairs.

Do UFOs exist?

Nothing exists unless I, personally, have seen it. That about wraps it up for God, the guy who refills the coffee machine and the Mackenzie Poltergeist.

FROM OSS, VICTOR TO DOUGLAS, ELLEN.

What a beautiful day it is out there! I cycled to work through the Meadows - it was like being in a Tampax commercial. Birds singing, sun shining, little old ladies doddering... I even stopped at the traffic lights. There was a young guy with an easel and paints by the side of the road and instead of shouting "Oi... arty-farty!... go and play football with the lads from the brewery instead of coming over all nish and Watership-Down with your Daler-Rowneys," I dismounted and stood behind him muttering "Hmmmm... interesting," in an encouraging manner. I even waved to the children at the primary school in Sciennes Road and got some interesting hand signals back.

We will have to go out for a few pints some night.

FROM DOUGLAS, ELLEN TO OSS, VICTOR. FROM OSS, VICTOR TO DOUGLAS ELLEN.

What? For all I know you're a one-legged, married serial killer. On the other hand, nobody's perfect.

FROM: OSS, VICTOR TO DOUGLAS, ELLEN. FROM: DOUGLAS, ELLEN.

TO: OSS VICTOR.

Then I need your phone number and timetable... plus four feet of anchor chain and a large vibrating egg.

FROM DOUGLAS, ELLEN TO OSS, VICTOR. FROM OSS, VICTOR TO DOUGLAS ELLEN.

My mobile is on the blink. The other things are in my bank manager's house. Quite busy this week though. On Tuesday night I'm going with my pals to the observatory to have a look at the comet. Apparently, you can see the tail very distinctly now.

I always appreciate a bit of tail.

Have you heard about it?

I have heard of it. Shumaker-Leavy 11 or Jackson Five or something like that.

Haley-Bopp actually. Rockin and rollin across the Milky-Way. They say a comet is how life started on earth.

I know. I was making a pun. Shumaker-Leavy 11 is actually a satellite.

FROM DOUGLAS, ELLEN TO OSS, VICTOR. FROM OSS, VICTOR.
How was your weekend?

The battle of Stalingrad was better than my weekend. Listen. My computer seems to have some sort of virus. Won't let me use the intranet system to get in touch with you. So we'll have to stick to emails. When are we going out for a drink?

Tuesday night?

FROM DOUGLAS, ELLEN TO OSS, VICTOR.
Didn't realise I was so busy this week. Can't make it. Am I a cow? Will I be dissed as I have dissed? I really don't think I've dissed out much diss.

FROM OSS, VICTOR TO DOUGLAS, ELLEN.
You haven't... and I am off on holiday next week so we will have to meet when I come back. Friday?

FROM DOUGLAS, ELLEN TO OSS, VICTOR. FROM OSS VICTOR TO DOUGLAS, ELLEN.

Forces of darkness are working against us. The power of the pound compels me to work (work and work). Attached is my schedule for next week. Read it and weep, baby cakes, then tell me if you are still actually interested in meeting up.

I am. And I still can't get through to you on internal mail.

Same here. I think this office is haunted. My console keeps swallowing one particular set of data I'm trying to enter. Could you input those bits for me, if I email it? Being my invisible shoulder to cry on, I am whining this to you. Okay senor shoulder, take a load off my chest.

Well... shoulder is not the part of my anatomy girls usually cry over but I'll certainly enter the data. And far be it from me to infer that you're just being lazy and trying to get me to do your work. So I've come right out and said it.

I think the ghost tours are at fault. It always happens after they walk past. You should get a job with them. Be my spy and see what they are up to.

That's not a bad idea, since my workload has suddenly doubled. I could wave to you as I go past. Or we could go out!

FROM OSS, VICTOR TO DOUGLAS ELLEN. FROM DOUGLAS, ELLEN TO OSS, VICTOR.
Wednesday?

Yesnesday.

FROM OSS, VICTOR TO DOUGLAS, ELLEN. FROM DOUGLAS, ELLEN TO OSS, VICTOR.

How about I meet you in Greyfriars Bar at 8.30? Is that satisfactory to your highly polished deadline Mondo?
Yours slaphappily,
O

Sounds like a plan Stan. My schedule is hardly highly polished, just dense and revered and feared, like kryptonite.
Yours super heroically,
Eve Plum.

FROM DOUGLAS, ELLEN TO OSS, VICTOR.
I still can't enter this particular set of data. I appreciate you doing it for me. Nobody else seems to work nights. It's gotten to the stage where I look forward to the tours. The stories are very droll. You should really consider getting a job there. You seem like a funny guy.

FROM OSS, VICTOR TO DOUGLAS, ELLEN. FROM DOUG-LAS ELLEN TO OSS, VICTOR
Visually, I'm hilarious. Still on for Wednesday?

Sorry! I can't make Wednesday now. Wanna go hout next Saturday?

Que time?

That twilight moment when slow segmented worms of time crawl languidly through the moth eaten memories of we children of the night.

Oh. About 9.30 then?

Sorry. Been listening to the tours again. The guides look like they're having a lot more laughs than me.

FROM DOUGLAS, ELLEN TO OSS, VICTOR. FROM OSS, VIC-
TOR TO DOUGLAS, ELLEN.

Aaaaaaaaaargh! Saturday is out. Am working an extra shift. I hope
you are doing better than me. I am a cold wet dog. Woof.

*Eh? You work Saturdays? We are most certainly going to meet at
some point.*

FROM OSS, VICTOR TO DOUGLAS, ELLEN. FROM DOUG-
LAS ELLEN TO OSS, VICTOR.

*What is this data you are giving me? I can't make head nor tail of
it. Entered the stuff anyway.*

My parents are flying in from the New World to visit me tomorrow.
That was unexpected.

You're American?!!!!

I am. I look and sound like Wilma Flintstone.

FROM DOUGLAS, ELLEN TO OSS, VICTOR. FROM OSS, VIC-
TOR TO DOUGLAS ELLEN

I hate being here. All I do now is sit around waiting to get a message
from you, a word from the great beyond.

*And the word for today is DOVECOT. How about 9.30 tomorrow in
Greyfriars bar?*

Unfortunately, the parental units have now arrived. From Ohio.
They don't approve of bars, unless they're used to cage young girls.

FROM OSS, VICTOR TO DOUGLAS, ELLEN. FROM DOUG-
LAS, ELLEN TO OSS, VICTOR.

I got to work late, I am very hungry and my work visa is about to expire. I am addicted to complaining. Especially when there is no one to tell me to stop whingeing.

Not to discard your emotional outpourings like bum fluff in a broken wind but... If your work visa runs out, how can you keep working here?

Good question.

FROM DOUGLAS, ELLEN TO OSS, VICTOR FROM OSS, VICTOR TO DOUGLAS, ELLEN.
Well... today is may last day and I am looking too bored for my own good, so I am being sent home early without any supper.

You're leaving TODAY? When?

After my shift. Goblins will usher me out if I protest.

Well... Are you having a goodbye bash? You inviting me?

Actually, when I say going... I mean going. My parents want to take me back to the States with them on Wednesday. And you should leave too. They are moving the Artificial Intelligence Unit to another building on the other side of Edinburgh.

So I heard.

FROM ROSS, VICTOR TO DOUGLAS, ELLEN. FROM DOUGLAS, ELLEN TO ROSS, VICTOR.

I have a solution. We tell your parents that you're pregnant with our child, so you can't leave Edinburgh cause you've got little Waylon Archibald Oss on the way.

Don't joke about that.

FROM DOUGLAS, ELLEN TO ROSS, VICTOR.
Things are really getting to me today, even though I'm no longer at work. Maybe that's because I am on my 4th Pepsi Max and 2nd Kit Kat. I'll be glad to exit the UK, I guess, but sorry to leave you all alone.
Love.
Ellen.

FROM ROSS, VICTOR TO DOUGLAS, ELLEN.
I went for an interview with City of the Dead Tours and was offered the job. Sounds interesting and I've always been fascinated with Greyfriars. Maybe that's why I work next door. But I couldn't wave to you if you've gone. So, even if I get the job, I don't think I'll take it. Thanks for the tip though.

You were right. The Intelligence Unit is moving across Edinburgh. But a change of scenery might do me good.

Say hello to your parents for me. We are no longer going to call the child Waylon. We are going to call it Dump Truck. This is equally un-likely to work.

FROM DOUGLAS, ELLEN TO OSS, VICTOR.
We'll meet some day, Oss. I promise. Go join the tours. I like to imagine you out in the graveyard, not rotting in some office on the other side of town. I can pretend I am watching from the window.

Ellen Douglas never replied to any more emails, so I asked the other workers about her. Turns out nobody by that name ever worked there. In fact, there was no night shift.
Go figure.

I never got the chance to follow it up. I was fired from the Artificial Intelligence Unit because of the data 'Ellen' asked me to enter in their system. I still don't know what the hell it was.

So I ended up working for City of the Dead, after all.

Is it a ghost story? I don't know. Might be.

Big O.

From the Journal of Donny Marigold

I knew that Robert Louis Stevenson often frequented Greyfriars. He wrote about the cemetery and even recounted the legend of how it was haunted by George Mackenzie.

At the height of his fame, Stevenson began to display some rather... odd tendencies. He claimed to have dreamt parts of his work and called the dreams that came to him 'Brownies', an old Scottish term for a supernatural being. Then one night he claimed to have been given a whole novel by these Brownies.

That book was The Strange Case of Dr Jekyll and Mr Hyde *and it's like nothing else he had ever written. It was like nothing anyone had ever written. For a start, it was a novella and he dashed it down in an astonishing three days and three nights. During this period his dreams turned into unbearable nightmares and he began to hallucinate.*

He gave the finished story to his wife to read, as she was the biggest influence on his writing and the love of his life.

She insisted he burn it. He did, then immediately wrote it again.

Unless you've spent your whole life living in the jungles of Borneo, you already know the plot. A respectable Victorian doctor called Henry Jekyll believes that everyone has a good and bad side, constantly at war with each other. So he invents a potion that separates the two and releases the bad egg known as Mr Hyde, who goes on a bloody rampage and eventually takes over his maker.

Not exactly Treasure Island *is it?*

The book was a massive bestseller, read all over the world, and it isn't hard to see some of the legends it influenced. The whole werewolf myth for one thing, where a decent and unwilling man changes into an uncontrollable beast. (Incidentally, the first modern werewolf story was written by Leitch Ritchie, who lived in Edinburgh as well).

It also influenced an obscure Austrian scientist called Sigmund Freud, who stopped conducting experiments on eel's testicles and put forward the theory that each of us is made up of a moral and law abiding superego and a base and savage id. That kick-started the science of psychiatry, a discipline that its practitioners have been struggling to get right ever since - usually for £500 an hour.

But a very different movement sprang up after the publication of Jekyll and Hyde. *It was inspired by a combination of Darwin's Survival of the Fittest and the Victorian notion of who the fittest actually were. Ignoring the fact that Stevenson's book was actually a warning, scientists and doctors from the upper classes decided they were morally, as well as intellectually, superior to everyone else.*

So they figured it was their duty to engineer a way to make everyone like them. Simple, eh? They called the movement Social Darwinism and it caught on big time. If it wasn't for the Nazi Party who took it to extremes by simply killing everyone who was different, it might still be going strong.

Or maybe it is. What is genetic engineering, after all, but the attempt to fundamentally change living things by adding and taking bits of genetic material away? What is Artificial Intelligence but an attempt to play God?

And what is it about Greyfriars that seems to inspire thinkers and writers to produce such fundamentally original ideas?

When I went to Daisy's that night I found an email from Ben Scott. This is what it said...

-25-

Ben's Story

Donny. This is the beginning of the last play I ever wrote. It was a horror story, never performed and I pretty much gave up writing after that. Didn't know what else to give you.
- Ben (Big Giant Head)

The stage is not well lit. Battling the darkness is a bed and a small bedside table. On the table, a candle flickers in the neck of a wine bottle. On the other side is a chair with a wooden ventriloquist dummy sitting on top.

A child enters, wearing a Day-Glo tracksuit. He runs to the bed and jumps in. He is followed into the room by his father, BAXTER. BAXTER is around 45 years old and carrying a large glass of wine.

BAXTER
Clean your teeth?

BEAN
Yes!

BAXTER
Say goodnight to Constance?

BEAN
Three times.

Bean is small and serious. It's hard to guess his age - it might be anywhere between 7 and 9. He sits up in bed like a stormtrooper on top of a Panzer.

BAXTER
Goodnight to you, Bean.

BEAN
Hey. What about my story?

BAXTER
It's awful late.

BEAN
So? You don't have to work in the morning. You're on benefits.
(BAXTER ponders this)
Mmmmmmmmmmmmmmmmm...
(He stalls)
A long time ago, in a building in this very graveyard there used to be an asylum, ruled by a tyrannical doctor.

BEAN
Heard it!

BAXTER
You haven't heard it. I'm making it up as I go along.

BEAN
(Suspiciously)
Sounds very like Star Wars if you really want to know.

BAXTER

I've only told you the first line.

BEAN
Is Darth Vader in it?

BAXTER
Yes. So is Napoleon and Lord Mountbatten. They're in the high se-
curity wing.
Anyway, the Doctor ruled the asylum with an iron hand.

BEAN
An iron hand!

BAXTER
And a rod of steel.

BEAN
And a tin of chicken

BAXTER
Right.
Because the inmates hated the asylum so much, they usually pretended to be sane just to get out of the place, which made the Doctor a
bit suspicious of his success rate. In a flash of inspiration, he hired the
people he had cured to run the asylum and gave them long white coats,
so he could tell them from the patients.

BEAN
Even Darth Vader?

BAXTER

Yeah. He wasn't happy about that. Since he was second in command, he insisted the staff all wear long black coats instead. Said it was aesthetically pleasing and made him feel more like himself.

Then the Doctor figured out his problem. Know what it was?

BEAN
Big itchy feet?

BAXTER
He realised he'd never be able to figure out who was really cured if he didn't know how it felt to be mad in the first place. After all, *he* was perfectly sane.

So he offered a fortune to any man who could show him how it felt to be mad. And he threw in his daughter's hand as an afterthought.

BEAN
Just her hand?

BAXTER
He was very possessive. But if prospective suitors failed, the Doctor had his staff bury them alive in Greyfriars.

BEAN
No way!

BAXTER
Way. And that put a few off. Then, one day, along came a young man called Ploughcatcher Jones. He told the Doctor.

"If you want to be truly crazy, your Medicalship, find me a photographer and an enormous gallery that's really long. Nothin fancy, y'know."

"I don't think I have anything like that." said the Doctor.

"What about the Covenanters Prison in the graveyard outside? That'll do the trick."

BEAN
(Caught up)
Why did he need the prison?

BAXTER
That's what the Doctor wanted to know. So he agreed. The picture taker was another problem altogether.

"Where am I going to get a photographer from?" he asked. "This is a nuthouse."

"There's one in ward seven," the young man replied. "He claims to be Lord Litchfield."

BEAN
Is that a relation to Lord Mountbatten?

BAXTER
They shared the same padded cell on alternate weekends.

So Darth Vader got the keys to the Covenanters Prison and handed them over to Ploughcatcher Jones. Jones set up two fifteen-foot speakers at the far end of the main hall. He made a tape of his favourite song, *Johnny and Mary* by Placebo - and then he looped the tape... y'know? So it would play over and over and over without stopping.

BEAN
What for?

BAXTER
So he would have something to listen to while he hung up all the pictures the asylum photographer had taken. He hung them on the front of the tombs.

BEAN
(Waving his hands)
Wait, wait, wait! What pictures?

BAXTER
That's what the Doctor's only daughter, Chlamydia, wanted to know. She was pretty curious. And curiously pretty, for that matter. So that night she sneaked into the Covenanters Prison with a torch and began to walk through it, looking at the pictures.
(A beat)
Each photo was of one of the horrible experiments her father had tested out on crazy children.

BEAN
(Dubiously)
The Doctor let the photographer take pictures of his experiments?

BAXTER
Ehhhhhhhh. It's possible the Doctor and the photographer may have been the same person.

BEAN
So the Doctor *was* crazy?

BAXTER
Who knows? *He* didn't and that's the point.

BEAN
This is complicated.

BAXTER

Isn't it just? Anyway, the Doctor's daughter tried to run to get past the images, but each picture was more horrible than the last. They sped by, faster and faster, until they looked like some disgusting splatter movie her father had directed. Sprinting along, she began to cry. Then she began to scream. By the time the girl reached the other end of the prison she had shrieked all her innocence away.

BEAN
She ran the whole length?

BAXTER
She was a doctor's daughter. She was pretty fit.
Talking of the Doctor. He arrived the next day knowing nothing of his child's hideous escapade the night before. Ploughcatcher Jones was there to meet him.
"All you have to do is walk to the far end of the prison," he said. "Bet you can't do it."
"Doctors don't bet," said the Doctor. And in he went.
But guess what? All the old photographs were gone. In their place were new ones. And these photographs were of the prison itself - taken from the far end. Nothing scary about that, huh?
(BEAN shakes his head vigorously)
But after walking for a while, the Doctor noticed that a tiny dot had appeared in each photograph and, with each successive picture, the dot was getting a little bit bigger. He could hear a noise now as well, thin and high. The farther into the gallery the Doctor walked, the bigger the dot became, and the closer he got to the sound.
Then, suddenly, he understood what he was looking at and what he was hearing.
The dot was the far-off figure of his daughter, running towards the camera. The sound was her scream.
It was on a loop tape.
(BEAN'S eyes are wide)

The Doctor kept walking till he got to the point where he could almost make out his daughter's weeping face. Almost see the look in her eyes. Then he turned back.

BEAN
Did it make him mad?

BAXTER
He wasn't very pleased about it.
So he didn't give Ploughcatcher Jones a piece of his fortune, or a piece of his daughter either. He imprisoned him in a stone chamber under a mausoleum in the Covenanters Prison - along with his looped tape and the asylum photographer - whose name nobody knows.

BEAN
Lord Litchfield.

BAXTER
Oh yeah.
In a way, Ploughcatcher Jones got the last laugh, even though he didn't feel all that much like laughing. Because the Doctor's daughter didn't want to be his daughter anymore.
So she changed her name, took her son far, far away where no one could ever find them and raised him to be a simple gardener. A shame, really, cause he hated gardening.

BEAN
What son? Where'd he come from?

BAXTER
I'm not going over the facts of life with you tonight boy.
Anyway, it doesn't matter.
(A beat)

What matters is that in Greyfriars Graveyard...

(Looking around)

There's a chamber hidden below a mausoleum. And inside, though nobody can hear it, is a scream that goes on forever.

The end.

BEAN

That it?

He is rather deflated.

BAXTER

That's it. Now go to sleep.

BEAN

Didn't really understand the story.

BAXTER

(After a pause)

No. Me neither. Goodnight.

He goes to the door.

BEAN

Bax...

BAXTER

Yeah?

BEAN

I got a story too.

BAXTER

Uh uh. One story a night.

BEAN
It's short!

BAXTER
(Drawling)
Sho's life, young-timer

BEAN
(Rapidly)
Once there was a boy who found a magic banana and it gave him three wishes that came true so he wished to be a king and a prince and to work on the Waltzers. Amen.

BAXTER
Yours is a better tale than mine. I should've known.

BEAN
Where did you get your story, dad?

BAXTER
I dreamt it. I dream it all the time.

BEAN
Do you ever dream about me?

BAXTER
Every night, kid.

He exits. Bean looks at a ventriloquist dummy sitting on the chair. It stares blankly back at him. The boy pulls a cover from his bed and throws it over the mannikin.

BEAN

(Calling out nervously)

Goodnight Baxter!

(Lying in the pool of spluttering candlelight, he begins to talk to himself)

-Say, you remind me of a man.

-What man?

-The man with the power.

-What power?

-The power of Hoodoo.

-Hoodoo?

-You do.

-I do?

-Remind me of a man.

-What man?

-The man with the power.

Never could finish it. Never will. Got my reasons.

Sorry kid.

Ben Scott

From the Journal of Donny Marigold

Daisy sat on the bed, watching a nature programme while I typed. She loved nature programmes. But I couldn't concentrate.

Partly it was because I wanted to kiss Daisy again. But I promised to give her time. Partly it was because of what I'd read.

Ben's story was obviously allegorical but it strongly hinted that he knew Doc Menzies. I couldn't approach him about it without giving away my own relationship with the wily old sod.

"You look lost in thought." Daisy had noticed me staring into space."

"I asked the guides to write horror stories," I said. "Naturally, I expected them to make stuff up, only they're all writing about themselves."

"So?"

"Don't you think that's a bit disturbing?"

"Perhaps we're all dead and haunt the place."

"That's not funny." Though I admit I gave the idea a moment's consideration. "I mean, how much do we actually know about Ben and the guides?"

"Maybe we should all learn more about each other." Daisy leaned forwards and turned off the TV. "Including you and me."

"I'm not sure what you mean."

"I haven't been entirely honest with you, Donny." Daisy pulled a sheaf of papers from under her pillow. "All of us have secrets, I suppose."

"Now I'm really not sure what you mean," I replied nervously.

"Another time." Daisy held out the manuscript. "Constance gave me this a couple of days ago. It's her horror story. She said I could read it. Took me a while but it's an eye-opener."

"Don't tell me?" I took the offering. "It's about her."

"It is." Daisy bit her lip.

"But also it's about Ben Scott."

-26-

Constance's Story

When I was a teenager, I took part in an anti-war march on Princes Street. Or maybe it was pro-war. I was on my way to buy shoes, so I was only in it for five minutes.

A police horse had done a poop in the road and me and my mates started taking bets on who would stand in it first. My money was on the guy on stilts dressed as Death. But it was a girl in a wheelchair who got stuck in the mess. My pals went wild, cheering and waving at her and I bet she ended up on YouTube.

That's when I decided to become an entertainer.

I always wanted to be rich and famous, and this seemed to be my best bet. So I made up a stage name and managed to get enrolled in Dunfermline Drama College. It used to be a polytechnic, teaching joiners and the like and they must have kept some of the old lecturers. I got taught wooden acting and also spent a lot of time pretending to be a tree.

My gamble paid off. Right after I graduated, I started on TV roles. I was 'woman in fish van' in *Taggart* and 'irate deaf-mute who falls over' in *River City*, though you can only see my feet waving in the air. Eventually I got typecast as 'body in bath' in a few crime series, on account of an uncanny natural ability to play dead, which is no mean, feat after hours lying in cold water.

That was about the time I met Ben Scott. He was working in the theatre where I had a small role as a traffic warden who gets murdered.

As well as helping run the place, he'd put on a few plays of his own. Even got a couple of books published, which impressed the hell out of me. They'd sold about five copies each, but he had talent and I suspected he was going to make it big someday. All he needed was the right subject matter.

Ben was living above Greyfriars Graveyard with his girlfriend and baby son Bryant, who he called Bean, for reasons he never told me. Ben's girlfriend was also a budding actress but hadn't got any further than me. Like a lot of graduates from Dunfermline Drama College, we were forced to back up our incomes in strange ways, daytime jobs being out of the question, in case we were called for auditions. Ben's girlfriend worked evenings as an exotic dancer and even asked if I wanted a gig. But I can't dance to save myself. Pretending to be dead is my thing.

So I helped look after Bean at nights while Ben stared at the computer muttering to himself. In return, he promised to write a big part for me in his next play

I even took the kid to one of my acting jobs, playing 'body found in dumpster' in an episode of *Cracker*. The director cast him as 'cute baby in pram'. He was in four scenes, got a bigger cheque than me and wasn't even a member of *Equity*.

Ben was a remote kind of guy. He didn't have photographs on his wall, had never owned a pet and couldn't remember to water plants.

Neither of us were successful in our chosen field but we refused to give up. The glass is either half empty or half full, you know?

In the end, we emptied and filled it quite a bit, which probably didn't help our careers. Nor Ben's relationship with Bean's mother.

Then, one day, Bunny Wunny Woo appeared.

"What the hell is that?"

It was upside down on one of the pine kitchen chairs, black candy-floss hair dusting the floor. Its head was too big for the wooden body and the jaw was twisted and splintered.

It didn't have eyes, only empty sockets.

"This," said Ben. "Is Bunny Wunny Woo."

A strange chill ran down my spine.

He'd brought home toys for his son before, but Bunny Wunny Woo was different. The broken body needed a lot of work to repair it.

Only Bunny Wunny Woo wasn't *for* Bean.

"I've got a great idea for a horror play," Ben said. "We could put it on at the theatre."

"I take it the dummy will feature heavily."

"Absolutely!" He held up Bunny Wunny Woo. "Ventriloquist dolls are innately creepy."

This one was. Nothing innate about it. Ben seemed pleased by that.

"I like him."

"I hate it."

"I'm going to fix him up. Learn how to do the voice."

"Ventriloquism?"

"Why not?"

"Where'd he get that stupid name?"

Ben pulled back Bunny Wunny Woo's collar, revealing a scrawny unpainted wooden neck.

"It's written on a tag."

He wiggled Bunny Wunny Woo's head at me. The broken jaw bounced slackly, held only by a couple of loose rubber bands. Ben spoke out of the side of his mouth.

How do you do?
I'm Bunny Wunny Woo
My eyes are broken
My jaw is too

But I'll get fixed and be good as new.

"Very impressive."

Ben began writing and the theatre agreed to perform his play. I argued *Bunny Wunny Woo* wasn't a very creepy name for a horror, but Ben was adamant.

"It'll get people wondering," he said.

"About your sanity?"

The plot revolved around a ventriloquist dummy that slowly takes over a couple. I played the girlfriend who, of course, ends up dying. Ben played the boyfriend who doesn't notice anything is wrong.

Nothing like a bit of typecasting.

Ben started to fix up Bunny Wunny Woo. He bought a large gooey rubber eye from the joke shop, cut it in half and glued the pieces into each empty eyeball.

"There we go."

Ben put his hand inside Bunny Wunny Woo's jacket. The jaw clicked open and shut like a little piranha, eyes wide and dead to match.

How do you do?
I'm Bunny Wunny Woo
My eyes are starey
My jaw is scary
But I'm not as hairy as my Auntie Mary

The jaw clicked open and shut. Ben's lips moved too, rather obviously. He looked at Bunny Wunny Woo's blank face and I looked at his.

"What? I'm still working on it."

The lines of his new play were good. Easy to learn, even if there were a lot of them. A week before the show, I had them three-quarters down. All the best actresses do it that way.

"You know I agreed to look after William tomorrow afternoon," I said as Ben paced the floor, biting his nails. "While I'm going over my lines."

William was my sister's boy, a quiet little thing. If I'm being honest, the kid was a bit slow. But I'd promised.

"Tell him not to touch Bunny Wunny Woo," Ben urged.

"I doubt he'd touch it if I gave him a barge pole."

"Constance, he's just a dummy," Ben said huffily. "What harm can he do?"

William arrived next afternoon. My lines weren't *quite* learned yet. Bunny Wunny Woo wasn't entirely fixed. Ben had gone for a walk because the flat wasn't big enough to contain his pacing.

William was no trouble to look after, though. He liked colouring books, so I had bought some crayons and a pad for him at the Spar. When he arrived Bunny Wunny Woo was sitting in Ben's favourite chair, legs sticking straight out. William gave a little jump.

Bunny Wunny Woo had splints fastened to his broken arms. Ben had applied glue to the snapped limbs and they kept everything in place while it dried. He looked like he was strapped in an electric chair, sitting like that.

I put a large tartan blanket on the floor for William to kneel on.

"Here's a colouring book," I smiled. "Aunt Constance's got some work to do, so she's going to the bedroom."

I went next door. Got my script out. Did a few vocal exercises and resisted the temptation to practise being dead. I couldn't work with Bunny Wunny Woo until his glue dried so I put an old sock over my hand instead.

Stand in for ventriloquist dummy. I knew how the sock felt.

I felt a tug at my leg. It was William.

"The big doll lookin at me." His eyes were tearful.

"The big doll can't harm you, honey."

"I don' like it. Scary, lookin at me."

"His name's Bunny Wunny Woo."

"Bun oh oh. Oh."

"That's right. Aunt Constance's a bit occupied right now."

"S'awright."

He turned and waddled off, back to the living room.

How do you do?
I'm Bunny Wunny Woo
With eyes to see
And a jaw to chew
Now we've gotten in a stew
You fixed me and I'll fix you...

There was another tug at my leg.

"Big doll talking to me. Scare me."

"William. Aunt Constance is very busy."

"Take doll away."

"What's the doll saying?"

"Don' know."

"Aunt Constance can't move Bunny Wunny Woo until his glue dries. He's not going to harm you."

"S'ugly. Scary."

"William. Go and get your blanket and bring it in here if you like, but you *can't* disturb Aunt Constance."

William looked tearful again.

"Tell you what," I said brightly. "Why don't you take your blanket and put it over Bunny Wunny Woo! Then you can't see him. And he can't see you."

William padded back into the living room.

I went over the lines again.

C'mon, he's just a dummy, what harm can he do to anyone?

Oh, fuck.

I dropped my script and ran to the living room, skidding on the polished wooden floor as I went.

Bunny Wunny Woo was sitting on Ben's chair, mouth open, staring with its dead fish eyes. William was on the floor colouring furiously.

Bean's crib was in the corner. His motionless body was covered by a large tartan blanket.

William didn't look up.

"Ugly doll can't see me anymore," he said.

From the Journal of Donny Marigold

"Holy hell." I put down the story. "Ben really did have a kid."

"And Constance almost killed it." Daisy hugged the pillow to her chest.

"That's a bit harsh," I said cautiously. "It was an accident."

"No wonder she freaked out when she saw that dummy." Daisy shuddered.

"What happened to Bean's mother? The story doesn't say."

"I asked Constance. Bean's mum took the boy to live with relatives in the USA and Ben hasn't seen them since."

"I don't blame her." I looked out the window at the lines of head-stones. "You wouldn't want to live over a graveyard after a near miss like that."

"Do you think Ben's punishing Constance? By keeping her around? Sleeping with her."

"Maybe he's punishing himself. One way or another, it's a pretty fucked up relationship."

"Not like us, eh?" Daisy had obviously mastered sarcasm.

"You and I are the most normal people in this entire company." I went to the kitchen and poured myself a glass of wine. Daisy had given up nagging and now kept a couple of bottles in her fridge just for me. "And we're both crazy as a box of frogs."

"I threw Bunny Wunny Woo in the bin. I don't want him anymore."

"I'm not surprised."

"Can I have some wine too?"

"You sure?" I stuck my head out of the kitchen door, surprised. "I thought you were teetotal?"

"I already had a couple." Daisy accepted a glass, took a swig and wrinkled her nose. *"Ready to do a lot of things I've never done before."*

"I'll drink to that." I sat down at the computer and raised my own glass.

"What do you mean?"

I spun in my chair and wine sloshed over my hand. I wiped it on my jeans and pulled out a cigarette. Then I couldn't stall any more.

"I don't think the tours are a healthy atmosphere for you." I ventured. *"Maybe you should think about quitting the company. Leaving the graveyard."*

"Eh? The guides are my only friends, apart from you." Daisy licked red wine from the side of her glass. *"Besides, where would I go?"*

I didn't have an answer to that. Instead, I logged on the internet and began to check my emails.

"I could get used to this." Daisy drained her drink. *"Can I have?..."*

"A cigarette? No, you can't."

"Another glass of wine, doofus."

I went to the kitchen and poured more. When I returned Daisy held out her notebook.

"I wanted to give you a proper story but I can't. I can't write."

"I never suspected the guides could either, but they've made a pretty fair stab at it."

"No, Donny." Daisy looked down, an action she rarely performed any more. With her hair still covering her face she thrust the notebook into my hand. *"I really can't write."*

"I'll be the judge of that."

"I know," Daisy mumbled through her hair. *"You've always wanted to be an author."*

I opened the notebook.

I do not remember anything veri wel before I com here. I no my dad and my mum were not geting along. One nite they had a fite and he beet her up. They were fiting about me I thinc but I don't

remember. He cut her reely bad. My mum was very prety. My dad cut her face until she was not prety ani more.

My dad went to prisin and I did not see him agen or go to visit him becos of what he did. My mum was different now. She never went owt. She did not speek to me ani more. One day she told me my dad was geting owt of jail soon.

That is whi I ran away from home. I changed my name so he cood not find me. I wus cald Daisy Menzies but I changed it to Daisy Lenin after the giy hoo wus in the band cald the beetels. He wanted world pees and everi one to luv eech other. I like being Daisy Lenin. Now I hav a howse and a job and a best frend.

This is whut I hav alwas wanted so it is not a gost stori. It is just my stori.

I felt tears well up in my eyes. Not cool. Daisy moved a lock of hair away and squinted up at me.

"I feel stupid," she said. "Why am I so stupid?"

"Stupid?" I took a long shuddering breath and held out my arms. "Daisy Lenin, don't you know how bloody special you are?"

She came off the bed like a coiled spring. With a whoop she landed on my lap, wrapping her legs round my waist and her arms around my neck. The swivel chair bent backwards and skidded across the floor with a flurry of squeaking castors, almost throwing us off. I clutched at her to keep from overbalancing and she buried her head in my shoulder, kissing my neck.

"I knew you would understand," she whispered. She clamped her legs tighter and, through the black tights, I could feel the heat of her body. That pretty much did it for me.

"I think you've damaged my knacks," I said feebly, trying to push her away. "I'm not a vaulting horse."

"You don't feel damaged." She giggled and wriggled harder against me. "Not that I have much experience in that department."

She leaned back, hands on my shoulders and looked me in the eye.

"Don't let anyone else see what I wrote. Promise?"

Her breasts, moulded into the tight charcoal sweater, were pressed against my chest.

"I promise." I reached out, tore the offending page from the notebook and stuffed it in my mouth. "I will deshtroy the evidensh."

I was trying every trick in the book. I couldn't let things happen the way they seemed to be going.

"That took me three hours!" Daisy pulled the soggy paper from my mouth. Throwing it away, she kissed me passionately on the lips. She jerked back, eyes sparkling.

"You taste like pencil."

"Daisy, wait." I took her face in my hands. "I want you more than you could possibly imagine. But you've been drinking."

"I only had four glasses of wine."

"That's four more than I've ever seen you drink before."

"What's wrong?" she said uncertainly. "You don't like it?"

"You kidding? I never want you to let go." I nodded towards the clock on the wall. "But I'm supposed to meet Ben in five minutes. His computer's playing up and I said I'd fix it."

"I know," Daisy grinned. "I thought I'd give you a way out if you wanted it. Me too, for that matter."

"I suppose you could stay where you are." I slapped her on the butt. "But that might embarrass him somewhat?"

"I got stuff to do too. Will you come back later?"

"Of course I will." I pulled her close and kissed her forehead.

Ben was out but had left his door unlocked. I let myself into his flat and began to work on the computer. All it needed was a bit of debugging, so I finished and checked my emails. There was one from Doc Menzies and one from Deek.

I opened the first and read the attachment.

My heart turned to ice.

-27-

Doc's Story

My dad was a therapist, as was *his* father. Perhaps it was cheaper to become one than hire one, though it has to be said, they were both loaded. In fact, they were always loaded. I helped carry on the legacy in both respects, becoming a psychiatrist and an alcoholic.

As a child, I was too afraid to ask my dad why he ignored me all the time and couldn't afford £200 an hour to engage his services in sorting out my feelings of rejection. So I turned to my gran for advice.

Granny Menzies was a formidably large woman, whose floral print dresses made her look like a field with legs. I swear to God, bees followed her around. I remember she always smelled flowery too, despite being able to down a bottle of Jack Daniels without taking the cigarette from her mouth.

"How old are you now?" she inquired. "Thirteen? Fourteen?"

"I'm ten."

"Then it's high time you learned about the family curse."

Lighting a Capstan double strength, she patted a basketball sized knee and I dutifully sat.

"Don't let anyone tell you this is just a legend," she warned before beginning her story. "Every word of it is true."

I couldn't imagine who might contradict her. Mum left when I was a baby and dad and grandpa didn't bother to speak to anyone except their patients.

"Could you stop bouncing me up and down?" I complained. "I'm finding it hard to concentrate."

"Just shaking loose the cobwebs," she cackled. "You'll need a clear head and a strong stomach for this story."

Here is the tale she told me.

In the 17th century, one of my ancestors was a highland mercenary known only as Mr Menzies, who fought in the 30 Years War. By all accounts, he was a terrible man who committed many atrocities during the conflict. One day, when a particularly vicious bout of pillaging was cut short by bad weather, Mr Menzies was approached by the Devil.

At this point, I felt I had to interrupt.

"The Devil?" Even at ten, I found this a tad hard to believe. "Are you sure?"

"He was red and had horns and hooves." Granny was unfazed. "Unless it was the front end of a panto cow, I'm going to stick with the Devil. Or a demon, at least."

I shut up before she started bouncing me again.

The Devil offered Mr Menzies a deal. He would enjoy long life and knowledge that would make him wealthy beyond his wildest dreams. Since my ancestor was already filthy rich from the spoils of war, his dreams must have been exceptionally wild. Or perhaps it was the kind of offer he couldn't refuse.

In return for the Devil's assistance, Mr Menzies had to make two promises. He had to swear that he would father a child someday and make sure his descendants all be buried in the same place.

"Seems like a pretty fair deal to me," I said.

"Auld Nick is like a credit card company," she replied sagely. "You'll always end up paying more than you expect."

At first, things went just fine. Mr Menzies returned to Scotland and bought a fine house in Edinburgh. He opened a bank account and stipulated the interest was to pay for future interments of his family in

Greyfriars Graveyard. He took a young bride called Grizzle and she bore him a healthy son.

Then the Devil came back and told Mr Menzies how the deal really worked.

I reside in you, he said. *And my line will continue to exist inside your son. Don't worry, I don't have anything catching.*

Mr Menzies protested vigorously.

Do I look bothered? the Devil shrugged. *You should have read the small print.*

I began to suspect granny was embellishing her tale a little, a trait I was to pick up in later years. But she'd had six whiskies by this point and wasn't in the mood to be interrupted.

When your son comes of age, I will make the same deal with him as I did with you, the Devil explained. *Long life, talent and prosperity. But he too must have a child, which must also be buried in Greyfriars. And so on and so forth...*

Mr Menzies could see a pattern emerging. Despite his flaws, he had once been a devout Catholic and didn't fancy the idea of his lineage being permanent carriers for the Prince of Darkness.

So he decided to kill his son and make it look like an accident. They didn't do things by half in those days.

He wasn't exactly a subtle man and when Grizzle found the child scaring seagulls off the roof during a thunderstorm, she suspected the worst. A local beauty, she deliberately began an affair with a fanatical young Covenanter called Thomas Weir, hoping she could entrust the lad to his care until she escaped her husband.

Weir was only too happy to oblige. Menzies was a hated Catholic, protected only by his vast wealth. The idea of spiriting away his child and indoctrinating the boy into the Covenanter faith was too good an opportunity to turn down.

In a black fury, Mr Menzies murdered his wife instead. Then he killed himself. Like I say, he wasn't a subtle man.

His plan was deceptively simple. By committing suicide, he denied himself a place in heaven, along with the atrocity he carried inside. And suicide victims couldn't be buried in hallowed ground, which would keep him out of Greyfriars too.

It would have worked if he'd bothered to cancel the payments to the church, but I suppose he had a lot on his mind - what with murdering his wife, making suicide plans and his only son living with the enemy while playing host to the embodiment of supreme evil. No Scottish church, even a Presbyterian one, was going to turn down the kind of money Menzie's legacy was offering. They buried him in Greyfriars without a headstone and hoped nobody would notice.

Gordon Menzies didn't turn out any happier than his father. It couldn't have been easy, becoming a protégé of the miserable Weir, who had become a preacher and now considered smiling to be a mortal sin. So when the Devil popped up and offered Gordon the same deal, he gladly took it.

"It's been that way ever since," Granny Menzies coughed, exhaling a huge cloud of dirty grey smoke. "How do you think your dad and granddad got so rich? They're both thick as platform boots."

"And that's why granddad hates dad and dad hates me?"

"Aw, he doesn't hate you, honey." Granny ruffled my hair. "He just can't stand to look at you."

"If Auld Nick comes for me, I'll refuse the deal," I said defiantly. "What's he going to do?"

"Make your life a living hell, I suppose." Granny shoved me off her knee and went to find another bottle. "Maybe your father's trying to prepare you for that."

I bet you're wondering if Beelzebub ever did come to make me an offer. Hard to say, really, as I spent most of my twenties and thirties in a drunken haze. But I did become obscenely wealthy and had a child of my own.

Daisy was a withdrawn and insular girl. Couldn't communicate or bear to be touched. Eventually, she was diagnosed as having Autism.

I wasn't going to accept that. I'm a fucking medical man and I knew it was something different. So I made up my mind to cure her. I read every article and study I could get my hands on.

Like Weir, I became a fanatic.

I restricted her diet. I forced her to read. I made her exercise and dance. I started to supply her with a cocktail of experimental drugs I obtained through a contact I had - a dodgy salesman for some big pharmaceutical company in Utah. She hated me for it and the improvements were negligible.

Then I had an idea for a truly radical therapy. Something so weird and wonderful I couldn't believe it would actually work. Yet, when I tried it out on other patients, there were remarkably positive results.

So I did the same with Daisy.

And, lo and behold, my daughter began to really change.

She started to speak properly. Gradually lost the strange monotone voice she had always used. Became properly aware of her surroundings. She was still quiet and withdrawn but I was elated.

Then everything started to go tits up.

I won't go into the details here - but it turned out my 'cure' had nasty side effects I hadn't predicted. When I attempted to correct what I'd done to Daisy, it was like something took her over. She broke free and attacked me with a carving knife. My wife, Hannah, tried to stop her and got carved up for her trouble.

Daisy wasn't aware of what she had done and still has no idea, so I took the blame. In exchange for my wife's silence, and her promise to look after our daughter, I signed my house and wealth over to her. She deserved that security now that she didn't have a face.

My wife hates me and Daisy for ruining her life and my kid thinks I'm a violent monster. I can't really blame either of them.

I guess I made a deal with the Devil after all.

From the Journal of Donny Marigold

My head was spinning. Doc's story was farfetched, to be sure. But all legends have a grain of truth, don't they? And there was one part of it I was certain he wouldn't make up.

He hadn't maimed his wife. It was Daisy.

I felt like I'd been punched in the face. She was no monster. Nothing would ever convince me of it. So what did that leave? A psychotic reaction? A nervous breakdown? Or something more sinister?

Could it be that The Menzies clan really had played host to something terrible over the centuries? And when each family member died, they were buried in Greyfriars along with their insidious passenger, strengthening the entity festering there.

I already knew Daisy Lenin had been diagnosed as Autistic, accurately or not. But this cast an entirely new light on her condition.

I wondered if she was possessed.

That might explain why she eventually headed for the place she was always destined to go. Greyfriars. Doc was in prison by then, so he couldn't stop it happening. That's why he contacted me and offered money to keep an eye on his daughter. More importantly, it's how he knew exactly where I'd find her.

What about Doc Menzies himself? If his story is true, there's something terrible in him as well. And what the hell was this 'radical therapy' he mentioned?

None of that mattered right now. I had intended to come clean to Daisy about my relationship with her dad. But how on earth could I tell her what she'd done to her mum?

I opened Deek's email next. I needed some sort of distraction and nothing in it could make me any more freaked out than I already felt.

I was sorely mistaken.

-28-

Deek's Story

I don't get it, Donny. Every time I try to write, this is what comes out.
-Deek

1635 1635 1635 1635 1635 1635 1635 1635 1635 1635 1635 1635
1635 1635 1635 1635 1635 1635 1635 1635 1635 1635 1635 1635 1635
1635 1635 1635 1635 1635 1635 1635 1635 1635 1635 1635 1635 1635
1635 1635 1635 1635 1635 1635 1635 1635 1635 1635 1635 1635 1635
1635 1635 1635 1635 1635 1635 1635 1635 1635 1635 1635 1635 1635
1635 1635 1635 1635 1635 1635 1635 1635 1635 1635 1635 1635 1635
1635 1635 1635 1635 1635 1635 1635 1635 1635 1635 1635 1635 1635
1635 1635 1635 1635 1635 1635 1635 1635 1635 1635 1635 1635 1635
1635 1635 1635 1635 1635 1635 1635 1635 1635 1635 1635 1635 1635
1635 1635 1635 1635 1635 1635 1635 1635 1635 1635 1635 1635 1635
1635 1635 1635 1635 1635 1635 1635 1635 1635 1635 1635 1635 1635
1635 1635 1635 1635 1635 1635 1635 1635 1635 1635 1635 1635 1635
1635 1635 1635 1635 1635 1635 1635 1635 1635 1635 1635 1635 1635
1635 1635 1635 1635 1635 1635 1635 1635 1635 1635 1635 1635 1635
1635 1635 1635 1635 1635 1635 1635 1635 1635 1635 1635 1635 1635
1635 1635 1635 1635 1635 1635 1635 1635 1635 1635 1635 1635 1635
1635 1635 1635

1635 1635 1635 1635 1635 1635 1635 1635 1635 1635 1635 1635
1635 1635 1635 1635 1635 1635 1635 1635 1635 1635 1635 1635 1635
1635 1635 1635 1635 1635 1635 1635 1635 1635 1635 1635 1635 1635
1635 1635 1635 1635 1635 1635 1635 1635 1635 1635 1635 1635 1635

1635 1635 1635 1635 1635 1635 1635 1635 1635 1635 1635 1635 1635
1635 1635 1635 1635 1635 1635 1635 1635 1635 1635 1635 1635 1635
1635 1635 1635 1635 1635 1635 1635 1635 1635 1635 1635 1635 1635
1635 1635 1635 1635 1635 1635 1635 1635 1635 1635 1635 1635 1635
1635 1635 1635 1635 1635 1635 1635 1635 1635 1635 1635 1635 1635
1635 1635 1635 1635 1635 1635 1635 1635 1635 1635 1635 1635 1635
1635 1635 1635 1635 1635 1635 1635 1635 1635 1635 1635 1635 1635
1635 1635 1635 1635 1635 1635 1635 1635 1635 1635 1635 1635 1635
1635 1635 1635 1635 1635 1635 1635 1635 1635 1635 1635 1635 1635
1635 1635 1635 1635 1635 1635 1635 1635 1635 1635 1635 1635 1635
1635 1635 1635 1635 1635 1635 1635 1635 1635 1635 1635 1635 1635
1635 1635 1635 1635 1635 1635 1635 1635 1635 1635 1635 1635 1635
1635 1635 1635

1635 1635 1635 1635 1635 1635 1635 1635 1635 1635 1635 1635
1635 1635 1635 1635 1635 1635 1635 1635 1635 1635 1635 1635 1635
1635 1635 1635 1635 1635 1635 1635 1635 1635 1635 1635 1635 1635
1635 1635 1635 1635 1635 1635 1635 1635 1635 1635 1635 1635 1635
1635 1635 1635 1635 1635 1635 1635 1635 1635 1635 1635 1635 1635
1635 1635 1635 1635 1635 1635 1635 1635 1635 1635 1635 1635 1635
1635 1635 1635 1635 1635 1635 1635 1635 1635 1635 1635 1635 1635
1635 1635 1635 1635 1635 1635 1635 1635 1635 1635 1635 1635 1635
1635 1635 1635 1635 1635 1635 1635 1635 1635 1635 1635 1635 1635
1635 1635 1635 1635 1635 1635 1635 1635 1635 1635 1635 1635 1635
1635 1635 1635 1635 1635 1635 1635 1635 1635 1635 1635 1635 1635
1635 1635 1635 1635 1635 1635 1635 1635 1635 1635 1635 1635 1635
1635 1635 1635 1635 1635 1635 1635 1635 1635 1635 1635 1635 1635
1635 1635 1635 1635 1635 1635 1635 1635 1635 1635 1635 1635 1635
1635 1635 1635 1635 1635 1635 1635 1635 1635 1635 1635 1635 1635
1635 1635 1635

-Part 5-

The Séance

There are things known and there are things unknown, and in between are the doors of perception.

Aldous Huxley

Peter had seen many tragedies, but he had forgotten them all.

J. M. Barrie. *Peter Pan*

From the Journal of Donny Marigold

What the fuck? The guides were a cheery bunch when I met them but they were changing, no doubt about it. True or not, each story they had given me was an unhappy one or hinted at some sort of mental illness.

Was that why Doc wanted the tales? To make some sort of diagnoses? After all, he's a psychiatrist. Yet, how could he have known there was something wrong with them in the first place?

And his story was the most frightening of all. I had suspected he was connected to the poltergeist somehow - but not that deeply.

I didn't expect to get more information out of him. He's more evasive than a greasy jackrabbit in a minefield. Luckily, I had another avenue. Someone else who always seemed to know more than he pretended.

Ben Scott

-29-

Next door to Ben's flat, Doc Menzies whistled *Peter and the Wolf* as he put his clinic back in order. Half a dozen empty beer cans lined the mantelpiece. Hauling a large cardboard box from the cupboard, he lugged it into the centre of the room.

He didn't hear Ben enter until a hand fell on his shoulder. Menzies spun round, his eyes bulging.

"Jesus!" He relaxed visibly when he saw who the intruder was. "You almost scared my panties off!"

"That's my job." Ben began setting out candles. "Here. I'll give you a hand."

They worked quietly for a while, used to each other's company.

"I'm warming to Donny, you know." Doc was rearranging the furniture. A circular table in the middle of the room. Five chairs around it, each evenly spaced to the inch. "Seems like a genuinely decent person."

"Yeah. *He's* never been in prison."

"That was uncalled for."

"I assure you, he has Daisy's best interests at heart," Ben said. "You won't even go near her."

"Think it doesn't hurt to stay out of her way?" Doc surveyed the room and gave a satisfied smile. "I'm working on it. And this séance is going to fix everything. Hopefully."

"I admire your diplomatic choice of words but we both know this is no séance. It's an exorcism."

Ben folded his arms and leaned against the wall.

"Is it likely to be dangerous, Doc?"

"Possibly." His companion took a candelabra from a cardboard box and plonked it on the table. "Probably."

"Why? We never had any hassle in the past."

"This is very different."

Doc grabbed some light bulbs from the box, stood on a chair and began to replace the ones in the chandelier overhead. He swayed alarmingly and Ben stepped forward, arms outstretched. Recovering his balance, Doc waved him away.

"Why don't we bring Billy Cream in to help again?" Ben asked. "He's a big guy."

"Billy's dead." Doc didn't miss a beat. "He committed suicide not long ago."

"Did he now?" Ben stuck a cigarette in his mouth and scraped a match down the wall. "You see him before he offed himself, by any chance?"

"I did." Doc glared at the black stripe on the beige paint. "I wanted to help him but he reacted... violently, despite being sedated. So, I tried something different."

Doc put in the last bulb.

"That didn't work either."

"You experimented on him?"

"Billy was my patient before he became my assistant." Doc got down off the table in a flurry of crackling joints. "I would never knowingly hurt a patient."

"And I'm not going to let you hurt my staff." Ben hesitated. "My friends."

"They're already hurting. It's only going to get worse."

"I don't see that at all." Ben took the cardboard box and stuck it in a cupboard. "They like their jobs and each other. They're proud of what they've achieved and make pretty good money."

"What they've achieved?" Doc massaged his back. "With all due respect, they could accomplish so much more. Instead, they're drawn to Greyfriars like moths round a flame. And the tighter they circle, the closer they come to being burned up."

"That's a mighty purty speech, Doc," Ben drawled. "Want to tell me what it means?"

"I take it you have everything at your end set up?"

"I'm not kidding." Ben stubbed out his cigarette on the windowsill and Doc tightened his lips. "I'm grateful for all you've done for me. But I want straight answers."

"You know how I operate. You always have."

"This is different." Ben folded his arms stubbornly. "Why these people? Why here? Why now, after all this time?"

"You're not going to like it."

"Really?" Ben's voice dripped with sarcasm. "You think?"

"You're not going to like me, either." Doc got another beer from the fridge and opened it. It gave an evil fizz and golden liquid oozed over his hand, dripping onto the floor. "Get a cloth. Quick!"

"Tell me the whole story, Doc. Or I'll cancel the damned thing."

"You better sit down." The man downed half the tin in one go and burped loudly.

"You too." Ben took a seat. "Before you fall down. Now out with it."

Doc sat heavily, looking defeated.

"The normal therapy we used on kids was very effective, as you know," he began. "But then I did something very stupid…"

Donny plodded up the stairs and into Daisy's flat. He took her by the arms and sat her on the bed.

"You sweeping me off my feet?" she laughed. Donny could see she was tipsy but ploughed on before his nerve broke.

"I know your father," he said.

The smile vanished.

"Doc was treating my brother, Sam." Donny continued. "Until he went to prison, that is."

"Why have you never told me this?" Daisy growled.

"Because you hate him." The boy clasped his hands together. "Doc contacted me from prison and asked me to visit. Told me you'd run away from home. Instructed me to look out for you and keep you safe. Offered me money and I took it."

"He's *paying* you to be with me?"

Donny had a whole speech prepared for this moment. Excuses. Explanations. Appeals to reason. None of it was enough.

"The money ran out long ago," he said simply. "I'm here because I want to be."

"You bastard." Her dismay was replaced by anger. "Give my keys back."

Donny placed them on the table. He was expecting that reaction but it was like giving away a piece of his soul.

"Now get out."

"I'm sorry," Donny said. "You've no idea how much."

"Just go."

Halfway down the stairs, he was accosted by Ben Scott.

"Take a seat, kid." Ben grabbed Donny and led him to the couch. "We need to talk."

The boy sat down and took off his coat while Ben poured them both a glass of wine. Donny's hands were shaking so badly he could hardly hold the drink. Ben lit two cigarettes and handed one over. It was an oddly intimate gesture.

"I see what you and the toots upstairs have, and it's a fine thing." He plonked himself down by Donny's side. It struck the boy that, no matter how many cigarettes Ben smoked, he always managed to smell as if he'd just had a shower.

"You fucked it up by telling her the truth, eh?" Ben glanced sideways at his abashed companion. "I reckon she'll forgive you, but it will take time. Best leave her be for a while."

"How could you possibly know that?"

"I was listening outside the door," he shrugged. "Sue me."

"You know Doc," Donny said, "Don't you?"

"We both do." Ben downed his wine. "You first."

It was time to bite the bullet.

"A year ago, Doc was treating my older brother, Sam Marigold." Donny saw no point in hiding things anymore. "Sam was a schizophrenic. He hallucinated. Heard voices. Nothing seemed to work, so my father hired a Doctor Menzies to treat him privately. He'd come to the house for the sessions and that's how I met him. He brought Daisy once, but she doesn't remember me. Seemed hardly aware of her surroundings and she had a strange monotone voice."

"She was a very different girl back then," Ben nodded, encouraging him to continue.

"One session was all it took. Sam told me that he finally understood what was wrong with him and Doc was going to fix it."

"Did he?"

"No. Doc got locked up soon after and had to stop treating Sam. One night I was supposed to be looking after him but I just couldn't cope. The strain was driving me crazy. So I went out instead. The police eventually found me in Greyfriars."

Donny finished his wine. Ben got up and fetched him another.

"When they brought me home, the stereo was playing so loud the walls were thumping, like the house had a pulse. My brother was hanging from the light in his bedroom." The boy choked back a sob. "I told my dad his nose had bled a little heart on the floor. It wasn't true. Just sounded more poetic."

He put out his cigarette and immediately lit a second.

"Dad hardly talks to me anymore. It was my fault and, besides, I look like Sam. I don't think he can stand to be in the same room as me."

"If it's any consolation, I know how you feel." Ben fetched the bottle of wine from the fridge and set it on the floor between them. "I can't bear to be in the same room as myself."

He gave Donny a lopsided smile.

"Which is difficult."

"Doc wrote to me from prison and begged me to visit," the boy continued. "When I did, he said Daisy had run away from home. Told me to look out for her and offered me money if I would."

He looked down at his expensive boots.

"A lot of money. He seemed to know she would head for Greyfriars and, sure enough, that's where I found her."

Donny took a deep breath and dropped his bombshell.

"I think it's because the entity wanted her here."

"Or..." Ben jerked a thumb at the wall. "It's because Doc's clinic was next door."

Suddenly Donny realised exactly where Ben was going to hold the séance and a shiver ran down his spine.

They sat in silence for a while, watching tendrils of smoke fill the room as if they were exhaling ghosts.

"Come clean, Ben," Donny said eventually. "What's your relationship with Doc?"

"A long and complex one. He's going to help me conduct the séance."

"What the actual fuck?" Donny's jaw dropped. "How the hell is *that* going to work? Daisy wants to go."

"Beats me. But that old bastard always has a card up his sleeve."

"I need to know everything. You owe me that."

"I will." Ben glanced at the clock on the wall. "But it's late. Get here bright and early tomorrow."

He wearily indicated for the boy to leave.

"I'm afraid I have another horror story to tell you."

From the Journal of Donny Marigold

I have no choice but to leave Daisy alone for a while, so I'm writing this in a notebook instead and, hopefully, I can enter it on Daisy's computer at some point. I'm desperate to talk to her but, if the truth be known, I'm too scared. Besides, I need to update updated my journal, adding in my fears.

There are a lot of them.

Ben has said he'll tell me everything tomorrow and show me proof nothing supernatural was involved.

Good luck to him.

It's time to put my new theory into words and see if I can somehow make sense of what I've learned. Which is comparable to building a jet engine with instructions from Ikea.

For assembling a wardrobe.

I still don't know what the Mackenzie Poltergeist is. I liked the idea of a pheromone cloud but it doesn't fit the facts. Instead, I'm going to concentrate on what it does.

The graveyard only existed from 1566, so there were no real records before that. In fact, nothing much happened in the cemetery until right after Grizzle's husband, Mr Menzies, got buried there in 1635.

Which had to be more than a coincidence.

The rest of the 17th century saw Greyfriars play a pivotal role in the destruction of Catholicism, then Anglicanism, then Presbyterianism in

Scotland. The National Covenant, George Mackenzie, the prison, Major Weir - all embroiled in an epic religious conflict. As if some strange influence, emanating from the cemetery, had it in for each successive bullish, inflexible denomination. And, finally, the fanaticism of religion itself.

As if the very Devil was at work.

Hard to swallow? I was going to run with it anyway.

Then came the 18th century. And a paradigm shift.

Now Greyfriars became the hub of a rational movement that led the rest of the world - the Enlightenment and its stars - like Burnett. Hume and Hutton. But science was too underdeveloped to be truly effective in providing real solutions to the philosophical questions being explored. Still in its infancy, it could only be nudged in the right direction.

It seemed to me the poltergeist was doing the nudging.

In the 19th century, Greyfriars changed again, becoming central to some of the world's most controversial literary works. Again, all were far ahead of their time. Shelly's Frankenstein. *Polidori's* The Vampyr. *Hogg's* Confessions of a Justified Sinner. *Dicken's* A Christmas Carol. *Stevenson's* Dr Jekyll and Mr Hyde.

Each book has two things in common. A supernatural theme and a delving into the very notion of what fundamentally shapes us. Alongside them come scientific bolts from the blue, like Chamber's Vestiges of the Natural History of Creation *and* Darwin's Origin of the Species *– the tome that wipes religion off the map as an explanation for how intelligent life came about, and rewrites mankind's perception of the fundamental principles of existence.*

By this point, I was seeing more than a mere horror novel coming out of my research. Not that I wasn't in good company.

I was thinking more along the lines of either a major scientific treatise or being locked up forever in a padded cell.

I believed I had uncovered a network of causal chains that changed world history. And the connection? Greyfriars Graveyard.

Or, more specifically, the Mackenzie Poltergeist.

So here goes.

I think the poltergeist has influenced visitors to the graveyard for centuries, waiting, like some paranormal Praying Mantis, for the right kind of minds to wander into its lair.

It was vindictive at first, attacking the religious structures that branded anything unknown as evil. But, increasingly, this entity began to push the boundaries of knowledge. Seeking explanations. Alerting the public to the existence of things beyond their ken. It stopped acting like a vengeful child and became a seeker of truth, following the driving force of all intelligent life. What am I and what is my purpose?

Until the 20th century.

Then the entity's influence vanished. In the 20th century, Greyfriars was central to nothing at all. Nothing for 120 years.

There are only two conclusions I can draw from my research.

Something happened to the entity at the end of the 19th century that forced it to become dormant.

Now, something has woken it up.

-30-

Donny turned up the next morning, trembling with anticipation. Ben indicated for him to take a seat. Without a preamble, he launched into his tale.

"I used to work for Doc, now and then, in his clinic," he said. "A bit of part-time cash."

"Didn't know you had any medical experience."

"I'm adept at making shit up." Ben shrugged. "As far as I can see, that's all you need."

"What did you do?" Donny screwed up his face. "Hold people down while he gave them electric shocks?"

"Actually, we tied them to a chair. I'm not kidding."

"Now I'm really intrigued."

"I supplied him with stuff from my theatre, mainly." Ben seemed reluctant to elaborate but Donny wasn't about to let it go.

"Did he dress up as Sigmund Freud and hit his patients over the head with a rubber chicken?"

"He did like props. Used that dummy, Bunny Wunny Woo, for disturbed kids to talk to, if they were too mucked up to confide in him directly. When he finally threw it away, I rescued it. Thought it might come in handy for a horror play I was trying to write."

Donny shut up.

Ben went to the window. There was nothing to see, so he stared at the wall instead. Donny saw that he was developing a bald patch, even through his shorn hair.

"Doc's methods were... eh... fairly unorthodox." Ben placed his hands on the sill and breathed softly on the glass. "But he was a very rich man and I was broke. So, when he went to prison, he offered to pay for the rental of his old premises, my flat and the empty one above. Plus funds to start up my own business."

"Ghost tours of Greyfriars?"

"Yeah. There was only one condition. He gave me a list and insisted I employ the people on it until he came back. He promised they'd be hanging around Greyfriars somewhere."

"Was Daisy on the list?"

"She was, though I hadn't met her until you introduced us," Ben said. "There was one name I recognised immediately. Billy Cream. He was an ex-patient who used to help out at the clinic until he became an ambulance driver. I don't suppose you ever came across him?"

Donny shook his head.

"I found another I couldn't employ." Ben continued. "That arsehole ned, Marky Cotter. But I keep a close eye on him. And there were three I never managed to locate. Vanessa Reese, William Anderson and Julie James."

"Don't know them either."

"I did pretty well, though." Ben had calmed down enough to return to his seat. "The last three are very familiar to you."

"You have *got* to be kidding me."

"Nope." Ben scratched his lip thoughtfully.

"Oss, Lee and Deek."

"Doc was an expert hypnotist," Ben continued. "With a very unique way of working. Borderline illegal, probably."

"That doesn't surprise me."

"He was a qualified hypnotherapist, but his powers of mesmerism went way beyond that. He used his talent to convince disturbed kids they had an evil entity inside," Ben ploughed on. "Then he would bring them back to his clinic a couple of days later and 'exorcise' the entity. Guess where I came in?"

Donny went pale.

"You organised props to make the exorcism look more authentic?" he ventured.

"You're a smart kid." Ben smiled approvingly. "The whole thing was utter guff, of course. But what do you know? It usually worked. He had a very high success rate."

Donny's hands began to tremble too. He placed them on the table in an imitation of his boss, wondering if it was for the same reason.

"Word got around and he ended up with a lot of wealthy clients. Rich people always have screwed up children."

"Don't I know it," Donny grunted.

"The parents paid through the nose for his services. What I didn't know, at the time, was that he had begun taking on charity cases for free."

"Like Oss, Lee and Deek?"

"Yup."

"Wait a minute!" the boy said. "If Doc is conducting this séance, he'll be recognised. That's going to be kind of awkward."

"They won't remember him. As I say, his powers of hypnosis were superb. He could bury just about anything in your subconscious and keep it from coming to the surface. He used numbers as triggers. One to reinforce his hypnotic suggestions, another to snap them out of it."

"I take it 1635 was the reinforcement trigger? It pops up too often to be a coincidence."

"Oh, you're smart."

"What went wrong, Ben?" Donny's head was throbbing. "Something obviously did."

"You remember Doc's story about the curse of the Menzie clan?" Ben looked longingly at the well-stocked fridge, then tore his eyes away.

"It's pretty much seared into my mind."

"Doc never really believed in it," Ben began. "But he figured out a unique way to use the story."

"He believed all right," Donny interrupted.

"I don't think you're an expert in what Doc thinks."

"Sorry Ben, but neither are you."

"Shut up. This is hard enough without you getting mouthy every few seconds."

"My lips are sealed."

"The story about the curse never left Doc. In fact, it gave him another idea."

Donny's sealed lips tightened perceptibly.

"There were a handful of kids he considered to be in far worse shape than the others. Children that needed stronger treatment in order to live a normal life."

"Like his own daughter."

"Yes." Ben went to the cupboard and opened it. He removed a thin sheaf of papers from a manila envelope and placed them on the table.

"Doc gave me his stuff to look after until he came back." He shoved the files towards Donny. "Here are the case notes from his initial interviews with Billy Cream, Victor Swift, Deek Elsby and Lee Watson."

"Aren't these confidential? Am I allowed to read them?" Donny looked at the papers warily. "Are *you* allowed to read them?"

"Considering the shit we're in, I hardly think it matters."

"Fair enough." The teenager scanned the files.

Billy George Cream (17 years)

Billy Cream is overweight and suffering from extreme obsessive compulsive disorder, along with a morbid preoccupation with death. He has a burning desire to help other disadvantaged children by doing social work or entering the field of medicine. This is not going to be possible unless he can defeat these overpowering handicaps.

Victor Swift (16)

Victor Swift is an awkward, lonely boy. His bipolar disorder makes it impossible for him to communicate normally with others. As a result, he has become a total recluse.

Imagining Oss now, Donny had to suppress a snort of laughter.

He badly wants a girlfriend, but it's just not going to happen. He is aware enough to accept this and has decided to go into IT, a profession he feels he can handle, as it would allow him to work on his own. But he isn't socially adept enough to hold down a job.

Derek Elsby (15)
Derek Elsby has cripplingly low self-esteem. His condition has developed into full blown depression with bouts of self-harm. Could not look me in the eye or raise his voice above a whisper.

He is fiercely intelligent and excels at school – particularly science. Would probably get a first at university if he ever got up the courage to actually go.

He won't, though.

Lee Anne Watson (16)
A clear case of childhood abuse, Lee has internalised her pain and become terrified of sexual contact. Yet all she really wants is a normal husband, home and family – an ambition she self-sabotages at every turn. Utterly lacking in confidence, I predict she will reject any normal treatment I offer.

So I'll have to fool her.

"I don't get it." Donny looked up, puzzled. "Deek, Lee and Oss aren't like that."

"Not anymore."

"Then they're cured." Donny accepted another drink. "What's the big deal?"

"Doc didn't treat them the way he did the other kids in his care. He tried something far more extreme." Ben lit a cigarette and Donny could see his hands were still shaking. "He was always an arrogant man. It's his biggest flaw."

"What did he do to them, Ben?"

The tour boss looked at the boy over a cloud of smoke.

"Ben," Donny repeated. "What the fuck did Doc do to them?"

Ben went back to the cupboard. Returned with a large notebook and opened it near the end.

"This is Doc's clinical diary. Look at this entry."

He placed it in front of Donny.

I knew my 'cure' would not work for the most profound cases I encountered. Most of my clients weren't ill, to be honest. They were rich, spoilt kids with rich spoilt parents. Their offspring weren't crazy, just unstable and nasty and I gave them the opportunity to wipe the slate clean and start again. But they'd make the same mistakes eventually because they're crap.

I hadn't been committed enough. Bit of quick hypnotherapy to implant the idea that they had a demon. One half-assed exorcism later, they'd go off, happy as Larry. Nothing was really solved.

I had to find a proper solution. I had to fix my daughter.

I needed to go deeper. Implant the hypnosis on a far more fundamental level. It couldn't just be a glib thing. If I was going to make it work, I had to believe in it myself. Hold up a mirror, if you like.

Take Billy Cream. He was never going to be sorted by my usual approach. So, when I hypnotised him, I supplied a whole back story, stretching back half a millennium. My granny's tale of the Menzies clan and the idea that our family were destined to become rich, confident and successful. I convinced him that I could pass the entity inside me onto him. Without that impetus, Billy would never have stood a chance of functioning normally.

Only I didn't exorcise the 'demon' this time. I left it inside him.

To go through life thinking you're possessed by a monster is not conducive to good mental health, so I buried the information deep in his subconscious. It was highly effective. Billy began to sort his life out. Learned to cope with the everyday situations that would have once defeated him. And he had no idea why.

Billy Cream thrived. He lost his shyness and his fears and eventually became my assistant. I kept up the normal therapy for most patients but, every now and then, someone came along who needed the same push as Billy did - just to survive in life.

Like Billy, they changed. Like Billy, they couldn't understand or remember why and didn't care. They were sorted.

So I did the same with my daughter. That's what it was always about.

Donny glanced up. "I could have told you that."

"Keep reading," Ben urged.

I had gone too far in my quest for authenticity. I don't know what possessed me.

I'd used the story of Greyfriars and the poltergeist. And what I implanted in them began to fester.

They all developed confidence. Turned into fully functioning members of society. And became utterly incapable of moving on. Tied to the graveyard for reasons they could never comprehend. Haunted by a curse that was never theirs.

Billy Cream was the first to crack, his desire to help kids becoming an obsession with ensuring they got to heaven. In short, he went mad.

I realised the rest would eventually go the same way, including my daughter.

In desperation, I tried to 'exorcise' Daisy. She was just a kid, so I didn't think to restrain her. But what I implanted in her was so strong, she fought like a maniac and tried to kill me. My wife, Hannah, intervened and Daisy carved her up.

She didn't remember the incident, naturally, so I took the blame and went to prison. Which meant, I was never able to complete the exorcism.

The others are still coping to some extent. It's even possible they've gained enough confidence to survive without any help from their subconscious ally if I remove it. Problem is, this notion is implanted so deeply in their subconscious, it is now part of their makeup.

When we exorcise them, they're going to fight us with every fibre of their being.

"I don't much like the 'fighting against it' bit," Donny said nervously. "Look what a little soul like Daisy did. Oss and Deek are big blokes. Lee isn't exactly tiny either."

"I'm with you on that. I'll figure something out. Hopefully."

"You said there was a trigger to bring them out of their hypnosis altogether." Donny picked up the notes again and looked for it.

"A much longer number than 1635, yes. Naturally, it had to be something that would never come up in conversation. Only Doc knows what it is."

"Then what's all this exorcism malarkey? Why doesn't he just snap them out of it?"

"He tried it on Billy Cream." Ben looked at the ground. "But it was like wiping a slate clean. Billy reverted to the person he used to be."

"And?"

"He committed suicide. The guy might have been fucked up but he'd had a taste of what normal life was like. Couldn't bear being his old self again."

"Jesus, Ben!"

"It means simply ending Doc's hypnotic suggestion isn't an option. Neither is leaving the guides to get worse." Ben stubbed out his cigarette. "We don't do the exorcism and Lee, Oss and Deek are going to end up in an asylum or jail."

"I'm not convinced you're right."

"How so?"

"I still think the poltergeist is real," Donny said. "You might want to consider that the guides really are possessed."

"I'm most certainly not going to consider it." Ben wagged a finger at the boy. "Stop that nonsense."

"I intend to find proof before this fake séance happens. If not, I'll help. Fair enough?"

"Knock yourself out," Ben sighed. "You've got a couple of days left to prove the entire scientific community of the planet wrong."

"I like a challenge."

"Then let me state *my* case first. It will change your mind, I guarantee it."

Ben beckoned to him.

"Come with me to Doc's clinic and I'll show you my bag of tricks."

From the Journal of Donny Marigold

I had painted myself into a corner. Accepted an impossible deadline to prove the existence of a supernatural entity that had managed to remain hidden for centuries.

I knew what it had done - but that paled beside what I didn't know.

I didn't know what it was.

I didn't know why it had vanished over a century ago.

Most importantly, I didn't know why it was back.

I was determined to work this out, and I still had a few ideas. I'd have another go at getting Grizzle to talk, for a start – though she was as good as Doc at sidestepping my questions.

Then Ben took me next door and blew my assumptions out of the water.

-31-

Ben and Donny let themselves into the clinic. There was a round table in the centre and the walls were lined with bookshelves. Ben fetched wine from the fridge and poured some.

"I swear you would find booze if we were suddenly transported to Antarctica." Donny took off his jacket and hung it on the back of a chair.

"This exorcism is going to be all smoke and mirrors." Ben showed the boy a box with buttons taped to the side of a bureau. "I press these and lights flash. Shit moves. Weird noises come from nowhere."

"How do you know how to do that?"

"From the theatre." Ben smiled proudly. "I used all sorts of special effects."

He pressed a button and a picture fell off the wall. Donny jumped.

"Cool! Can I have a go?

"Stop mucking about. We're talking about my guides' sanity."

"OK. Doc's story is very plausible, but it doesn't explain everything that's been going on." Donny retorted. "Take the stories I had the guides write, for instance."

"The stories *Doc* wanted written," Ben corrected. "He wanted a snapshot of their mental state and it doesn't look promising, as you saw."

He waved at Donny to continue.

"But, go ahead. Get all the weird out."

"Lee's story indicates she's beginning to hallucinate. I accept that. And Deek's is off the chart." Donny sat down with his drink. "Can you explain the mysterious ghost girl emailing Oss?"

"They were *emails*. They could have come from anyone." Ben scratched his head awkwardly. "All right... they came from me. His work was going to relocate Oss and I needed him to stick around."

Donny remembered the binoculars on Daisy's windowsill. Ben must have been able to see right into the Intelligence Department windows. Keep an eye on everything Oss was doing. He slapped his forehead.

"The data entries that got him fired. They came from you."

"1635, repeated endlessly. I knew he wouldn't question it."

Ben waited.

"What about the tourists?" Donny continued. "So, they bump each other around." The teenager picked his way carefully. "But they have marks on their skin that look like handprints. Lots even collapse."

The teenager sat back with a smug grin.

"Explain that."

"It was me," Ben replied evenly.

"Eh?"

"Look at this." The tour boss opened a cupboard. Donny could see a large metal tank with a nozzle attached.

"It's for spraying weeds. I nicked it from the council shed at the other end of the graveyard." Ben patted the cylinder. "Got Deek to give me a couple of pointers in chemistry. Turns out, if you add antiseptic to this type of weed killer, it will produce a massive allergic reaction on human skin."

"Oh… you didn't."

"Yup. I spray it every now and then on the walls of the Black Mausoleum." It was Ben's turn to look self-satisfied. "People touch the stone, scratch themselves under their clothes. Instant blisters, leading to a handprint on the skin. It's odourless but, in that confined space, the fumes make people dizzy and confused. Knocks out the more susceptible ones after about ten minutes."

Donny's eyes widened.

"Is that why birds keep dying near the entrance? Is that why there's no cats in the graveyard anymore?

"Probably." Ben looked guilty. "I think it poisons them."

"Oh my God." Donny thought back. "The knocking on the walls of your flat. The exploding vase. The stopped clock. They were your *special effects*."

"They were."

"Fuck me. Why would you do that to the guides?"

"I didn't know they were sick at the time, did I?" Ben replied defensively. "They frighten the tourists so much more effectively if they believe in the poltergeist."

"You sir," Donny raised his wine in admiration. "Are a complete and utter bastard."

"Why, thank you." Ben clinked his glass. "I try my best."

They began to laugh. At first, it was just a fit of the giggles but it escalated to an almost manic pitch. Ben wiped tears from his eyes and Donny held his sides in pain. When the merriment had subsided, the tour boss rested his chin on his hands.

"Convinced now?"

"Getting there. Just remember, there's two sides to every story." Donny put on his jacket again. "The poltergeist may not be back, after all. That doesn't mean it never existed."

"God, you're a persistent bugger. Where are you off to?"

Donny glanced out of the window.

"I want to talk to an old friend."

From the Journal of Donny Marigold

Ben isn't as bad a guy as he thinks.

He's looked out for me, Daisy and the guides and he's doing what he thinks is best for them. He genuinely believes Doc tried to fix those kids for altruistic reasons. That his old boss is trying to correct the mistakes he made so everyone can lead a normal life.

Wrong.

I doubt Doc is even slightly interested in their welfare. If he can cure them, he can do the same for Daisy. It's that simple.

But Daisy isn't like the others. They had social disorders. Hers was something more. In my opinion, she was already possessed and whatever was inside her didn't take kindly to his interference. It wasn't something Doc implanted. It was already there.

He simply doesn't learn from his mistakes.

If he tries to exorcise Daisy again, fuck knows what will happen.

I decided to have one last go at talking to Grizzle.

-32-

Donny made his way to the back of the graveyard, carrying an electric lantern.

Grizzle was crouched in the farthest corner of the graveyard, hunched beneath a skeletal willow tree. She was dressed in the City of the Dead tour outfit, complete with a full-length leather coat and a silver topped cane, cradled in the crook of her arm. She didn't move as Donny approached, didn't flinch or blink when the lantern was held in front of her face.

Her dark hair was swept back into a severe ponytail and bright red lipstick glistened like a scar in the halogen light.

"Hi, toots."

"Been a while." The girl placed the cane on the ground and unfastened her jacket, revealing an angry scar between her breasts. "Thought you were ignoring me."

"A lot has happened recently." Donny sat down in front of her, placing the lantern between them.

"Fallen out of favour, perchance?" The ghost took a knife from inside her jacket and played with its tip. "So, you come crawling back here."

"Cynically put. But I guess so."

Grizzle held up her hands in front of her face. When she parted them, Donny was looking at Daisy's image. He kept his expression neutral, not without some difficulty.

"Happy now?" Grizzle asked.

"Nice trick, but you still have the ponytail," he admonished. "She'd never wear a ponytail."

To Donny's surprise, the apparition laughed.

"You're not really the wife of Campbell Menzies," Donny said. "So, who the hell are you?"

Grizzle sniffed disdainfully, got up and strolled away. The boy picked up the lantern and followed.

"Damned if I know," she replied eventually. "I'm sure you're familiar with the feeling."

"What do you mean by that?"

"I'm not evil, though." She deflected the question. "I'm just misunderstood."

They skirted a tombstone and continued down the hill, Donny keeping the light aloft, so he could see the terrain.

They reached the farthest end of the graveyard from the Covenanter's Prison, under Ben's window.

"My favourite spot." She lay down on the grass. "I'd like to go to heaven but being with you is as close as I'll ever get."

"You believe in heaven?"

"Got to believe in something, don't I?" Grizzle patted the ground beside her. Donny hesitated, then lay down as well.

"Ben says there's no entity attacking tourists in Greyfriars." He rolled over on one side and squinted at his companion. "Claims it was all him and he was pretty convincing."

"I agree," his companion said. "Sure, you bring in a lot of tourists but the Mackenzie Poltergeist never needed help before."

"True," Donny acknowledged.

"It may have existed once, but it's gone. After all, the deal it made with the Menzies clan has fallen through."

"How so?"

"They were all supposed to be interred in Greyfriars, weren't they? Yet, this hasn't been a functioning cemetery for well over a century. Nobody gets buried here anymore."

Grizzle sighed.

"I guess that wasn't the answer you wanted."

"Nobody likes to be proved wrong, I suppose." Donny rubbed his temple. "Listen, I have to go. I'm cold and puzzled and more than a bit depressed."

"Please stay a few more minutes," the ghost said forlornly. "It's lonely here and I don't have anyone but you. But I can't really have you, can I?"

"No." Donny squeezed his companion's hand in return. "I love Daisy Lenin."

He reached out and touched Grizzle's cheek.

"I'm sorry things turned out the way they did. And please stop looking like her."

"Took you long enough to admit it." Grizzle turned back into herself. "I guess my time is up. It's been a lot of fun, though."

Donny smiled gratefully. He put his arms round the ghost of his past and rested his head on its chest.

"Goodbye, my friend."

They lay in the darkness and looked at the heavens. Beautiful pinpoints that seemed to offer the promise of undiscovered worlds, if they hadn't been impossible to reach.

Donny stayed until she faded away.

The boy was leaving Greyfriars when he remembered what Grizzle had said.

This hasn't been a functioning cemetery for well over a century. Nobody gets buried here anymore.

He stopped, got out his phone and pressed speed dial.

"Little late to be ringing wee D," Deek's sleepy voice muttered down the line. "I might have been in bed with a hot chick."

"If I thought there any chance of that, I wouldn't have called."

"Touché." Deek accepted the jibe. "What do you want?"

"You're a whiz at biology and chemistry," Donny said. "Time to find out just how good."

From the Journal of Donny Marigold

Sometimes you don't see the wood for the trees.

From the mid-17th century to the end of the 19th century, the Mackenzie Poltergeist was active in the graveyard. It appeared to certain people and gave them ideas that they would never have thought of on their own. Tried to advance its own knowledge by expanding the imaginations of visionaries who were in a position to spread those notions.

But, if it wanted to influence intelligent or famous people, why haunt a place where those kinds of visitors would be few and far between? Why not hang out at the National Library down the street or the Royal Mile which is always mobbed?

What does a cemetery have that you don't find anywhere else?

It has bodies.

Greyfriars has more people packed into its soil than the fields at Flanders. From the mid-16th Century to the end of the 19th century it saw the influx of thousands of corpses a year. They had to stuff the damn things into the ground to get them to fit.

It's a reservoir of DNA.

What would need something like that to exist?

A virus.

The Mackenzie Poltergeist wasn't supernatural at all.

It was a fucking disease.

It may have come about through Transmutation, sparked to life in 17th century Germany by a comet hitting a swamp, infused with thousands of newly dead villagers. This vast genetic soup generated an entirely new kind of viral life.

It got into Campbell Menzies the way any disease would, through the many wounds on his body. He carried it back to Scotland and, when he died, it was transferred to yet another genetic reservoir.

Greyfriars Graveyard.

For over two hundred years, this viral entity was supplied with a continuous supply of fresh corpses, including geniuses like Burnett, Hogg and Hutton. Hell. The place is stuffed with world leaders in their fields. Men like Joseph Black, who pioneered thermodynamics, discovered magnesium, bicarbonates, latent heat, specific heat and carbon dioxide. Or Robert Sibbald, physician and botanist, first Professor of Medicine at the University of Edinburgh, Geographer Royal, founder of the Royal College of Physicians and creator of Edinburgh's Royal Botanic Gardens.

Fuelled by these titans, it acquired the DNA it needed to evolve and interact with human hosts. Gained the ability to present ideas to men like Dickens or Darwin. Perhaps by entering their bodies through cuts or lesions as well. And each generation of the Menzies clan kept it topped up with a fresh injection of the original strain.

Thanks to Deek, I figured out what changed.

In 1879, two tons of corpses from St Giles' cemetery were transferred to Greyfriars, dumped on the topsoil and spread around. New genetic material, you might think. Enough to start another wave of fantastic occurrences.

But these bodies were different. They were mixed with vast quantities of Quicklime.

Deek told me that Quicklime is also known as Calcium Oxide.

As a compound, it has many functions. But, in the old days, it was used during epidemics and plagues to fight the spread of disease.

Two tons of quicklime would deal a virus like the Mackenzie Poltergeist a powerful blow. That might only have been a hindrance if the corpses had kept coming.

It never happened. New cemeteries were springing up on the outskirts of Edinburgh and, after 1879, Greyfriars became an unused relic.

I checked every date on the surrounding headstones. No one was interred here in the 20th century. Not even the Menzies clan.

The Entity's fuel supply was gone. It was an ex-poltergeist. And it never came back.

Everything happening now was trickery by Ben Scott and that should have been enough to satisfy me.

But I was still missing something.

-33-

The guides sat quietly, reading Donny's new tour script.

"That's some story." Ben finished and removed his glasses. Donny hadn't known he wore any. It made him look older and more vulnerable. "You have quite the imagination, young sir."

"The poltergeist influences famous people for generations and then vanishes until we wake it up again." Oss punched the air. "I can so sell that to the punters."

"Except for the virus bit." Lee sounded unsure. "I prefer a good old-fashioned spirit."

"Like Jack Daniels and Coke?"

"Yes, hun. Except, according to Donny, it's gone."

"No need to mention *that* bit."

"I'm not making it up," the teenager broke in. "I think it's what actually happened."

"Donny is describing a HERVE," Deek said.

"Want to try that in English?" Lee laughed.

"A human endogenous retrovirus."

"Still went over my head."

"A viral parasite that has a symbiotic relationship with its human host. Better?"

"Not much."

"Species of the families Adenoviridae, Asfarviridae, Iridoviridae, Papillomaviridae, Polyomaviridae and Poxviridae can infect vertebrates.

"Nope."

"Jesus. Do you know how to boil an egg?"

"No need to be rude."

"The problem is, viruses can't be self-aware or communicate with their host." Deek abandoned his attempts to educate Lee in the finer points of biology. "Sorry, Donny, but that's impossible."

He sat next to the teenager and nudged him.

"I mean, it's brilliant, Wee D. Truly inspired. But it goes against every scientific principle I know."

"Oh yeah?" The boy folded his arms defiantly. "And when Darwin came up with his theory of Evolution, how many people said it was impossible? How many respected scientists, for that matter?"

"Pretty much all of them," Deek conceded.

"I'm with Donny." Constance took a swig of wine from the nearest bottle, not bothering to get herself a glass. "I think he's damned well right."

"Aw, don't be so gullible," Ben sighed. "It's clever but it's nuts."

Constance slammed the bottle down and glared out of the window.

"Donny, you're amazingly smart but you're just a kid. You're hardly Charles Darwin."

"What do I have to do? Grow a sodding beard?"

"Get a grip, lads," Oss said placatingly. "Does it matter if Donny's right or not?"

"How do you mean?"

"The poltergeist, if it exists, never does us any harm. And it makes the tours a heap of money." He spread his arms. "It doesn't make any difference if it's real or a figment of people's imagination. Am I right?"

"You are," Ben agreed. "Though I never thought I'd hear myself say that."

"Then let's party."

"I forgot to mention. The séance on Thursday?" Ben got up and walked over to Constance. "I got an experienced medium to lead it. May as well try and do it properly."

He put his hands on her shoulders and squeezed.

"His name is Doctor John Menzies."

Ben looked directly at the boy, daring him to say anything.

"Cool beans," Lee giggled. "This is going to be a lot of fun."

"Yeah. It'll be a blast." Ben let go of Constance. "But I'm going to cut the evening short now. I'd like to talk to Donny."

"No problem, boss." Deek downed his glass. "Who's for the pub?"

"Sit yourself down, kid," Ben said when the guides were gone. "We need to have another heart-to-heart."

"Again?" Donny sulked. "Why do you keep ambushing me?"

He picked up the nearest glass of wine and downed it. Had no idea who it belonged to and didn't care.

"I explained everything," Ben said angrily. "So what's this nonsense about the poltergeist being some kind of virus? The guides have to believe it's a phantom for the exorcism to work."

"It's not nonsense." Donny was equally adamant. "I'm close to an answer."

"I gave you the bloody answer."

"Which is completely plausible. Just testing out an alternative idea, that's all."

"Luckily, they didn't believe it. Did you really expect they would?" The tour boss ran a hand down his face. "Can't you just trust me and play along?"

"I do trust you." Donny hung his head. "I don't trust Doc."

When he looked up again his eyes were filled with hurt.

"How about having some faith in me? I'm not one of his nutty patients."

"Then stop acting like it." Ben slapped his arm contemptuously. "We have a bunch of gullible tourists who have been let down by science and religion and are desperate to believe in the paranormal. They'll latch onto any tiny excuse to justify that."

"Supernatural beings exist," Donny protested. "I was talking to a ghost called Grizzle last night. Not that she was much use."

"That's because you were talking to yourself."

"I told you. I can see dead people! They gave me the stories for the tours."

"You looked up those stories on the internet or in the library." Ben came and sat on the couch next to Donny. "You're worse than our punters. Desperate to believe in life after death. It makes you feel better about your brother."

"You leave Sam out of this!"

"I can't. I've been putting off this moment." Ben put his arm around the boy's shoulder. "Dreading it, in fact."

"What are you talking about?"

"Your brother was a lively and intelligent boy with a bright future. And he didn't kill himself. He died in a traffic accident."

"Don't be stupid!"

"Oh, God." Ben's knee jiggled apprehensively. "Doc Menzies never treated your brother."

"Of course he did!" Donny tried to struggle away. The tour boss tightened his grip.

"He treated *you*."

"What?" Donny fought harder but Ben wouldn't let go.

"*You're* the one who heard voices and suffered from hallucinations. And you went downhill rapidly after your brother's death."

Donny forced his arms from Ben's grasp and began to punch him. Ben grabbed the boy's wrists and enveloped him in a bear hug.

"I'm so sorry," he whispered. "You're like my own son, you know?"

"You're lying!" Donny yelled, trying to get loose again.

Ben wrestled him down on the couch until he was on top of the writhing body. Donny kicked and screamed and cried but the bigger man used his weight as leverage until the teenager stopped moving.

"Doc's treatment turned you into a fantasist." Ben's grip tightened. "It's how you cope with your condition. You don't see ghosts and your father isn't a jet-setting banker. Doc took on your case for nothing because you live in a crappy council house in Niddry and your dad is an alcoholic who doesn't know what to do with you."

His voice cracked.

"You don't even have a computer, which is why you use Daisy's and mine to write your journal."

Donny felt bile rise in his throat.

"You haven't got a private tutor." Ben pressed on. "You don't go to school because you're not sixteen years old. You're eighteen."

"Why are you saying this to me?" Donny whimpered.

"You were the last name on Doc's list, boy," Ben whispered into his ear. "I have the file to prove it."

"I wouldn't remember Doc if I was his patient!" the boy cried. "You said so!"

"You don't remember him treating you. But when Doc contacted you from prison, it jogged your memory, so you visited him out of curiosity. He spun you a fine old tale, revolving around your brother being in his care. You couldn't come to terms with the truth, so you bought into his explanation. But it was a lie."

A tear ran down Ben's cheek.

"Donny is the one who died, kid. Your name is Sam Marigold."

Ben held him until his crying subsided.

"I'm such a fucking screw-up." The boy wiped his eyes. "You must hate me."

"Never."

"I'm so sorry." Donny poured himself another glass of wine. "Sorry for crying like a girl, too."

"You wanted to be somebody else. So you convinced yourself you were." Ben smiled wanly. "I can certainly see the attraction in that."

"You're not mad?"

"Why should I be?" Ben winked at him. "I'm the one who's setting up a fake séance for the guides."

"My little brother was awesome," Donny said. "A fun person. A guy people admired. Everything I wasn't. He was going to be a writer."

"I figured that."

"After his life ended, the best tribute I could think of was to become him."

"You're all these things now, Donny."

The boy's eyes widened.

"You all right, kid?"

"You called me Donny."

"If you want to be Donny Marigold, who am I to argue? I'm not going to tell anyone and neither is Doc."

"I can't hide this from Daisy. The only truth left I have is that I love her. But she'll never speak to me again if I come clean."

"I wouldn't be so sure." Ben put his arms behind his head and stretched. "Why shouldn't we try be who we want?"

He glanced at himself in the mirror.

"Most of us never do."

Donny bit his lip.

"If that were true, I'd be calling you dad."

It just came out. He couldn't help it.

Ben's eye twitched. He took an enormous drag on his cigarette and squinted through the smoke.

"That's enough wine for tonight." He snatched the half-finished glass from his young companion's hand. "You need a bit more rest than you're getting. I've been keeping you up too late."

Ben ushered Donny to the door. As he was about to leave, he put his arm round the boy's shoulders and gave him a self-conscious hug. Donny turned and pressed his face against Ben's chest. The man kissed the top of his head.

"Goodnight Bean," he said tenderly.

Donny didn't correct him.

For the briefest of seconds, they had the relationship they both craved.

From the Journal of Donny Marigold

Fuck sakes. I'm mad as the rest of them.

Convincing myself I was my own brother. Talking to imaginary friends and pretending they're ghosts. Making up a fake entity to justify my actions.

My heart is broken and so am I. I love Daisy but I doubt she will ever look at me again, once the truth comes out.

I'm one of Doc's ex-patients so of course I'm obsessed with Greyfriars. Everything fits at last.

Fits just a bit too well.

I know. I know. The ravings of a lunatic.

But I can't let it go.

When he was a boy, James Matthew Barrie's 13-year-old brother, David, died in a skating accident. David had been their mother's favourite and she effectively denied James a separate identity, dressing him in his dead brother's clothes and calling him by his sibling's name. James even pretended to be David to please his mum.

Moving to London, he wrote Sentimental Tommy *and* Tommy and Grizel *about a manipulative youth growing up in the slums - who becomes a compulsive fantasist - with tragic results.*

But J M Barrie's most famous creation is Peter Pan, *a lonely boy who can imagine things into existence. According to psychologist Rosalind Ridley, the story raises many post-Darwinian questions about the origins of human nature and behaviour.*

In the late 1870s, right before quicklime was dumped in Greyfriars, Barrie lived in Edinburgh and attended its university. There he became good friends with Robert Louis Stevenson and Arthur Conan Doyle. He also suffered from stress-related illnesses all his life.

The last hurrah of the Mackenzie Poltergeist? Or me clutching at straws?

Two sides to every story, I guess.

So, why is Barrie's story so much like mine?

-34-

Daisy was sitting in her flat, sipping wine. Everyone else was downstairs but she still couldn't bring herself to face Donny. She felt too hurt. What other lies had he told?

She glanced at the computer. Donny's journal was on that. She'd always wanted to read it but respected his privacy. Only, he'd betrayed her trust, hadn't he? Why shouldn't she look?

Problem was, she didn't know the password for his files.

She inched over and sat at the PC. Typed *Daisy* into the box.

Incorrect password.

"I suppose it was too good to be true," she muttered.

Then something leapt, unbidden, into her head.

She entered 1635.

The online files opened. She clicked on Donny's journal and began to scan the entries. Halfway through, she ran to the bathroom and threw up.

When she came back, she continued to read to the end. As she was finishing, Ben knocked on the door.

"Donny's just left," he said. "He's hurting pretty badly."

"He's not the only one," Daisy replied. "I just read his diary."

"Fuck."

"I know everything."

"I wish that were true." Ben fumbled nervously for a cigarette. "But Donny just found out a rather horrible fact himself a few minutes ago."

"Hit me with it." Daisy looked utterly defeated. "Nothing could make me feel any worse."

"You better sit down."

When Ben finished, Daisy fumbled for her phone.

"You should go," she said. "I have to talk to Donny."

"Good." The tour boss opened the door and paused. "You've both been dealt a bad hand and, right now, you need each other."

Donny was walking home when he got a text from Daisy.

Get up here. Right now.

He got a night bus back. Taking the steps two at a time he stopped and hesitated. Then he knocked and the girl let him in.

She was drinking. And smoking too. The place smelled stale and musty.

"You've been living the high life," he said tentatively, unsure how to start the conversation.

"Damned right." Daisy was dressed in black as usual but now she had really taken on the role. Her fingernails were glittering ebony and her eyeliner thicker than normal. "Figured it was time to start enjoying myself."

"Wow," he said nervously. "You look positively gothic."

"Help yourself to the booze."

Donny went to the kitchen and got some wine of his own.

"You've hidden things I should have known." Daisy clinked her glass against his. "That wounded me."

"I know."

"Will you promise never to do it again?"

"No."

"Excuse me?" Daisy looked shocked.

"I will never lie to you again and I will never break a promise." Donny put a hand on his heart. "But I will not tell you everything. It's the best I can do."

"That's remarkably honest," the girl admitted. "Especially when our relationship is hanging by a thread."

"I'm afraid that thread is going to break," Donny said. "My name isn't Donny Marigold. It's…"

Daisy put a finger to his lips.

"Sam Marigold." She looked him in the eye. "Ben told me."

"Ah." Donny took a deep breath.

"I also read your diary," Daisy continued. "So I know my dad didn't hurt my mum. That it was me."

The boy went white.

"That what you're refusing to divulge?" the girl asked.

"Daisy, I didn't know how…"

"I understand and I forgive you. I'll have to make amends to both of them, somehow."

"You didn't know what you were doing."

"I'll deal with it later. Let's get to the most important thing you wrote." Daisy put her hands on either side of the boy's face.

"You said in your diary that you love me. Is *that* a lie?"

"No. I can't imagine life without you and I don't want to."

Daisy smoothed down his hair and took a deep breath.

"Then stay with me tonight."

"Are you sure?" Donny couldn't tear his gaze away.

"At the moment," the girl lamented. "It's the only thing I am sure of."

Next morning Donny made coffee and toast. Plonked it down onto a table next to the bed and sat on the chair staring at his sleepy partner.

"Why are you up so early?" she groaned. "What time is it?"

"After eleven." The boy grinned. "You're a sound sleeper."

"Was last night OK?" Daisy asked shyly propping herself up on one slim arm.

"Depends on what you mean by OK." Donny took a slice of toast and grinned. "If you mean 'was it the greatest night of my life?' the answer is a definite yes."

Daisy gave a beaming smile and reached out for her coffee. Donny passed it to her.

"What about you?"

"It was fine. Until we got into bed."

The boy's face fell.

"After that, it was amazing."

Donny gave a mock gasp of relief.

"You don't regret it?"

"Not at all. Never will." Daisy reached out a slender arm. "Am I not getting any toast?"

"I thought you didn't eat bread?"

"As you can plainly see, I'm trying new things."

"Here you go." Donny handed her a slice. The girl hesitated, then took a big bite.

"I'm a good cook, aren't I?"

"I haven't had bread in years." Daisy chewed with obvious relish. "You could have dipped it in rancid fat and I'd still enjoy it."

"I'm going to quit the tours after this exorcism." Donny took a sip of coffee. "I want you to come with me."

"When I've straightened out things with mum and dad."

"Good. I'll get another real job. I've been saving up too."

He leaned forward to peck her on the forehead. Daisy grabbed the back of his head and kissed him passionately.

Donny's phone buzzed and he pulled it out of his pocket.

"It's Ben. He needs me to go get keys cut for the new guides." The boy sighed. "Bloody slave driver."

He stroked her face gently.

"Gotta go or I'll find myself back in bed again."

As soon as Donny had gone, Ben Scott walked in and glanced at the unmade bed.

"Hmmmm. Donny's not just back in your *flat,* is he?"

"Don't make any jokes."

"Shame. I've got a good one about three greyhounds in a bar," Ben chuckled. "Why did you ask me to send Donny off on an errand?"

"My dad is going to be conducting this exorcism. Right?"

"You really do know everything, eh?"

"I had a long chat with Donny last night."

"Then, yes, he is. Want a coffee?" Ben went into the kitchen. "He's going to test it out on Oss, Lee and Deek first. Partly cause Doc still has no idea how to approach you."

He emerged a few minutes later with a steaming mug.

"I'll sort that," Daisy said. "I want Donny and I to be exorcised too,"

"You are Doc's world and Donny is special to me." Ben picked at his lip. "The last time your dad tried this kind of thing, it went spectacularly wrong."

"You mean me maiming my mother?"

"Eh… Yes." Ben sipped the brew, steam obscuring his expression. "We won't perform it on you and Donny unless we know it works."

"That's pretty cold. Using the guides as guinea pigs."

"I'm not proud - but it may turn violent and I don't see the sense of risking everyone."

"We're a family, Ben," Daisy scolded. "We're doing this together."

"Donny won't like it." Ben exhaled a long stream of cigarette smoke.

"He'll do exactly what I say."

"I suppose he will. Kid's in love."

"So am I." Daisy smiled.

"Now get on the phone and tell my dad to come up here."

From the Journal of Donny Marigold

I came in through the bottom entrance to Greyfriars. My heart was singing but my head was buzzing. Daisy had accepted everything and I loved her even more, if that were possible. I skirted the massive hole in the ground with a little skip.

Then stopped.

I rarely came down here in the daylight, as this was the dominion of Marky Cotter and his crew. And, at night, the area was just a pool of ink. Now I could see it properly.

The trench was half filled in and a coffin was missing. It might have been that way for days. Even months. The workmen had used an excavator to dig the hole and would surely use the same method to cover it. But there were no tracks.

This was done with a shovel.

Why was it only half filled, though? Lazy as they were, council workmen would have finished the job.

The last piece of the puzzle clicked into place.

What would the poltergeist need to gain strength in a defunct graveyard?

Fresh bodies.

I grabbed a spade from the council shed and began to dig.

Sweat gathered under my clothes and my breath erupted in short puffs of condensation. Finally, I stopped, heart pounding in my chest.

"Oh, fuck." I sank to my knees and began to scrape the soil.

"Jesus Christ."

-35-

Donny burst into Daisy's flat.

"Some serious shit is going down..." the boy skidded to a halt.

Daisy was sitting on the bed, wrapped in her father's arms, their eyes red-rimmed. Ben loitered by the window, looking awkward.

"Family reunion," he said. "I'm stood here like a bit of a spare prick, so feel free to give me a hug."

"Hi, Doc," Donny panted. "Sorry, but this can't wait."

"Hello, boy," Doc tisked. "You certainly know how to spoil the moment."

"I found bodies at the bottom of the graveyard."

"That's hardly unexpected."

"These are fresh and not supposed to be there." The boy burst into tears. "I think they've been murdered."

Doc and Ben glanced at each other.

"C'mon, we talked about this."

"For fuck sakes, I'm not lying! That's all done with." He held up grimy hands. "Not hallucinating either, before you start."

"Show me." Daisy kissed her father's cheek and beckoned to her boss. "C'mon, you two."

She got up and took Donny's hand.

"Christ, she's really changed," Doc whistled. "Okay-dokey. Let's see what the fuss is about."

An hour later they stood in a trench, wearing high-vis vests and hard hats and carrying shovels that Ben had purloined from the council sheds. It was bitterly cold and the few hardy visitors strolling around, ignored them.

So far they had found three bodies, partially decomposed, lying at awkward angles. One was in a broken coffin.

"I'm no expert, but these sure as hell look recent to me," Ben said. "And they haven't been buried with any kind of ceremony. They were tossed in."

"You reckon it was Marky Cotter and his gang?" Donny asked. "They're nasty pieces of work, but I never thought they'd go that far."

"I'm not sure it was them." Ben pulled a watch off one decaying wrist. "This is a Rolex the size of a sundial. They'd have taken it, for sure."

"We have to call the police." Donny was trying not to gag.

"We can't," Doc said. "You already know who the main suspects are."

"None of the guides could have done this," Ben objected. "They're good people."

"Who are far from being in a normal state of mind. Besides, these bodies must have been killed and buried at night, when the graveyard is locked, or someone would have seen. Only your staff have the keys."

"It wasn't me." Daisy's face was ashen.

"Me neither." Donny sat down heavily. "But... would I even remember?"

"I refuse to even consider that." Daisy knelt beside him. "You're not capable."

"Cover the bodies up again," Doc commanded. "We're doing the exorcism tomorrow night. If it's successful, this will never happen again."

"What about these sorry fuckers?"

"Call the police and this is what will happen." Doc tossed Ben a spade. "Your tours will be shut down. If the cops find DNA evidence implicating one of the guides, they'll get life in prison for a crime they had no control over. Even if they don't, I won't be able to do the exorcism and that may mean more killings."

He began to shovel earth over the corpses.

"What's done is done. For now, our priority is making sure nobody else ends up here. Agreed?"

One by one, they nodded.

"Then get working, before some nosey bastard wanders over to see what we're up to."

Later, they sat in Ben's flat, drinking wine.

"I want you to do the exorcism on all of us, dad," Daisy said finally. "Not just Lee, Oss and Deek."

"That's not practical."

"I'm not going to be treated differently from our friends. I won't have them be my test subjects."

"This isn't favouritism, baby." Doc opened a packet of Pringles. "If they react as violently as you did, we'll have a battle on our hands."

He stuffed a handful of crisps into his mouth.

"I'd rather not have you rip my throat out just after I got you back."

"We'll be there as backup, then." Donny insisted. "If it works, we're next. Right away."

"You have my word."

"I'm a bit traumatised by this turn of events, so I'm going to bed." Daisy held out her hand to Donny. "You coming?"

"I... eh..." The boy looked at Doc, mortified. "I don't..."

"My daughter has become quite the little firebrand," the man said softly. "I'd love to take all the credit for that, but I suspect you've done more for her than I ever could."

He crumpled up the tube and tossed it in the bin.

"On you pests go, before I turn all macho. But get some proper rest. We have a hell of a night tomorrow."

"We will, sir. I promise." Donny was grinning as they walked out the door.

When they got upstairs, he sat down at the computer.

"You're going to update your *diary*." Daisy poured them both wine. "Feel free to include my foxiness once you actually notice."

"I'm Googling missing people in Edinburgh," Donny blushed. "If I can find out their identities, I might have a clue as to who those bodies are. And who offed them."

"Bit of a passion killer," Daisy draped her arms around his shoulders. "But I guess it's quite important."

"Look at this." Donny tapped the screen.

Relatives Appeal for Information on Missing Exotic Dancer

The family of Julie James have appealed for the woman to get in contact with them. Miss James, who went under the stage name Rachel Rouge, was last seen in the Jekyll and Hyde Bar, where she worked as a pole dancer, on the 15th of September. She had been fired that evening but her parents insist it would not have made her suicidal.

"We need her to contact us," her mother said. "If she has moved somewhere else, we simply want to know. We love her."

Edinburgh & Lothian's police are investigating the disappearance.

Donny swallowed hard. Julie James. One of the names on Doc's list.

"I think I saw her in the graveyard the night she vanished," he said. "So did Oss."

Daisy drew in a sharp breath.

"Keep going."

They found others. John Walters III, a pharmaceutical salesman from Ohio who disappeared on a business trip to Edinburgh.

"None of the entries mention Greyfriars," Donny closed down the search engine. "But I'm willing to bet they were bumped off here."

He scrolled down.

"Then there's David 'Ando' Anderson - a small-time dealer and junkie found dead in the cemetery with a head wound."

"Any idea who did it?"

"Not a clue. They all seem unconnected and there's no evidence they knew of each other's existence."

"I feel so bad for these people. Couldn't we leave an anonymous tip for the police?"

"Not if one of us did it." Donny shook his head. "The important thing is to make sure it never happens again."

He kissed Daisy's hand.

"Can't write my book now, though," he said. "Or we'll *all* end up in jail, as accessories after the fact."

"So, make it a work of fiction. Horror novels seem to be par for the course in this place."

"Maybe." Donny pondered this. "But I'll have to wait a long time, just in case."

"I'll remind you in fifteen years or so. Once you're a successful author."

"Still intend to be around after all that time?"

"You can't get rid of me," Daisy grinned. "I'm your muse."

"Then let's go to bed and you can do musey things."

"Want me to dance around naked waving a scarf?"

"Wasn't exactly what I had in mind."

"Good." She kissed the top of his head. "I'm a terrible dancer."

From the Journal of Donny Marigold

After Daisy had fallen asleep, I stared at the ceiling, turning every-thing over in my head.

Everything I thought the entity had been doing recently had turned out to be the work of Ben Scott. I had accepted that. But I'm sure it still exists in Doc Menzies. He's host to the original strain of virus. A virus that creates causal chains.

What chain could Doc have caused without even realising it?

And there it was. Plain as day.

Doc sets up his clinic, in Greyfriars, of all places. Uses the legend of his own ancestor for a new therapy. That leads to him 'curing' a bunch of kids, including his daughter. Only it goes wrong.

That leads to Doc being imprisoned, giving his ex-patients time to get obsessed with the graveyard. That leads to the tours being founded - bringing us all together, including me and Daisy. That leads to the graveyard becoming a huge tourist attraction, with huge amounts of people for the entity to interact with – should it ever resurface.

Then one of Doc's patients begins to kill people and bury them here.

This leads to fresh DNA being deposited in Greyfriars. The quick-lime has dissipated by now, so new DNA could allow the poltergeist to make a comeback. All it needs is the right spark to ignite it.

Oh, Christ.

The virus in Doc is using him to engineer the entity's resurrection.

-36-

The guides were seated around the table in Doc's clinic. Donny was stationed outside the door and Daisy was in the graveyard, much to her annoyance.

"You expect them to come flying through the window?" she complained. "They're mentally unstable, not superhuman."

"I'm not taken any chances," Ben grunted.

"This is Doctor John Menzies," The tour boss introduced everyone. "The medium who will be conducting our séance."

Doc sat serenely, ignoring everyone, already playing his part. He had chalked a pentangle around the table and lit candles twinkled on every piece of furniture.

"It's your night off but you're all wearing tour costumes." Ben looked around. "That's a bit tragic."

"It was my idea, hun." Lee beamed. "Wanted to get the atmosphere right."

"You look like the bloody *Cure.*"

Doc coughed loudly.

"Before we get started." He spread a set of cards across the table. "There are a few rules I should emphasise."

"Three Kings are highest, then three Aces, then running down accordingly," Oss deadpanned. "After that, it's a running flush, a run, a flush and then a pair."

"These are Tarot cards." Lee thumped him on the arm. "Take this seriously."

"No, they really are playing cards." Doc scooped the plastic rectangles back up and expertly shuffled them. An Ace of Spades rose from the middle of the pack, seemingly on its own. "They'll function just as well."

"I've never seen a medium do that before," Deek said appreciatively. "You must be a large."

"Let's not use labels, especially not that one." The man was unruffled. "I've actually lost weight."

"Sorry."

"Especially since any old con man can fool the public into thinking they're in touch with the spirit world."

"What are you looking at me for?" Ben snorted.

"We are about to call up some very dark forces and all we need are the right incantations." Doc began to place the cards on the table, one by one, face down. "I happen to know these incantations."

"Klaatu Barada Nicto?"

"Come in number 666." Deek cupped his hands like a megaphone. "Your time is up."

"Settle down chaps," Ben tisked. "You're the ones who wanted this."

"That was before we found out nobody could get stuck into the booze until it was over."

"You all drink too much, anyway. You must have livers like window cleaners' sponges."

Constance stood by the window, refusing to join in the banter, visibly nervous about the deception they were about to perpetrate.

"Constance will act as my assistant," Doc said. "Ben will chair the proceedings."

Ben lounged against a bureau in the corner and opened a can of lager with a happy sigh. The guides glared at him.

"What? Chairing is thirsty work."

"My rules cannot be broken." Doc began to turn over the cards. "We must all hold hands and not let go, no matter what happens. That is vital. It creates a protective chain that cannot be broken without the direst consequences."

The guides reached out for each other.

"Damn," Deek complained. "I'm sitting next to Oss. Can you swap places with Lee, mate?"

"There's three of us, babe. It doesn't matter where you sit."

"Christ on a bike."

"I been scratching my knacks, by the way." Oss leered.

"I'm going to throw up."

"We have to make absolutely sure you won't step outside the pentangle." Ben held up a bunch of plastic ties. "Constance will fasten your wrists to the chairs.

"Say *what* now, hun?"

"That's kinky in a bad way," Deek agreed.

"How about we just promise?"

"It's not negotiable," Ben warned. "We have to do this right."

"Don't you have a rope to go around their waists?" Doc snapped. "How are they going to hold hands?"

"Fuck." Ben frowned. "I never thought of that. I could look in the cupboard if you like."

"You can fasten our wrists to each other," Lee said. "That's as far as I'm willing to go."

Doc hesitated, then nodded. The guides reached out for each other.

"You do the honours, Constance." Oss relented. "Wouldn't be the first time a beautiful woman has tied me up."

"Then called the police," Deek sniggered, offering his wrists.

Once they were all bound together, Constance stepped back.

"I'm not happy about this." She put on her coat. "I'm going outside to keep Daisy company."

She marched out before Ben could protest.

"I never figured she'd be so superstitious," Oss said.

"She's right to be cautious," Doc warned. "You have to take what is happening as real or we are doomed. Sorry to be melodramatic, but it's true."

"Yeah, come on guys," Lee scolded. "I'm totally up for this."

"The sooner it's over the quicker you can start drinking," Ben added. Oss and Deek fell silent.

"Everything in this world and the next has a mathematical equivalent," Doc's voice was low and soothing. "Some say the number of God is the Golden Number or Divine Proportion."

"I have a divine proportion…" Oss began.

"I have designated us individual numbers for tonight." Doc broke in. "Including myself. 1, 6, 3 and 5. Collectively 1635."

"That's my PIN number," Lee giggled. "Probably shouldn't tell shifty buggers like you."

"Eh? It's my PIN number too," Oss said.

"It's the number to unlock my phone." Deek raised his eyebrows. "What's going on here?"

"Just a trick." Doc smiled reassuringly. "But it works and we can summon the poltergeist with the same sleight of hand."

He began to speak in a low sonorous voice, Ben immediately recognised. It was the one he used in hypnotherapy sessions.

"1635. You will hold on to each other," His tone deepened further as he spoke. "You will not let go, no matter what transpires."

"I need to scratch my nose," Deek said nervously.

"I call on the power of darkness to reveal itself to us," Doc continued "I summon the spirit of the graveyard to convene in this room."

Ben slid his hand under the bureau and pressed a button on the effects box hidden there. The chandelier on the ceiling began to flicker on and off.

Lee gave a moan.

Doc's voice rose in volume as he began to chant.

"Hear these words, hear my cry. Spirit from the other side. Come to me, I summon thee. Cross now the great divide to the numbers 1635."

In the corner of the room, Ben rolled his eyes. The guides paid no attention, staring raptly at Doc.

"I command the spirit we call Mackenzie to appear. I challenge Him to reveal His secrets and speak to us through me."

Ben pressed another button. A loud knocking reverberated through the room. Even Oss shuddered this time.

"I command your presence demon," Doc roared. "By your name, I know you and when I call you by that name you are bound to me. To enter me and speak through me."

The table began to vibrate. This was no trick, Ben realised, but motion caused by the guides shaking. He pressed a final button and a vase of flowers on the windowsill exploded in a shower of glass, water and torn blossoms.

Lee screamed and Oss began to whimper. Deek had his eyes tightly closed, teeth gritted.

Doc slumped forwards over the table. Then he sat bolt upright as if he had been electrocuted.

When he spoke again, his voice had changed completely, a throaty growl loaded with menace. Ben shook his head in admiration. His conspirator's talents never ceased to amaze.

"I am Mackenzie and I am here." Doc's head lolled across his shoulders. "What do you want of me?"

-37-

That was Ben's cue. He got to his feet and put hands on his hips.

"Why are you haunting the graveyard?" he said with all the authority he could muster. "Why are you hurting the people who go there?"

"I am ANGRY."

Lee began to cry.

"What angers you?"

"There are those who have trespassed on my province."

"Who are the usurpers?"

"They have sought refuge from me in 1635." Doc's voice grew even harsher. "This I cannot allow."

Deek, Oss and Lee were transfixed, no longer aware of their surroundings.

"They reside in those I see before me." Doc gurgled theatrically. "I wish to take back what is mine and mine alone."

The guides were swaying now, keening softly to themselves.

"If I cast out the demons from my friends," Ben said. "Will you take them back into yourself and swear to do these people no harm?"

"I will accept what is rightfully mine and depart," Doc intoned.

Ben had to admit, he was putting on quite a show.

"Is everyone here agreed?" he asked the guides.

"Fuck, yeah," Oss whispered, eyes screwed shut.

Ben drew himself up to his full height and put on his best tour voice.

"I command you, unclean spirits, whoever you are, along with all your minions now attacking these servants of God, by the mysteries of the incarnation, passion, resurrection, and ascension of Our Lord Jesus Christ; by the descent of the Holy Spirit; by the coming of our Lord for judgement, to leave the bodies of the unfortunate souls that you have infested and cursed."

He moved round the table laying his hands on the heads of each guide.

"I command you, moreover, to obey me to the letter, I who am a minister of truth, despite my unworthiness; nor shall you be emboldened to harm in any way these creatures of God, or the bystanders, or any of their possessions."

"The spirits are now leaving 1635!" Doc cried.

Oss's eyes popped open, fastening on Ben with a baleful malevolence that made the hair stand up on the man's neck. The guide's face twisted into an evil sneer and he ground his teeth together, saliva pooling in the corner of his mouth. Lee drew in a shuddering breath and began to laugh, a guttural hysterical cackling torn from her throat.

Ben stepped back, clasping a hand to his mouth. Deek's lips were pulled back like a rabid dog and Oss struggled to rise from his seat, the muscles of his neck stretched and taut.

"Leave now!" Doc shouted again. "I command you in the name of Mackenzie!"

"Depart, then impious one, depart, accursed one, depart with all your deceits!" Ben pushed Lee roughly back into her seat.

The guides were spasming now, still clutching each other's hands. Spittle flew across the table as they snarled and spat and cursed. Ben looked in horror at Doc, noting something near to panic in his ally's eyes.

Lee surged sideways and bit Oss on the shoulder.

"Bitch!" Oss head-butted her in the face and wrenched at the ties.

Chairs went flying as the three struggled to their feet, howling in unison. They tried manically to pull away from each other, putting all their strength into the action.

"Do something, Doc!" Ben shouted. "Look at their wrists!"

The ties had buried themselves so deeply into the guides' flesh that they could no longer be seen. Blood was washing over their arms in spurts and still they yanked at each other.

"Don't break the circle!" Doc commanded.

Deek turned and slammed into Lee, his teeth snapping, inches from her throat. The movement pulled Oss over and they landed in a writhing heap, rolling out of the pentangle, the girl on the bottom.

"Help me boss!" she shrieked.

"Out unclean spirits!" Doc pointed to each of them. "Out now!

"Fuck this." Ben ran into the kitchen and emerged with a small knife. With quick strokes, he began to slice through the ties.

"Stop it!" Doc hurried round the table and tried to haul him away. "It's a trick!"

"Get off! These things are going to cut through a fucking artery."

Ben cut the last tie.

Oss punched him in the head and he staggered back, dropping the knife.

Deek grabbed the blade, spun and plunged it into Doc's leg. The man howled in agony and limped away. Lee flung herself on his back, grabbing handfuls of hair and viciously twisting.

Ben tried to intervene but Deek and Oss slammed into him and he went down, both men on top, clawing at their boss with feral intensity.

"You are *so* bloody fired!" Ben lashed back. "Donny! Help us!!!"

Doc elbowed Lee in the ribs, knocking her sideways. Lee cackled and raked pointed nails down his face.

"Aaaaargh!" He grabbed the girl by her lapels and slammed her head on the table. Ben was wrestling with Deek and Oss in a pile of black leather and flailing arms, trying to keep the blade away.

The door burst open and Donny barged in. Taking in the scene at a glance, flung himself on Oss and Deek

Standing on a flat gravestone, Daisy watched in horror through the window.

"Get in there and do something," she shouted to Constance. "I'll fetch help."

She turned and ran.

-38-

Marky Cotter and two of his mates were crouched round a paraffin heater in one of the larger tombs. They were dressed in dirty tracksuits and baseball caps covered their greasy hair. They passed half bottles of cider and a joint to each other as they talked.

"It's no right, is all ahm sayin. Ye cannae even hae a wee smoke ony mair without some fat yank fuck poking his Nikon in, eh? It's them tours that's done it."

"Dinnae bloody complain." Marky shot back. "We've done awright off them. Instant alibi, know? We kin do whit we like."

The others laughed in agreement.

A shadow fell across the doorway and they looked up.

"What the…?"

Daisy stepped into the mausoleum.

"I need your help," She begged. "Please!"

"Fuck right aff, doll," Marky sneered. "I'm no obliging some stuck up cunt."

"Suit yourself." Daisy slapped him across the face with all her strength. "Been wanting to do that for months, you scabby twat."

She took off, sprinting for the clinic.

There was stunned silence. Then the trio were on their feet.

"BITCH!"

"After that bird, lads," Marky ordered. "Truce is over. She's dead."

They switched on their torches and streamed from the tomb.

Prison had made Doc fit and wiry but his leg was bleeding profusely and Lee seemed indestructible. Deek and Ben would have been evenly matched if the tour boss hadn't been out of shape and almost thirty years older than his opponent. And Oss was far larger than Donny.

Yet the guides' main advantage was the complete abandon with which they fought. They kicked and clawed and bit, screaming with unfettered rage.

Constance flew through the door, slipped on the blood and crashed into Lee, both going down in a tangle of arms and legs. Doc scrambled over to the other battle and prised the knife from Deek's hand.

"Don't make me use this," he hissed, pressing the point into the man's cheek.

"Do it." Deek laughed and wormed onto his back, grabbing Doc by the neck.

Donny struggled to his feet and ran round the table.

"Get this crazy bastard off me!" Constance grunted, trying to keep Lee's nails from her precious face. "Donny! Donny!"

The teenager stepped over them and opened the cupboard door. Pulling the weed killer tank from the darkness, he tucked it under his arm and lifted the nozzle.

"Lee," he said. "Check this out."

The girl looked over Constance's shoulder, eyes pinpoints of hate.

Donny blasted her in the face.

Lee recoiled with an animal howl. Constance arched her back and hefted the girl off, then lay gasping and sucking in lungfuls of air. Lee retreated to the kitchen and Donny crossed to the next struggle. Seeing what was coming, Ben rolled onto his stomach as a stream of foul smelling liquid covered Deek. With a shriek, the guide wrenched himself away, slamming a foot into Ben's back as he rose. He stumbled after Lee, shaking his head like a rabid dog, sending acid droplets in an arc around the room.

Donny turned towards Oss but his prey reacted with astonishing speed. Flinging Doc clear across the table, he too headed for the kitchen. Donny blasted him with weed killer as he ran past.

The kitchen door slammed shut.

"We've got them trapped." Doc tried to rise and then collapsed with a groan. "I think I need medical attention."

"There's Aspirin in the kitchen," Ben wheezed. "Also plenty more knives. They're not trapped. They're regrouping."

"They each got a lungful of your concoction," Donny said. "It should knock them out in a few minutes."

"Then. if you don't mind, I'm going to sit this round out." Constance backed into the bathroom and locked the door.

"Thanks for your support, baby." Ben began to inch toward the open front door. "I say the rest of us beat a hasty retreat."

"That's not an option." Daisy dashed in, perspiration running down her face. "We got company."

Seconds later, Marky Cotter and his crew entered the room.

"Anyone in the graveyard not coming to this shindig?" Doc remarked amicably, fastening a plastic tie around his injured leg. "You're just in time lads."

"We're here to cut the wee fucker who dissed us," Marky snarled. "This time nothing's gonnae stop us."

"How about £1,000 in cash for each of you?" Ben said. "Doc here's got it in his safe."

"Ah've suddenly decided to reconsider," Marky whistled softly. "Ye certainly know how tae push mah buttons, big man."

"Whit do we have tae do?" His companions nodded enthusiastically.

"Any second, three people armed with knives are going to come through that door." Ben pointed to the kitchen. "I want you to subdue them."

"Nae problem." The quartet pulled flicknives from their back pockets.

"Without bloodshed, please."

"Aw, fur fuck's sakes. We're no getting chibbed, if that's what your askin."

"Make it £2,000 each."

"Consider the job done." Marky tucked his flicknife away.

"There's rope in the cupboard to tie them up," Donny said. "Spotted it when I got the tank."

"I forgot that was there," Ben blushed and Doc shot him daggers.

The kitchen door opened and the guides stepped out.

"C'mon tae fuck," Marky stammered. "This is no right."

The trio's faces were blistered, raw and peeling, as if they had been flayed. In their black attire and long leather coats they looked like they had just emerged from hell. Lee was carrying a carving knife, Deek had a pair of bone knives and Oss gripped a cleaver. Each were wheezing like steam engines.

"In a *clinic*, Doc?" Ben backed away. "You fancy yourself as Jamie Oliver or something?"

"Ahm no takin those raj bastards on," one ned hissed. "They're pure monsters."

"Dinnae be such a pussy," Marky retorted. "For two grand, ah'll square go the Earl of fucking Hell."

"That's just what you're doing," Donny muttered.

Deek, Lee and Oss glared at their opponents, tongues lolling from cracked lips. Each waiting for the other to act first.

"When I give the signal," Doc whispered to Donny. "Get Daisy out of here.

"What signal?"

"This." The man raised his arms in the sign of the cross.

"Why do you still linger here?" he shouted. "Your place is in solitude; your abode in a nest of serpents. 1635, this matter brooks no delay."

"No, Doc!" Ben shouted. "Don't keep this up."

The guides charged.

The neds reacted first, running forwards and upending the round table. As the guides skirted it, Marky grabbed the weed sprayer tank and slammed it into Oss' side. It didn't even slow him down. His companions leapt on Lee and Deek, trying to wrestle them to the ground.

Donny grabbed Daisy and sprinted for the door, almost yanking the girl off her feet.

"I can't leave my dad!"

Donny didn't reply. He pulled the girl through the open door and slammed it shut behind him.

Oss swiped at one ned with the cleaver and the boy hopped away, leaving Lee free. Deek sank a knife into the other's hand and he let go with a screech.

"For the last time, unclean spirit, leave these poor creatures!" Doc had backed into a corner.

"Stop it!" Ben begged. "They'll kill you."

Sure enough, the guides headed straight for the man, arms windmilling. Ben dived away from the swinging blades and the neds started forwards again.

They were too late.

"Oh my," Doc sighed as his adversaries reached him. "You really do have the Devil inside you."

They fell on him, chopping and slashing, ignoring Ben as he desperately tried to pull them off.

Blood spurted up in fountains.

Marky and the neds ran forwards joining in the fray, kicking and punching. Finally, Donny's spray took effect and guides collapsed, unconscious, in a pool of gore.

"Tie those mad bastards up," Marky commanded.

Doc lay on the floor, most of his face gone and his body hacked to pieces. Ben knelt and felt for a pulse.

"Dinnae bother, big man. He's well and truly dead." Marky crossed himself. "I'll still be wanting paid, though."

Ben sat heavily, shaking his head. Eventually, he spoke.

"Let's make it £3,000 each, Marky. That's all I've got."

"Fur whit?"

"Take Doc's body and bury it in the pit, near the tomb where you hang out. I'm not having my guides go to prison for this."

"Aye, right. I'm no going back tae juvie for any amount."

"It's a damned graveyard." Ben ran a hand down his face." Who's going to know?

"Fair enough." Marky motioned to his companions. "You two get moving. I'll stay tae make sure we collect the cash."

"How do we ken you winnae double cross us?"

The flicknife appeared in Marky's hand.

"Get it done, wankers. Mah pal's in mourning, so show a bit of fucking respect."

"Ok, boss. We'll move him oot the windae, so's naebody sees."

The neds lifted Doc up, opened the window and unceremoniously pushed him through. Then they crawled after the body and dropped out of sight.

"Get a mop and let's clean up," Marky said. "Idle hands and aw that."

The toilet lock clicked and Constance emerged, her makeup streaked with tears.

"You kin help too, blondie. Time ye did something useful."

Ben's mobile rang and he held it to his ear.

"Keep her away until I tell you, Donny," he said brusquely. "This is something Daisy doesn't need to see."

-39-

They worked in silence until all evidence of the battle was gone. Marky went into the kitchen, opened the fridge and helped himself to a beer.

"I'll make masel a wee sandwich while I'm at it. I feel you two need some alone time, eh?"

"I can't believe they're just going to dump Doc in a pit." Constance put away the mop and bucket. "We should report this to the authorities."

"He was recently released from prison. Didn't have any friends or anyone to miss him. Except Daisy."

"I was talking about the morality of the situation, you dick. We're covering up a damned murder."

"It's not the guides' fault." Ben glanced at the unconscious trio, now tied to the table legs. "They didn't know what they were doing."

"Are they badly injured?"

"I checked. Nothing broken. When they wake, they'll have bruising and a mild concussion at worst. Maybe some breathing problems."

"Better call Donny and Daisy, then."

Donny edged in, holding Daisy's hand. They took in the scene with wide eyes.

"Where's Doc?"

Ben shook his head.

"My dad's dead, isn't he?" Daisy said matter-of-factly.

"I'm afraid so."

"Was it Lee, Oss and Deek?"

"They... eh..." Ben groped for words and gave up. "Yes. It was."

"I don't hate them. I don't even blame them." She laid a hand gently on Lee's head. "I tried to do the same thing once."

The kitchen door opened a crack and Marky stuck his head out. Daisy gave a start.

"Yir safe, doll," he reassured her. "We got nae beef anymore. No after this."

He pointed to the guides.

"We tried oor best, but yir right. Those three were aff their fuckin nuts on somethin."

Daisy flopped down on the couch and put her head in her hands, tears dropping through the veil of hair. Constance and Donny sat on either side, unsure of how to comfort her.

To their surprise, Marky came and knelt in front of the girl.

"Life an death, doll," he said. "They're both pish, know?"

Daisy looked up.

"You make the best of things ye can, eh? Me I'm an angry bitter cunt. Got something rotten inside me. So I take drugs an fuck people over. That's how I deal wi it."

He took her hand and squeezed.

"Dinnae be like that, though. Yir paw died savin you. I seen it with mah ain eyes. Move on, or it wasnae worth his effort."

Daisy nodded.

"I'll be aff, big man." The youth glanced over his shoulder at Ben. "But keep yir word aboot the money or they'll be anither body in the graveyard tomorrow. Get me?"

"I want you to stay awhile." Daisy lifted her head. "Please."

"Ahm no the most sociable type." Marky looked surprised. "But I'll hang around fur a bit and make anither snack. I dinnae eat too well normally."

He patted Daisy's arm and retreated back to the kitchen.

"You buried Doc in Greyfriars?" Donny asked quietly.

"I'm trying to stop our friends going to prison." Ben made a slicing motion with his hand. "Let's leave that discussion for later."

"You were right," Daisy said. "It was the sensible thing."

Donny lapsed into angry silence.

"So what now?" The girl wiped her eyes. "Finish the exorcism?"

"Aw, now's not the time." Donny put his arm around her. "You need to…"

"I hardly knew my dad. For most of my life, I wasn't aware of too much, remember? And then he went to prison." The girl sniffed loudly and regained her composure. "Haven't got much to mourn, to be honest."

"I don't know how to finish the exorcism without Doc," Ben said wretchedly. "I can't do his bloody hypnotism thing."

"Did you memorise the trigger to snap them out of it entirely then?"

"Didn't need to." Ben pointed to a laptop in the corner. "Doc recorded it in case things got out of hand. Everything happened so fast we never got the chance to even switch it on."

"Then use it now."

"It'll put the guides back to the way they were. They won't be able to lead normal lives. Look what happened to Billy Cream."

"Our normal lives are well and truly over," the girl pointed out. "One way or another."

"I guess so."

"Wait until we've left, Ben." Donny tugged at Daisy's arm. "Or it will change us back too."

"No. You have to stay."

"You don't have to worry about us," Donny stammered. "We're going to move away and start a new life. You'll never hear from us again."

"I don't want to go back to the way I was," Daisy agreed. "I'm not that person anymore."

"It's the people you're becoming Doc was worried about."

"Ben. You *cannot* do this," Constance pleaded. "They have a future ahead of them."

"He said *everyone* would get worse." Ben sounded less and less sure. "He was right about everything else."

"Donny and I can cope." Daisy clasped her hands together. "We're not crazy. We can beat this."

"I'm wi them," Marky shouted from behind the closed door. "Even if I dinnae have a clue whit yir talkin aboot."

Ben hesitated.

"And what about the poltergeist, Donny?" he sighed. "You think your theories sound *sane* to anyone?"

"I believe them." Daisy leapt to his defence.

"Then you're obviously as warped as him."

"I think he's right too and I've said so before." Constance cracked her knuckles. "Want to try calling me nuts? Cause I'm really not in the mood."

"Then convince me," Ben said.

"I looked up missing people on the web and found the people I think are buried here," Donny said. "A travelling pharmaceutical salesman, a stripper and a junkie. No obvious connection to each other or Greyfriars, so the police wouldn't think to look here."

"I presume the connection is they're in a pit a couple of hundred yards away."

"Exactly. The entity is gone and Greyfriars is no longer a functioning graveyard, so there was no chance of it returning." Donny paused dramatically. "Unless it had a fresh supply of DNA and the original virus."

"Which could only happen if more bodies were buried here," Ben nodded. "Including Doc. I see where you're going."

"Doc caused this chain of events," the boy said. "Subconsciously, I suppose, which is beyond ironic. It was all done to make sure he was buried in Greyfriars and his only child would get pregnant."

Ben raised an eyebrow.

"Donny and I had sex," Daisy blushed. "It was kind of spur of the moment and we didn't use protection."

"We've just given the poltergeist everything it needed to make a comeback." Donny clenched his fist. "You press that keyboard and you'll be finishing the job. The tours will continue, with new guides, and bring in more people. I'll never be able to get Daisy out of its reach and the virus will start a new causal chain to make sure she gets buried here too."

"So we're slaves to some organism, which uses our intelligence to plot and plan. That how you see it?"

"No. That's how it sees *us*."

"You're outnumbered three to one, Ben," Constance said. "Let them go."

"You're forgetting one vital point." Ben swallowed hard. "Someone killed the people buried at the bottom of the graveyard and it had to be one of the people in this room. I can't have it happen again."

"It wasnae fucking me." Marky strolled out of the kitchen. "This is the first I've heard aboot it."

He gave Ben a withering look.

"I winnae be spreadin the word neither. No if you had us stick yir pal on top of them. We'd get the blame fur sure."

"It wasn't you. The guy in the coffin had an expensive watch. You'd have taken that."

"Damned right."

"You won't believe me, boss," Donny whispered. "But you're playing into the poltergeist's hands."

"You're right." Ben nodded. "I'm playing into its hands."

"*Why?*"

"Because Doc screwed up." He gave a heartfelt sigh. "For the sake of argument, let's say the poltergeist is real. All it wanted was for the Menzies clan to carry on and provide it with a home. What's wrong with that?"

"Nothing, I suppose."

"Exactly. But Doc followed his family legend to the letter. Implanted the notion that you had a demon inside. That you were guided by an *evil* entity. Evil."

Ben moved towards the computer.

"Doc said, if the exorcism failed, everyone he'd hypnotised would eventually go bad because of that - and no amount of wishful thinking would change it. Daisy may be destined to end up in Greyfriars, but I don't want you to be the one who puts her there."

"Bollocks! All you care about is keeping your money-making operation going." Constance tried to cut him off - but Marky pulled her back.

"Sorry, hen. Guy's a total arse. Still, he's paying me, know?"

"I never believed you were a terrible man until now," Daisy said miserably. "It's not because you don't understand how other people think and feel. It's because you don't try.

"Doc is dead," Donny agreed. "What happens next is on you, Ben."

"It seems to me, your poltergeist is the only hope we have left," Ben insisted. "I'm going to reset everything and pray it finds a way to start over."

He hit the enter button and Doc's voice emanated from the speakers, low and soothing, reciting the secret number to end their hypnosis.

16756426. 16756426. 16756426. 16756426. 16756426. 16756426. 16756426. 16756426. 16756426. 16756426. 16756426.

It was on a loop.

-40-

Donny and Daisy waited. Ben held his breath.

"Nothing's happening." They looked at each other, smiles slowly spreading across their faces. "We're OK!"

"So it would appear." Ben let out a long exhalation. "Billy Cream must have been a one off."

He spread his hand magnanimously.

"See. Never doubt the boss man."

He pointed to Lee, Deek and Oss, still tied to the table legs and snoring quietly.

"You two head to Daisy's. I still have this lot to contend with."

He slapped Donny's head as the pair moved past.

"And buy some bloody condoms."

He went to the safe, withdrew an envelope full of cash and handed it to Marky.

"You better take off, as well."

"Cheers big ears." Marky gave him a salute. "Geis a shout next time anithir of yer twatty ideas goes aff the rails. Ah can always dae wi mair dosh."

He left with a cheery wave.

"Get a cloth, Constance," Ben said. "Let's clean these guys up."

Ben carefully wiped the blood from Deek, Oss and Lee's faces.

Deek's eyes shot open.

"What the fuck happened?" He cried. "We were doing the séance and then... nothing."

Oss and Lee began to come round, their groggy expressions changing to panic.

"What happened, hun?"

"I don't remember anything," Oss groaned. "Where's the weird doctor guy?"

"Calm down," Ben said. "Things got a little out of hand, is all."

"My head's throbbing," Lee winced. "And my wrists are cut to pieces."

"Menzies got a little overenthusiastic and you all went slightly insane. He's probably in the pub by now, laughing about it."

"*Why?*"

"He wanted to see how much he could push things. Told me to think of the cash we'd make if could make real punters go crazy."

"Fucking moron," Oss moaned. "I'm gonna need therapy after this."

"I wouldn't recommend that." Ben frowned. "Anyway, I fired him. I guarantee you'll never see the guy again."

"Then why is his voice still droning on with a bunch of numbers?"

"Sorry. Part of the séance." Ben switched off the computer. "Things have been rather hectic."

"Is he telling the truth?" Lee asked Constance suspiciously.

"Of course," Constance lied. "*Was* a bit hairy though."

"Why do I have a lump the size of a football on my noggin?" Lee was unconvinced. "How come you're covered in bruises?"

"My face is all blistered." Deek was touching his cheeks gingerly.

"Mine too, hun."

Oss got up and looked in the mirror.

"Jesus Christ!" He sat down quickly again.

"You owe us an explanation, boss."

"You freaked out so much, you got into a bit of a barney and we had to subdue you. A squirt of weed killer seemed the fastest way."

"Excuse me?"

"What's done is done," Ben snapped. "We're never going to speak of this again, do you understand?"

"But I look like a fucking Orc."

"DO YOU UNDERSTAND?"

The guides lapsed into sullen silence.

"I've called taxis," Constance interrupted, holding up her mobile. "They'll pick you up outside. Tell the drivers to take you to Accident and Emergency to get those injuries looked at. You might have concussion."

"Remember to keep the receipts," their boss added. "The tours are suddenly a bit light on funds."

The guides shakily stood. Lee laid a hand on Ben's arm to steady herself and put her mouth close to his ear.

"We don't want to know the truth," she whispered. "Do we?"

"Someday, perhaps. Not now."

"You're a good guy."

"I'm not. Get going."

Helping each other along, the guides staggered out of the door.

"I don't suppose this is the most appropriate time to bring it up." Constance picked up a bottle of wine from the cabinet and took a swig. "But I'm quitting City of the Dead."

"Under the circumstances, I can't say I blame you."

"I'm leaving you too." The woman bit her lip. "I can't stay here forever, out of guilt."

"I thought you loved me?"

"Love is like a colour, B.S. It has to match its surroundings. Everything here has gotten too dark for me."

"This is kind of a bad time," Ben said morosely. "I'm feeling a bit fragile."

"There's ever going to be a good time?"

Ben took out a cigarette. Lit it. Nodded slowly.

Constance kissed his cheek.

"Can I keep the leather jacket? I like the leather jacket."

"Sure. Have the cane too."

"Take care, Ben Scott."

"You too, baby."

She kissed him again. On the lips this time.

"I'll see m-m-my own way out."

"Sorry?"

"I'll see m-m-my own way out."

"You're talking funny." Ben looked puzzled. "You OK?"

"Of course, I'm fucking not. I probably have post-traumatic stress."
She picked up the cane and left.

Ben sat alone, drinking wine and chain smoking.

He hadn't told his staff the whole story, as usual.

Billy Cream hadn't reverted to his old self immediately. It had taken a week or so before he killed himself. A week of torture as he slowly succumbed to his old ailments. Gave in to his own demons.

Lee. Oss. Deek. Donny. Daisy. Marky. They'd all go the same way.

He stared at the ceiling. It was too late to reverse what he'd done, even if he knew how. At least the killer would never strike again.

But something else was nagging at him. What the hell had happened to Constance's speech?

"No." The cigarette fell from his lips.

He opened the bureau and pulled out Doc's files. Began to rifle through them. He found Marky Cotter's entry and glanced at it.

Mark Cotter (12)

Cotter has had a difficult life. He is small in stature and remarkably sensitive. He is also extremely timid. However, he lives on a rough housing estate and has been bullied mercilessly ever since he was little. As a result, he is paranoid, distrustful and scared of his own shadow. He won't even go outside.

Casting it aside, Ben kept digging.

And there it was. Like all Doc's files, he had read it before. Now he was seeing the words in a different light.

Vanessa Elizabeth Rees (12)

Vanessa Rees is a girl filled with fear and mistrust. She was taken into care because her father was an amphetamine addict and drug dealer who abused her terribly. Her mum, an exotic dancer, turned a blind eye to her daughter's plight. Vanessa hates them passionately.

She wouldn't even talk to me until I used my ventriloquist dummy as a go-between. A lot of damaged kids are like that.

She is obsessed with achieving fame and fortune – an obvious attempt to gain independence and self-respect. Unfortunately, the poor soul is fat, with bad acne and a serious stammer, so that's a no-go.

She is my test case. If I can use my new therapy to cure a girl like this, I may be able to help Daisy.

The poor soul is fat, with bad acne and a serious stammer.

"Fuck."

The paper trembled in Ben's hands as he remembered what Donny had told him.

I looked up missing people on the web and found the people I think were buried here. A travelling pharmaceutical salesman, a stripper, and a junkie.

Drug dealers, junkies and strippers. The people Vanessa loathed. Ben hadn't even seen the clues in Constance's own story.

I have always wanted to become rich and famous and this seemed like my best bet. So I made up a stage name and enrolled in Dunfermline Drama College.

Constance was Vanessa Reese.

"I should have known," Ben moaned. "Who the fuck is actually called Constance Storm?"

Of course, Doc hadn't recognised her. Why would he? Last time he had seen her, she was a fat ten-year-old with acne. Since then her skin had cleared up, she had lost weight, dyed her hair and changed her name. And she was cured of the stammer.

Ben thought about Bean's mother, who earned part-time cash working in a strip joint. How Constance had sabotaged his relationship with her. It seemed she had gone onto bigger things.

"It's a shit world, Mr Poltergeist." He toasted the graveyard. "If you're real and trying to change that, I'm on your side. You have your work cut out, though."

He downed the drink in one.

"Just try not to be such a cunt doing it."

Daisy lay on the bed, curled into a ball, crying softly. When Donny put his arm around her, she flinched.

"I'm sorry," he apologised. "Wanted try and comfort you."

"I'm starting to feel like I don't want to be touched. It's weird."

"I'm changing too." Donny let go. "It's like parts of me are drifting away, just as I'd finally become whole.

"Because I complete you?"

"I thought you didn't watch movies?"

"That's from a *movie*?"

"I never can tell when you're being serious."

"We had time together." Daisy struggled out of her clothes. "Better than nothing, eh?"

"We can fight this," Donny insisted. "We don't have to be beaten by some fucking bug that lives in a tomb."

"It moves in mysterious ways," Daisy laughed forlornly. "Maybe we'll live on in Greyfriars. Like some strange version of heaven.

"Always look on the bright side."

"Aren't you going to get undressed?"

"I wasn't sure you'd..." Donny grimaced. "Y'know? The touching thing."

"I love sex with you and this is probably my last chance." Daisy smiled. "So put out or shut up."

"I love you Daisy Lenin."

"I know."

"That's from *Star Wars*. You sure you don't watch movies?"

"Will you get naked?" She pulled him close. "I want to go out with a bang and not a whimper."

"That's funny."

"Words can't convey how I feel about you, Donny. Which is a good job. I suppose."

Daisy climbed on top of him.

"I better get used to not talking again."

-Part 6-

The Book of Revelations

Those who were seen dancing, were thought to be crazy, by those who could not hear the music.

Friedrich Nietzsche

Next year he did not come for her. She waited in a new frock because the old one simply would not meet, but he never came.

"Perhaps he is ill," Michael said.

"You know he is never ill."

Michael came close to her and whispered, with a shiver,

"Perhaps there is no such person, Wendy!" and then Wendy would have cried if Michael had not been crying.

J. M. Barrie. *Peter Pan*

From the Journal of Donny Marigold

Oss, Deek and Lee never came back to the tours. Ben helped them sign on for unemployment benefits and gave them money for a couple of months' rent. But he hasn't been to see them since and I doubt he ever will. He isn't the kind of guy to get sentimental over the trauma of others. I'm not sure he knows how to handle anything but loneliness. I've never understood how his mind works.

Marky Cotter disappeared with the cash and his former mates are still looking for him. Constance vanished too, though Ben refuses to talk about her.

I've begun to suffer from hallucinations and hear voices that aren't there. I am taking anti-psychotic pills but they make my head fuzzy. Typical. The one time I really need Doc, he's no longer around.

But I understand my illness. I'm a Schizophrenic with a dose of paranoia thrown in. Best I can do is hang in there and try to lead a normal life.

This is my last entry, as I am giving up writing. It's hard enough for me to distinguish fantasy from reality without adding fuel to the fire.

I still believe I was right but can never bring that up or I really will end up in a padded cell. Instead, I am learning about science for I hope to sit exams and go to college. Deek is giving me pointers but he's difficult to converse with and no longer raises his voice above a whisper. Oss keeps himself to himself and Lee has managed to get a job at Mac-Donalds. She says she likes having a uniform, even if it isn't leather.

Daisy stayed on in Ben's flat for a little while but she is no longer able to cope on her own and hardly recognises me.

I cannot bear to think about that.

-41-

Hannah Menzies opened her front door. She was wearing sunglasses, despite the overcast skies.

Her eyes widened.

A man stood on the path, dressed all in black. Behind him was her daughter. Daisy was wearing a plain grey tracksuit and her hair was tied back in a ponytail. In one hand she held a hard-backed book and a pair of night vision goggles dangled round her neck. Hannah made to shut the door.

"I'm called Ben Scott," the stranger announced.

The woman faltered.

"I know that name."

"I used to work with your husband."

"Doc's work is no longer a concern of mine." Hannah refused to look at Daisy.

"I found this girl wandering around Greyfriars Graveyard." Ben pushed her forward. "She refuses to speak but she was carrying a letter."

He thrust a typewritten sheet, one he had composed himself, into the woman's reluctant hand.

To Hannah Menzies. 25 Hansfield Lane, Edinburgh.
Dear Hannah.
My experiment failed, so I'm going away. You can have your daughter back.
Your real daughter.
Goodbye.
Doc.

"Curt to the point of rudeness, as always." Hannah crumpled up the missive. "Did you see my husband?"

"Didn't even know he was out of prison," Ben lied. "We haven't spoken in a long time."

"He was always a secretive one." Hannah's lip curled, a motion made all the more pronounced by the scar pulling up one side of her cheek. Ben tried not to stare.

"I don't think the kid should be walking around on her own, to be honest." He jerked a thumb at his silent companion and rolled his eyes. "I don't want to sound mean, but she's a little bit... eh... simple."

"That's rich coming from someone dressed like a fifteen-year-old Goth," Hannah bristled. She pushed Ben out of the way and stood before her daughter, breathing hard. Daisy clenched her fists and stared at the ground.

"Do you know who I am?" Hannah removed her glasses.

Daisy dropped the book. She reached out and gingerly put her arms round the woman's waist. Hannah's wavering hand hovered in the air then rested on her daughter's head, soft as a butterfly landing, ready to be snatched away.

"You're my mummy." The voice was slow and monotone, but it held no doubt. Daisy reached up and touched her mother's face, tracing the line of her scar. Hannah closed her eyes but didn't pull away.

"Pick up your book, precious."

She folded the sunglasses and put them in her pocket.

"Thank you for returning my daughter, Mr Scott. Can I give you something for your trouble?"

Ben shrugged.

"You could look happy about it."

The woman's hand rose involuntarily to her face. Then it dropped.

Hannah Menzies smiled.

Ben returned to his car. Donny was sitting in the passenger seat.

"She needs her mum," Ben said. "We can't look after her anymore."

"We could."

"The old Daisy would hate that and you know it."

"Doesn't make things any easier."

"Maybe she's happier in her own world," Ben replied, brightly. "Hannah might buy her a dog."

"She didn't want a dog. She wanted a life."

"I know that."

"And the others? You haven't even visited them."

"What would I say? I'm just a painful reminder of what they lost."

"That about sums you up." Donny fastened his seat belt. "Training new staff to take their place?"

"Show must go on, kid."

Ben rested a hand hopefully on the boy's shoulder.

"You seem to be doing remarkably well, though. If you like, you can have Daisy's flat and keep working for me. I'll make sure you're OK."

"I'm never setting foot in the graveyard again." Donny folded his arms. "I'll get another job. I intend to take night classes and then go to university."

"To study what?"

"Virology."

Ben closed his eyes and gripped the steering wheel tightly.

"Sounds good."

"I know. Crazy Donny."

"Not what I meant."

He reversed out of the driveway and drove the boy home.

"You should start writing again," Donny said. "Tell my story. Be warned, though. The poltergeist won't want you to."

"Why not? It seems to be a total publicity hound."

"It appeared to people for centuries and gave them ideas. But it never once told them why or what it was. It left that to their imaginations. The Devil. A Demon. An Entity. A Poltergeist. Depended on the era."

He laughed miserably.

"But I worked it out. And I know what can destroy it."

"I suppose ole Mackenzie wouldn't care for that knowledge to be made public." Ben turned onto the ring road. "Nor am I keen to divulge the role we played in covering up four killings."

"Make it a horror novel, then. As you pointed out more than once, nobody will believe it."

Ben lit a cigarette and Donny rolled down the window.

"Do it for me. The fucker chose us to bring it back, then expected us to fade away. We don't deserve to be forgotten like that."

"I won't forget you."

They arrived at a shabby street, graffiti daubed on some of the walls. The tour boss pulled up and opened the glove compartment.

"Your last wage packet." He handed the boy an envelope.

"How much is in here?"

"Enough. Don't let your dad see it."

"I'm not in a position to say no." Donny tucked it into his pocket "Doesn't mean I've forgiven you."

"I'm well aware. Stay safe, eh?"

Donny opened the car door.

"Bye, boss man." For a moment it seemed like he might lean in and embrace Ben. Then he stopped himself

"You take care. I mean it."

"You know where to find me." Ben tried one last time. "Look, kid. I only did what I thought was right."

"I'd like to believe that." Donny got out of the vehicle. "But there's two sides to every story."

He slammed the door and walked away. Ben watched until the boy entered his dilapidated front gate.

He didn't look back.

"Bye, kid. Love you."

Ben drove back to Greyfriars alone.

-42-

He spent the rest of the day cleaning out Daisy's flat, whistling *Peter and the Wolf* to himself. Under the bed he found a silver heart on a chain. He wondered if Daisy had misplaced it or hid it there deliberately for him to find. Once he was done, Ben went downstairs, switched on the computer and poured himself a glass of wine.

He opened Donny's journal and read every entry. When he was finished, he began to punch the keyboard, battering it until his fists bled. He picked up a crystal paperweight on the desk and threw it at the wall. It exploded in a crescendo of sparkling shards.

Poor kid. He'd never given Donny the benefit of the doubt. Worse than that, Daisy was right. He hadn't even tried.

Ben looked down at his bloody hands. Instead of washing them, he stormed out of the flat and into Greyfriars, locking the gate behind him.

There were no humans, but every headstone was lined with the jagged silhouettes of perched birds. Crows. Sparrows. Seagulls. Finches. Eyes sparkling like neon jewels in the darkness. The tour boss stood frozen, breathing loud and ragged.

"Fuck you," he finally rasped. "This is *my* graveyard."

He marched through the dark to Doc's last resting place and knelt down. Wormed torn knuckles into the soil.

"All right, Mackenzie," he said. "If you're real, you'll damned well show yourself. If not, I'll fill that weed killer tank full of industrial-strength antiseptic and spray the whole damned graveyard. Tonight and every night, starting with this spot."

His arms began to tingle, the sensation spreading throughout his body until he was shuddering violently. Stars exploded before his eyes, melting into mental algorithms, causal chains of astonishing complexity unfolding in his head.

Finally, he understood.

For centuries, people had produced magnificent illustrations and explanations of the way the world worked. How the beat of a butterfly's wing might eventually cause a tsunami in some far country.

The virus was an integral part of that thought mechanism.

External influences were filtered through human biology until they sparked a chemical reaction in the brain. Individuals interpreted this as experiencing events then making choices.

The virus had become a part of that biology, mapping its environment down to the last neuron. Could predict exactly how the host would react to *any* situation. Men's thoughts were no more than scuttling rats in an organic maze. A maze the virus could navigate more efficiently, sending those thoughts in a new direction.

Ben gave a sigh.

Free will, man's most cherished notion, was an illusion.

The realisation had nearly broken some and drove countless others mad. Some denied or tried to work round it, setting geniuses like Hume, Darwin, Stevenson and Conan Doyle down previously unimagined paths. All buoyed by one flicker of hope.

That their incredible ideas must have come from a supernatural or divine being - one that defied natural laws. Even the scientists couldn't see an alternative and it, literally, put the fear of God into them.

Ben ran a hand through his hair. No wonder the poor bastards were so mixed up. And so wrong.

The first viruses weren't discovered until 1892.

The 'entity' they encountered *wasn't* outside natural laws. It was simply a facet of man's desire for knowledge, unconsciously discerning a pattern they were tentatively following and providing shortcuts.

The virus had no more autonomy than its host. The universe was a train on fixed tracks, carrying every living thing with it. Any new discovery it instigated was simply part of the scenery.

Ben pulled both hands out of the muck and rolled onto his back.

"Fucker," he sobbed. "I was hoping you'd show me how to win the lottery."

He finally made his way back to the flat. He felt hollow but, then again, he always had. He'd never considered himself more than a ghost in the mechanism of his own life, so was neither surprised nor comforted at knowing he couldn't have acted any other way.

Doc wanted to cure his daughter. His passenger had engineered the best shot he had until Doc's actions threatened its own existence. He never stood a chance of succeeding.

Donny would try the same thing but the entity was programmed, like all living things, to put its own survival first. Ben had no idea whether the two aims would mesh, for he had pulled his hands away before he saw the patterns. If he couldn't change things, he didn't want to know.

But he was smart enough to make a prediction of his own.

"Donny Marigold made one of the great scientific discoveries of all time," he muttered. "And nobody will ever accept it. They'll simply say he's mad."

He lit a cigarette and looked out of the window.

"Word of advice, Mackenzie," he admonished. "Be a bit more subtle when you impart information. Most people can't handle the truth. They like a happy ending."

Ben paced up and down until he had stopped shaking. Poured another glass of wine. Sat at the computer again.

Dozens of plots and ideas for books buzzed around his head. A gift from the entity, perhaps. Or the residue of briefly glimpsing a million causal chains. After all, there were two sides to every story.

He was grateful for that, at least. He'd always wanted to be a writer.

He mentally filed them away. There was one story he had to tell first.

"Donny asked me to finish his journal and I will," he said to the graveyard. "But you already know that. Do your worst."

And he began to type...

Father Figure

Epilogue

Around the time the tours started, an unemployed woman named Joanne Rowling would sit in the Elephant House café, overlooking Greyfriars, writing about supernatural beings existing among unsuspecting humans. Below her was the narrow alley of Candlemaker Row, with its novelty witchcraft shops - the perfect Diagon Alley. Across the cemetery stood castle-like Heriots, once a school for orphans. Greyfriars contained the headstone of Tom Riddle, the true name of archvillain, Lord Voldemort. Rowling's story concluded with Voldemort's soul being trapped in Limbo for eternity. His legacy and bloodline, however, lived on through his daughter.

Her *Harry Potter* books became the bestselling series of all time.

Though names have been changed, City of the Dead is a real Edinburgh tour company, owned by J A Henderson. In 2003, he completed *Father Figure* in his house overlooking Greyfriars, which doubled as the tour office. The flat then burned down, destroying the manuscript, his computer files and backup drives.

He eventually moved to Australia and, in 2020, wrote *Father Figure* again. When he finished, the Covid-19 virus shut down his tours and a fire destroyed the Elephant House café.

The Mackenzie Poltergeist is still active, with hundreds of recorded 'attacks' on visitors to the graveyard. Regarded as the best-documented supernatural case of all time - nobody knows what it really is.

And Edinburgh, once more, leads the world in scientific achievements - particularly green technology, cloning, DNA and viral research.

Bacteria or viruses could be to blame for illnesses once thought to be caused by genetic or sociological factors... These include Prostrate Cancer, Obsessive Compulsive Disorder and Schizophrenia.

Priya Shetty. *New Scientist Magazine.*

Profound changes in behaviour are observed following infection of the central nervous system by some viruses. Irritability, insomnia, hyperactivity and learning disability are some of the behavioural disturbances that have been described in both humans and animals with central nervous system infection.

A H Mohammed. *National Library of Medicine.*

The virus like components of the human genome amount to almost half of our DNA. This would once have been dismissed as mere 'junk DNA' but we now know that some of it plays a critical role in our biology. As to the origins and function of the rest, we simply do not know... I propose that plague viruses also interact with their hosts in a more subtle way, through symbiosis, with important implications for the evolution of their hosts.

Frank Ryan. *New Scientist Magazine.*

Just suppose that Darwin's ideas were only a part of the story of evolution. Suppose that a process he never wrote about... has been controlling the evolution of life throughout earth's history.... At the root of this idea is overwhelming recent evidence for horizontal gene transfer – in which organisms acquire genetic material 'horizontally' from other organisms around them,

rather than vertically from their parents or ancestors. The donor
organisms may not even be the same species.

Mark Buchanan. *New Scientist Magazine.*

Bacteria aren't just isolated cells, or even isolated populations,
but multi-species communities that communicate with each other
and, crucially, us. We are almost certainly, more intimately con-
nected with the bacteria that inhabit us than we ever would have
believed.

Hayley Birch. *New Scientist Magazine.*

Researchers showed that slime mould could solve a maze. Much
speculation followed that these single-celled organisms were dis-
playing a rudimentary form of intelligence – one that might
ultimately underpin our own.

New Scientist Magazine.

[Physarum plycephalum] can sense and react to its environment
and even solve simple puzzles... Somehow this single-celled or-
ganism had memorised the pattern of events it was faced with
and changed its behaviour to anticipate future events.

That's something we humans have trouble enough with.

Justin Mullins *New Scientist Magazine.*

ABOUT THE AUTHOR

Jan-Andrew Henderson (J.A. Henderson) is the author of 40 teenage, YA, adult and non-fiction books. Published in the UK, USA, Australia, Canada, and Europe, he has been shortlisted for fifteen literary awards and is the winner of the Doncaster Book Prize, the Aurealis Award and the Royal Mail Award.

www.janandrewhenderson.com

www.ingramcontent.com/pod-product-compliance
Lightning Source LLC
Chambersburg PA
CBHW051603100726
47898CB00001B/206